How the World Works

KIRSTEN SUTTON

Cataloguing-in-Publication information for this title is listed with the National Library of Australia.

Published in Australia by Kirsten Sutton and InHouse Publishing.
www.inhousepublishing.com.au

Printed in Australia by InHouse Print & Design.

Note from the Author

This story contains my impressions,

of global affairs, and world history.

It is not supposed to be pinpoint accurate,

and it is not supposed to

stand up to scrutiny.

The reader should be free

to make up their own mind, about history,

politics, finance, and war.

This story contains, just a few of my ideas,

about how the world works.

Dedication

Dedicated to all the courageous doctors,

nurses, and paramedics

who save people's lives, every day.

Dedicated to everyone associated with the space race.

And dedicated to my heroes, David Attenborough,

Simon Reeve, and

Brian Cox.

Chapter 1

It was an eerie Friday night. It was so still so quiet and dark. The only noise was the sound of the moths, as they flew around the dim streetlights.

The clouds had come over, and the sky was black. There was no moon or stars. The smell of rain was in the air, but it was holding out for the moment. The humidity was the prelude to the storm, and the storm was predicted later on tonight.

As Hayden walked home from the hospital, he neared his apartment building, and saw something in the corner of his eye.

If he was any more tired, he would have missed it completely. Or should he say, he would have missed *her* completely.

It wasn't particularly that he saw her. It was more that he *felt* her lying there.

There was just a girl. She was lying down near the banister, by the far right, of the stairs. That's why he almost missed her. She was situated at the furthest edge, away from the street light.

It was as if she was *trying* not to get noticed.

She had long red hair. With an oval face, and white skin. She was wearing a white singlet top, blue jeans, and a black jacket. She had a small black bag with her.

Her eyes were closed, but she kept making whimpering noises, as if she was in the middle of a nightmare. There was also a bottle of alcohol. A passionfruit cruiser. It looked like it slipped out of her hands. It was laying on the steps.

She looked about seventeen. Her delicate hands were wrapped against her chest, as if she was cold. She was wearing black work boots on her feet. They didn't quite match her outfit.

She *did* however look pale. She was clearly weakened, and her skin was covered in perspiration.

Hayden walked over to her.

He didn't have to be a med student to know there was something wrong with her, but since he *was* a med student, he should probably go figure it out.

This could have been a case of alcohol poisoning, but it didn't feel like it.

He put his hand across her forehead. She didn't have much of a fever. He checked her pulse, which was fast, but not too out of the ordinary.

He was leaning down over her, as she opened her eyes. She stared at him.

Her eyes were calm. She wasn't afraid.

She seemed fairly indifferent, about the fact, that there was something wrong with her.

"What wrong?"

"It hurts." She said breathlessly.

"What hurts?" He asked concerned.

"My tummy." She mumbled.

The girl doubled over. She curled up in a fit of pain.

"Your appendix." He told her. "I should call an ambulance."

The girl shook her head. "No. It's not my appendix."

Hayden looked around, distracted. "Are you sure? You look really sick."

The girl shook her head, again. "No." She looked up into his eyes. "I don't need an ambulance. I know what's wrong with me."

"Are you in withdrawal?" he asked her, grasping at straws.

She looked up at him again. Seemingly amused by his second diagnosis. "No." She clarified. "Not withdrawal."

Hayden looked around. He didn't know what to do.

"I can't leave you here." He told her. "I'll have to take you up to my apartment. I'm a medical student. I can help you."

She nodded at him feebly, as if she was humoring him.

She probably didn't think he knew what he was talking about, but he didn't really care what she thought.

He didn't wait for her reply either. He picked her up.

She didn't weigh much, but she was heavy enough, for someone who was so tired. Hayden needed a good shot of adrenalin to pull him into shape.

He found the strength somewhere, to hold on to her. He carried her up the stairs, through the lobby, and on the elevator.

He walked her to his front door, but it was an almost excruciating test of endurance.

It was a struggle to put the key in the lock, and hold her up, at the same time, but he managed it.

"I'm going to put you on my bed and examine you." He told her timidly, although she didn't protest.

She nodded again, but her face was going a slight trace of green. She was really sick.

He put her down, on his bed, and stepped back.

She looked like sleeping beauty in the new millennium, with makeup, and hip clothes.

Hayden took out his Sphygmomanometer and stethoscope from his desk draw. He checked her heart beat, and blood pressure, which were both normal.

She appeared healthy, except he could smell the alcohol on her breath.

He didn't know what he was dealing with. In the hospital, you could never diagnose someone until you got their vitals, their temperature, and their whole medical history.

Hayden slightly lifted the girl's shirt, and pressed his fingers into her belly, at the point where her appendix would be.

She didn't flinch. It wasn't her appendix.

Then he felt it.

His power kicked in. His hidden power. His extreme heightened sense of empathy, and the telepathic abilities, that he was born with.

The reason he wanted to be a doctor, because he was so susceptible.

He had this power, and had kept this secret, for most of his life.

This girl was suffering from… extreme period pain.

"Far out." Hayden yelled out. He *literally* fell back on the floor, because he could feel her agony.

Hayden closed his eyes. He ached all over because she did. He could feel the weakness in her, because he felt himself, getting weaker. Her heart beat was strong. She was a fighter, but there were issues. Her digestive tract was a mess.

He gave himself a minute.

Then he tried again. He put his hand on her stomach.

He thought he knew what was wrong with her, but he was incorrect. She was not having a miscarriage. There was *no* sign a baby was, or had been, inside of her.

Hayden tried to clear his mind, and delve deeper. The girl was mentally strong. She was halfway blocking him out, without even trying to.

He was starting to get tipsy from *her* alcohol consumption. Then he figured it out.

Hayden had got the information he needed. He let go of her, and then fell on the floor again.

He waited till the pain dispersed, from his mind and his body. He laid there for a moment, coming to terms with her ordeal, and his cross to bear.

The girl had been sick like this for a long time. With various symptoms. She had coeliac disease.

He sat on the chair by the bed, and watched her whimpering with painful cramps that came and went. It was one of the unfortunate side effects of the disease.

For females, one of the symptoms of coeliac disease was severe period pain. That was why more women, were diagnosed with the illness, than men. Many people, like Kara, didn't know they had the disease in the first place. This was one of the telltale signs.

The cramps were incapacitating her.

Hayden waited and watched.

The girl just breathed in and out, as she laid on the bed. A look of anguish on her face.

It was an unscrupulous amount of suffering. Then her expression lightened. The pain started to ease. The cramps started to come further apart. He noted the pain in her face, and then relief, and then the pain again.

The whole thing felt so surreal. She kept staring at the wall. So disorientated and weak. She was just counting the contractions till it subsided. She had done this many times before.

Hayden just sat and watched. There was nothing else he could do. There was no medicine that could help her. The painkillers would be too little, too late. She had already got through the worst of it.

He watched over her, till the pain calmed, and she fell asleep.

Chapter 2

Hayden woke up early, even though he was so tired. He woke up on the lounge chair, in his bedroom, with an intense feeling of incomprehension.

The chair he had been sleeping on, was by no means an uncomfortable chair, but it was *not* the most comfortable place to sleep.

His body was stiff and sore. He was still wearing his jeans, and blue sweater, from yesterday, but there was a blanket over him.

The blanket was warm. It felt peaceful in the room, but there was a scent he was unfamiliar with. The strange feeling wouldn't seem to go away.

It was the girl.

He realized it finally. There was a girl in the room, and she was awake.

She was sitting up in bed, looking out the window. As he moved, to straighten up. She turned her attention towards him.

"Hi." Hayden said, blankly.

She nodded at him, modestly. "Hi."

He looked her over. "Do you know where you are?"

"In your apartment." She said simply.

"Yeah." Hayden acknowledged. "You were sick last night."

She nodded. "Yeah."

"I was worried about you."

She smiled, faintly, at him. "You carried me all the way up here"

"You weren't very heavy."

"Heavy enough."

"I hope you don't mind." He asked, concerned. "I didn't want to leave you out there."

"No." She shook her head.

"You were shaking the whole time. You were in pain."

The girl shrugged. "I just drank too much last night. I was drunk." She lied.

"You can't be old enough…"

"I'm nineteen."

"Oh." He said, awkwardly.

"Yeah. I'm an adult." She told him flatly.

She looked at him curiously, for a moment. Studying his facial features. "I'm glad you didn't leave me out there."

"Yeah I'm glad I didn't either." Hayden almost blushed. "I was worried about you." He said for the second time.

"You didn't have to be, but thank you." She nodded at him again. "Thanks Hayden.

Hayden did a double take. "How do you know my name?"

"I've seen you around."

"Do you live here?"

"No." The girl shook her head. "My best friend does though."

Hayden nodded. "And your name." he asked suddenly.

"It's Kara." She smiled. "Kara Cooper."

Hayden nodded, and studied her back.

The girl was pretty, but she also had a lot of character, and personality, in her features. There was a grace and beauty in her demeanor, and even in her gait, as she sat up in bed.

The girl had something about her, and it wasn't just her vibrant red hair. She was beautiful, and confident, and clearly smart, but it was more than that.

Hayden thought about it, and suddenly he became distressed at what had transpired last night. He worried about what she would remember.

"When I touched your stomach last night." He jumped in, trying to explain. "I just wanted to see if you had any tenderness in the abdominal area." He continued. "You were uncomfortably pail. I thought... I mean... I was worried that your appendix might have ruptured."

"I know what you were doing." Kara said astutely.

"Oh." Hayden said again. "Ok" he nodded hesitantly. "What were you doing out so late at night?"

"I just finished work. I finished early, because I didn't feel well."

"Where do you work?"

"A bar." She was being evasive.

"You're a bar maid."

"Yes."

"Why were you drinking?" He asked her.

"Is there something wrong with that? I told you I was over eighteen." She tried to explain.

"No, why were you drinking when you felt sick?" He pushed her.

"I don't know." She said evasively. "I guess I just felt a bit fluey. I thought the alcohol might make me drowsy." She lied again.

"But you said you were in pain. You wanted the pain to go away." He tried to clarify.

Kara shrugged, and then blushed. "Who knows what I say when I'm drunk." She deflected the conversation. "I was just being stupid."

Hayden withdrew slightly. "Yeah." He shrugged his shoulders. "Ok."

Kara sat up, and leaned towards him. "I know it doesn't make sense." She looked at him thoughtfully. "You picked me up last night. Anyone could have come by. Anyone could have come by and done anything to me."

"Well, late night revelers, around here, don't have the best of intentions." Hayden said awkwardly.

He said that, but he immediately regretted the remark. He didn't want to scare her.

"I thought it was for the best." He tried to change the subject, quickly. "You put the blanket over me last night."

"You looked like you were cold." She told him.

"It did get cold last night." He agreed. "When the wind picked up. Before the storm." He looked her in the eye. "Did you hear the storm last night?"

"I heard the thunder, but I was just drifting off." She commented.

Hayden looked away. She was still being evasive.

As he looked back at her. She was staring back at him.

Her stare was curious and intense. It was making him uncomfortable, not the least because he was drawn to her.

"Excuse me. I have to use the bathroom." He said quickly. He said it to fend off the awkwardness, but it was also extremely true. He got up to leave the room.

He had no idea what to say to her next.

Chapter 3

Hayden took his time in the bathroom.

He was washing his hands, in the sink, when a noise pierced the bathroom, so suddenly, that he jumped back, and almost fell over.

It was a mobile phone ringing.

It wasn't Hayden's mobile phone. His phone almost never rang. It belonged to the girl. The girl in his bed: Kara.

She was beautiful, and when he found out she was nineteen, she became even more beautiful.

He probably had a crush on her, but it didn't matter. His crushes rarely went anywhere.

Kara's phone was just a discrete, black, flip phone. It was sitting on the cabinet bench. She must have left it there, when she was rummaging around last night.

The display said it was 'Greg Calling'.

Hayden didn't want to touch it. He let it ring out.

When her phone stopped ringing. The display said that she had five missed calls.

She was a popular girl.

Hayden took the phone with him, and headed for the kitchen. He needed a cup of coffee.

In the mornings he liked to absorb the sensation of hot water scolding his throat. He liked it black, and strong. No milk. No sugar. Just an uncorrupted shot of caffeine. To jump start his nerves.

As he finished the coffee. Her phone was vibrating again. This time it was 'Corey' calling.

Hayden thought about it for a moment. This was how the other half lived. The popular half. Maybe it was important.

He started walking the phone to its owner, but suddenly there was another noise. It was behind him. At the doorway. Someone was knocking on his front door.

He looked at the phone in one hand, and the front door in the other direction. He knew he had to answer it.

It turned out to be Randy, his neighbor.

"Hey." Hayden answered, slightly suspiciously.

"Hey." Randy looked him up and down. "I locked myself out of the apartment, again. Do you have my spare keys?"

Hayden rolled his eyes.

Randy had a talent for locking himself out of his apartment. Usually, though, it was two o clock in the morning, when Hayden was fast asleep, and about to have an exam the next day.

Randy never gave Hayden the time of day, unless he locked himself out of his apartment. He was a twenty-three year old, self-employed, gardener, and full time womanizer.

Randy looked disheveled, and hung over. He always looked like that, at times like this.

He was handsome though, and he knew it. He was almost six foot tall, with blonde hair, blue eyes, strong jaw line, and he had rock hard abs. He spent most of his time at the gym. Fine tuning his body, to fat, ratio. He was buffed and over confident. As such, he was incredibly obnoxious.

"I'll go get them."

Hayden tried to tip toe, back into the bedroom, because the spare keys were in the desk draw. He rummaged, carefully, through the contents, and finally got his hands on them. The girl sat up in bed, and watched him.

Suddenly Randy appeared in the entrance to the bedroom, behind him.

"What the hell." Randy jerked his head upwards, as he saw Kara. "Are you holding out on me Hayden?"

Hayden sighed, and let his head drop. "No." He said distracted. "It's not what it looks like."

"It looks like you have a girl in your bed!" he grinned slyly. "Sorry, man, didn't mean to interrupt."

Randy stared blatantly at the girl's physique, under the covers. He was checking her out.

"Sorry." He whispered to the girl, obnoxiously.

Kara raised her head, slightly, to acknowledge him, but she didn't look impressed.

Hayden held up the keys. He walked out into the lounge room and shook his head. "Here." He said finally. "Here are your damn keys alright." He said annoyed.

"Who's your friend?"

Hayden ignored the question. He walked across the hall, and physically opened Randy's front door.

"Come on Hayden, spill." Randy piped in. "That girl is hot."

Hayden shook his head. "She's just a friend."

"A friend?" He grinned. "Well, she's a friend who's definitely sleeping in your bed."

"I'm just helping her out." Hayden said. "I slept on the couch last night."

"Why? What's the problem? Gee whiz Hayden." Randy smiled fiendishly at him. "You're really no fun at all, are you?" he hesitated for a moment. "Well, you should definitely tap that. You could use a piece of *that* action."

"You have no tact at all, do you?"

"Not when it comes to this." He commented fiendishly. He put his arm around Hayden, and took him into his confidence. "Stop over thinking it Hay. That's what you do. Just get in there and do it!" He let go of Hayden and staggered into his own apartment. "Anyway, I swear I've seen that girl before. Don't leave it too long. Lest I get to her first."

"She's not your type Randy." Hayden said bluntly, without knowing what Kara's type was.

"They're *all* my type." Randy argued. He slapped him on the back again. "Nice seeing ya buddy."

"Wait Randy." Hayden called out to him. "Can I ask you for something?"

"You want to borrow a condom?"

Hayden rolled his eyes. "My exams are in two weeks. Can you not bother me until then?" He asked meekly. "I can't handle you knocking on my door. At all hours. Especially when I'm trying to study."

"It's not my fault." Randy said defensively. "Penny deliberately steals my keys. She thinks it's funny." he pleaded.

Randy was talking about Penny Johnson. His longtime girlfriend, but only one of the girls that he was currently 'tapping.'

"She steals them, because she doesn't trust you." Hayden rephrased.

"Something like that." Randy acknowledged. "Don't worry Haydo. I won't bother you again. Just close the deal in there." He encouraged him, before he closed the door.

Hayden stared again at the phone in his hand. The girl had just received a text message.

He slowly walked to the kitchen and filled a glass of water. He wondered if he looked as disheveled as Randy did.

Chapter 4

Hayden wondered back into his bedroom, and looked upon the girl. "Hello." He said softly. His tone of voice, came out awkward, although he was trying to be smooth.

"Hello." She said back.

She waited for a moment, and watched him. She was waiting for him to say something more substantial.

"So…I didn't ask before…" He tried to get the words out. "Are you feeling better this morning?"

The girl didn't answer him straight away. She looked at him cautiously.

Hayden clarified. "You said you felt sick yesterday."

Kara looked directly into face, then finally nodded. She scanned his face, with her eyes. Eyes that were almost turquoise. "Much better."

Hayden cleared his throat. "I'm sorry about the interruption before. That guy's a dick"

"I'm sleeping in your bed, Hayden. I'm pretty sure, *I'm* the interruption."

"No. You're not." He said quickly.

"But you don't know me." She ventured. "You took a chance on me last night."

Hayden shrugged his shoulders. "Always glad to roll that dice." He laughed softly. "You didn't rob me, or anything, this morning."

Kara giggled. "You're funny."

"Not too funny." Hayden commented.

He turned to Kara, and held out the glass of water. "Would you drink this?"

"I'm not really thirsty." She said politely.

"If it was up to me." Hayden tried to tell her, gently. "I would have had you on saline drip, hours ago." He held the glass out, closer to her. "Would you mind, for me?"

Kara took the glass, and drunk it. She must have been thirsty after all, because she drunk the whole thing in one go.

"Thank you."

Hayden changed his tact. "I have your phone." He said trying to sound casual. He held it out towards her. "It was in the bathroom." He informed her. "It's rang a few times, since I picked it up."

Kara took the phone, and then looked at it for a moment. She put it down on the bedside table. "Ok thanks."

Hayden stared at her. He stepped forward. "Do you mind if I check your pulse." He didn't wait for her reply, or her consent, before he did it anyway.

He grabbed her arm, and felt her pulse.

He counted the beats against his wrist watch, but what he was really doing, was getting a sense of her.

She was exhausted. The cramps were now minor, but her body was weak and drained.

Her mind was peacefully engaged, however, she felt too tired to have much morale. If anything, mentally, she was toying with him. She was shrewd.

"It's fine." He let go of her arm and stepped back.

"Good." She said, somewhat confused. "I Hope I'm not in your way, here." She said quickly. "You're probably busy today."

"No." Hayden said, and then ignored the comment. "Do you want me to run you a bath?" He asked suddenly.

Kara froze. Completely caught off guard. "You wouldn't mind?"

"Not at all." Hayden nodded.

She was sweaty and sticky. A bath was exactly what she needed right now.

Hayden had sensed it, when he grabbed her arm. He turned around and walked into his adjoining ensuite bathroom and started to run a bath.

It was half way full when she walked in.

She looked at him enquiringly, with her turquoise eyes. Then politely sat down, on the toilet seat.

"You will want to get out of those sticky clothes." He said quietly. As he turned off the tap.

He stared at her for a moment. Then he was about to leave, when she spoke again, softly.

"Will you help me?"

Hayden stopped in his tracks. He didn't expect that.

"I feel like every ounce of strength, in my body, is gone." She explained to him, as she leaned helplessly, against the back of the toilet.

Hayden stepped towards her. He felt caught off guard. "Yeah. I can do that." He replied slowly, trying to sound casual again.

She nodded.

He went to her, and kneeled down at her feet.

Kara's eyes flicked over him. She continued watching him, curiously.

She lifted her arms, then held them up in the air. Hayden lifted her singlet top over her head.

She was wearing a pink, and white, lace bra. Hayden paused and left it in place. He went for her jeans. He unhooked the top two buttons. Then he looked at her again.

She simply nodded, as if it was ok.

He unzipped the zipper. Then Kara lifted herself up slightly. He pulled her jeans down, and they came down over her legs, over her feet. Then he put them aside.

She sat there, diminutive, in her underwear.

She was clearly waxed, and her body was trim and taunt. Nothing to be embarrassed about. Not that she seemed to suffer emotions, like embarrassment.

She was just breathing in and out, just staring at him.

Hayden looked in her eyes. "You can take it from here?" He asked her.

She nodded. "Yes." She was looking deep in his eyes.

Hayden couldn't look away, even if he wanted to.

"I'm sorry I'm such a mess." She said to him, meekly.

"No. It's fine." Hayden stammered. "I've seen pretty much everything in the emergency room. This is nothing." He commented off handedly.

Kara nodded, then laughed weakly. "You've seen much worse than me?"

Hayden shook his head, doubtfully. "No, I mean, I've seen the human body. I …didn't mean… you look beautiful… I just meant to say…."

"It's ok." She smiled at him.

Hayden turned around, eager to give her some space.

"Wait" he said suddenly. He walked out of the ensuite, and into his walk-in wardrobe.

He returned quickly with a pile of folded up clothes. "Here." He said, showing her the clothes. "This is a t shirt, and trousers. My mom left them here once."

The T shirt was at least a stylish one. He put the clothes down on the vanity, next to the sink.

Kara watched him closely. "Thank you."

"You're welcome."

Kara looked in his eyes. "Last night… I could have got caught in the storm. If you didn't save me."

He smiled awkwardly. "I didn't save you. I just helped you out."

"I think you saved me." She said earnestly.

"I didn't… It was nothing… You're welcome." He said quickly.

"You don't know, what a good guy, you are." She told him tenderly. Her eyes bright, with adoration.

Hayden shrugged, and turned around. "I'll give you your privacy." He mumbled, as he stumbled out of the bathroom, embarrassed again.

As he left, he walked straight into the other, bigger, bathroom.

He desperately felt the need to shower, shave, wash his hair, clean his teeth, put on zealous amounts of deodorant, and aftershave.

Then, when he was finished. He felt so much better.

He slowly walked to the kitchen, and got some cereal, and milk. He sat down at the kitchen table, slurping up his Sultana Bran

It was almost, half an hour, before he saw the girl again.

She reemerged slowly, in his mom's pink blouse, and blue trousers. Her hair was wet, but she had it up in a towel.

The girl looked thoroughly refreshed as well. She looked, somehow, more at peace.

She walked in, and sat down, at the table across from him.

"How are you feeling now?"

She smiled "Good…Thank you… Much better."

Hayden nodded, and looked down at her mobile phone, on the table. He had collected it from the bedroom, when it started ringing again, incessantly.

He pushed the cell phone across the table.

"Last time it rang, you had seven missed phone calls."

She put her hand on the phone, and grinned. "I must be popular this morning."

"You must be." Hayden noted.

"What did Randy want before?" She asked suddenly, changing the subject.

Hayden almost choked on his sultana bran. "You know Randy?" He asked quickly

Kara nodded her head. "Who *doesn't* know Randy?"

A pang of jealousy flared up in Hayden. The two of them must have been in the same social circles. The same social circles that Hayden knew nothing about.

"He wanted his spare keys." he finally answered, and then sighed. "You know his girlfriend always steals his keys. She always tries to protect him."

"Penny Lane" Kara said exasperated. "Always so hopeful."

"How do you know them?"

"I see them at work sometimes." She said dismissively.

"Oh, that's right. You're a bar maid. Where do you work?"

Kara didn't answer. She flipped her phone open, and started reading the text messages.

She finally finished. Then she started typing something in her phone.

"You said your name is Hayden Manning right?" She asked out of nowhere. "What's your phone number?"

Hayden was taken aback. He briefly wondered if he should give her his number. She was still basically a stranger, and he generally avoided distractions in life. At least until he made it through med school, and by distractions, he meant other people. He wasn't even on Facebook.

Hayden didn't even tell Kara that his last name was Manning. Nor did he that his first name was Hayden. She seemed to know everything, like the teenage detective, *Veronica Mars*.

Kara looked at him with an infinite amount of compassion.

Hayden carefully took the phone out of her hand. He hesitantly entered the numbers into the log that Kara had set up for him.

Kara smiled. She looked around for a second, then took hold of a pen, and a conveniently placed notepad, that were both sitting on the table.

The notebook was one of his subject notebooks, from university. She didn't care. She just started writing on the next available page. She wrote down her name, and number, on it.

"I have to go." She said softly. "But would you call me?"

Hayden was caught off guard again.

"Yeah." He finally answered, trying to sound aloof. "Of course."

She smiled again. "Good."

She got up, collected her belongings, put her hair towel back in the bathroom. Then she walked out, and left.

No goodbye, no nothing. She just left.

Hayden wasn't sure how to take that.

Chapter 5

K ara was at work.

She poured her Bacardi rum shot, put the bottle back down on the rack. Then she looked into the face of the customer she was serving.

The guy had dark hair, a light complexion, and he had a nice grin. He was cute, but not as cute as Hayden.

She was thinking about Hayden, again, for the millionth time. Which she had been doing, constantly, for the last two weeks.

He always seemed to be there, in the back of her mind.

It was like the name, Hayden, was always on the tip of her tongue, and that was confusing. She didn't usually go for guys like him. She usually went for the richer, cooler, more sophisticated model.

The fact was, though, Hayden wasn't just any guy. He was an important. He was going to be a doctor, and more to the point, there was something about him. When he touched her, she felt like she was floating.

She gave him her number, but he hadn't called her back.

That clearly meant he wasn't interested. Which hurt, a lot.

Kara brushed her hair aside. She hooked her hand up, to the customer's hand. "Here's your change darlin'" She said smiling at him.

Flirting with cute customers was her signature move.

"Well, thank you." He said back, with a smile and a twinkle in his eye. She could have got his number if she wanted to, but he was just one of many.

Kara watched him walk away, and smirked to herself. She really loved her job sometimes.

It was still slow at the moment. She looked around the bar, and checked out all the customers.

She could see what they were made of. Or at least, see what they were capable of, on a night like this. Sometimes it was like working in a circus, and all the drunken idiots were the performers.

There was another reason that Kara started to think about Hayden now. His neighbor, Randy, had come in the entrance of the Joker club, twenty minutes ago.

He was a thorn in Hayden's side, but Hayden didn't know it yet.

Kara stood behind the bar and watched him move around the club. He moved with a triumphant ease, because he thought he was the hottest guy in the room, and he acted accordingly.

Randy had that classic combination of confidence and arrogance. A mentality that was so common, to guys like him. They walked around as if they owned the place.

Kara was actually the one who belonged here. She had worked *this* hottest, inner city, nightclub, for over two years now.

Her friends called her Kara54, like the movie, because some of the staff were just as infamous as some of the clientele.

Kara54 was based on Studio 54. The hottest night club that ever stood.

Studio 54 had been in New York City. A city Kara had visited, when she was sixteen. When her parents actually had money. Right before they lost it all.

Kara was busy serving the growing crowds, when Randy finally came over, to order his drink.

She nodded at him, but he barely looked up at her. He was sifting through the wad of cash in his wallet.

She carefully reached across the bar, to grab the bottle of *Jack Daniels*.

"Is this what you're looking for?" She held the bottle up, and looked Randy directly in the eye. "This is what you drink isn't it?"

Randy raised his eyebrows. "I knew I had seen you before." He told her. "The bar maid at the Joker club." He looked behind her, and checked out his own reflection in the mirror. "How could I have missed that?"

"I don't know." She shook her head. "You're here all the time."

"Well, I don't really notice the help."

Kara smiled. "Yeah, I'm sure you don't." She smirked. "Not when you're busy spending that trust fund of yours."

"How do you know I have a trust fund?" He asked.

"Everybody knows." She said flatly. "Everybody knows because you brag about it." She nodded at him, again, knowingly. "Let me assure you." She suggested. "The girls on your arm: They are always so aware of it, too." She grimaced. "I hope you don't think they like you for your mind."

"I please them in other ways." He grinned. "You're a feisty little thing aren't you?" he continued. "Whatever does Hayden see in you?"

Kara breathed in deeply, and resentfully.

"So...Kara..." Randy continued. He seemed pleased that he remembered her name. "Are you even friends with Hayden? Because I've been watching, and I haven't seen you around lately. Not since that *first* day I saw you...in his bed" He smiled at her. "I've taken the time to keep watch."

"What did you do? Install a video camera, outside his front door?"

"I was just curious." Randy shrugged. "I mean, I was really happy for the guy. He had a friend."

"He does have a friend." Kara defended him.

"Well, the way I heard it. You ran off on poor Hayden, before he even got a chance to speak to you."

"He told you that?"

"Well he seemed pretty upset about it. When I talked to him."

"He did?" Kara said softly feeling a pang of guilt. "But I told him to call me?"

"He's too shy Kara." Randy told her. "All he saw was your back, as you walked out the door. *And...*" He continued, mischievously. "He told me, you were being evasive."

"I was sick that night. What was I supposed to say to him?" Kara said exasperated. "Does he tell *you* everything?" She staggered. "I was going to go see him again. I *wanted* to see him again. I just thought he'd call."

"Of course he didn't. He's too clueless. Why didn't you call him?"

"I have just been busy." Kara said, defensively.

"Well why bother? That's a lost cause if ever I saw one." Randy grinned again, obnoxiously. "You should detour to my place. I can entertain you in ways that Hayden never could."

Kara cringed. "Do you want me to pour this, or not?" She asked, nauseated.

Randy smiled. "Sure, and poor one for your pretty little self."

"No thanks."

"Surly you can sneak one."

Kara looked at the bottle for a moment. She hesitantly poured the Jack Daniels into two shot glasses, and decided to take his offer.

She picked up the glass. Threw her head back, and skulled one for herself. Then she pushed the other one, across the bar.

Randy watched her closely. Then he drunk his own shot.

"So Kara... You obviously didn't meet Hayden here. He doesn't drink" he paused "Or go out."

"It's none of your business where I met him." She said defensively.

Randy put the money down on the counter. It was a fifty dollar note "Two more."

"Two more for you?"

"For us."

"Believe me Randy, there is no us. Nor will there ever be."

"That's a challenge I'll take on." He replied. "Just pour it anyway. I'm sure I'll find someone else."

"I'm sure you will." She said snidely. "Probably someone who *isn't* your girlfriend." She sniped at him.

"We're not exclusive." He said annoyed.

Kara rolled her eyes. However she did as she was told. She would certainly take his money.

"I'm sure Hayden could use a good friend." She said hopefully. "Have you ever even invited him out for a drink?"

"No." Randy scoffed. "My stock would plummet, if I was seen out with that guy."

"That guy? Are you kidding? You have no idea what you're talking about." She yelled at him. "You didn't notice how good looking he was under all that insecurity? You know he's going to be a doctor right?"

"Hey Kara." A voice came from behind her. Out of nowhere. "This is a bar, not a social hour."

Kara had to think. "Actually a bar is a social hour."

She turned around and saw her manager Corey. He was shaking his head at her, but not in a bad way. Corey adored her.

Corey was a newly married man, but he would cheat on his wife in a second, if Kara battered her eyelids, in his direction.

Corey was looking incredulously at Randy. He couldn't understand why Kara was bothering to indulge this guy, and usually she wouldn't. Corey had seen Randy's type before. They all had.

"She was just pouring me another drink." Randy answered him.

Kara flicked her hair again. It was hot under these lights, in the bar. She turned back to her boss and smiled mischievously at him. "Just give me a second." She told him cautiously.

Corey nodded at her. Then he walked off, to serve another customer.

"Sounds like you like Hayden." Randy teased her.

"I do."

Randy reached over to her. He flicked a few loose strands of her hair, over her shoulder.

Kara flinched, and repelled backwards from him.

"No I mean like 'like like'."

Kara laughed softly. "Is this high school?" She frowned for a second. "Look, Hayden is import ok. He's in medical school. I'm just a barmaid. What would he want with me?"

Randy was caught off guard.

"Oh my gosh. Don't tell me *you're* the one who is insecure." He grinned at her. "Give the guy a break. He wants what every guy wants. You really think he's too good for you?"

"I know he bet the bank on becoming a doctor. When he graduates, there will be girls all over him."

"You really don't know him very well, do you?"

"Do you?" She asked defensively.

"I know him. He's sensitive. He couldn't get a girl like you, to save his life."

"You have no idea what you're talking about. You have no idea how many girls out there would kill for a guy like that. When he's ready. He'll get whichever girl he wants."

"You mean he's not ready yet? I know he's older than I am."

Kara shook her head. "I don't care how old he is." She said annoyed. "He is my friend. So just shut up." She said frustrated, because he wouldn't listen to her. "I actually have to serve the other customers you know." She told him, exasperated.

She picked up the money from the bar, and went to the register. She held out the change.

"Keep it." He told her, trying to act suave.

Kara nodded, feeling slightly off balance. She put the change in the tip jar.

"Are you going to drink this?" He asked, leadingly. There was still a second drink, sitting on the counter.

Kara shook her head. "No."

"Alright Kara." he winked at her, and picked up both glasses. "I'll definitely see you later." He left, dramatically, walking away.

Kara felt so confused again.

Hayden must have thought she had walked out on him.

He didn't know that she liked him. She had to fix this. She had to see him again.

Chapter 6

Hayden felt kind of lost, as he sat in the break room, at the hospital.

He sat back, on his uncomfortable, off-white, plastic chair, and stared into space.

He cradled his cup of coffee in both hands, and leaned so far back, in the chair, that he was practically staring at the ceiling.

It was rare for him to have lunch in the actual lunch room. Usually he went to the subway down the street, or the McDonalds, a block away.

When he did have lunch in the hospital break room, he kind of felt antsy. He tried to avoid any in depth conversations about himself. He was embarrassed, because he didn't have much to talk about.

He was thinking about Kara now, but he didn't know why. He had been thinking about her for about two weeks now, but he hadn't called her yet.

He wanted to call her, but something always stopped him. Every time he would start to dial, he would lose his nerve, and hang up the phone.

He knew Kara probably had a boyfriend. Her boyfriend was probably the 'Corey' that had called so many times on her phone. Although it had not always been the same name, on her display.

He didn't know why she had been so curious or cagy around him.

He didn't know why she asked him to call her.

He didn't even know anything about her, because she had never told him anything. All he knew was that the girl was evasive, and shrewd, and probably not good for him.

He *should* have felt disappointed, and moved on with his life. After all, she got his number too. She didn't call him.

It didn't matter anyway. This was all too much of a distraction.

Today was his last day on work experience, and his exams would start on Monday. He needed to focus.

Hayden sipped his coffee, it was going cold.

"What are you thinking about?"

Hayden looked up. There was a nurse by the coffee machine. She had just appeared there. Then just as quickly, she had asked him a question.

"Oh." Hayden sat up, with a start. Trying to get his mind off the girl. "This is my last day on prac, at the emergency department, this semester." He told her. I was wondering what kind of review they are going to give me."

The girl smiled. "A pretty good one. I would think." She said warmly. "You always seem to get the right diagnosis."

Hayden looked away, embarrassed. "Thanks for saying that."

"No, it true." The nurse told him. Her name was Melanie. She stared at him admiringly. "You're better than most of the doctors around here."

She grinned at him, and changed the tone in her voice. "You know, I didn't even know you were in medical school until you started *treating* patients, and not wheeling them around." She shook her head. "You're pretty stealthy, Hayden." She told him, mischievously. "An orderly by night, and a doctor by day."

Hayden shrugged his shoulders. "Med school is expensive, so I need that job."

"Yeah, but you never talk about yourself, and you always sneak around like a mouse, so no one can ever get to know you." She continued.

"I've always been quiet." Hayden shrugged. "There's not really much to know about me." He tried to explain.

"You're probably a lot more interesting than you think you are. I assure you." She started to explain. "A lot of guys think they *are* interesting, but they are not. Just ask my ex-boyfriend." She said ironically.

Hayden looked up, startled. Was this a regular conversation, or was she hitting on him?

This girl, Melanie, had a boyfriend very recently. His name was Ian. She talked about him a lot. She talked a lot, about a lot of things.

She changed the subject. "So what kind of doctor do you want to be when you finish med school?"

Hayden laughed to himself. "A good one." He said bluntly.

Melanie laughed.

"I don't know." He told her, and sighed to himself. "I want to be an ER doctor, but I also want some experience in surgery." He sighed. "I want to play the field."

"Really?" Melanie commented. "Can you do that?"

"Probably not." He shrugged. "I probably can't have it both ways. I haven't made up my mind yet." He told her contemplatively. "I'm only in my fourth year of medical school. I do my official rotations next year." He shrugged. "I'd like to be part of the doctors without borders program, at some point."

"Yeah?" she asked surprised. "So you want to be one of those humanitarian doctors?"

"I hope so." Hayden shrugged. "I don't know what's involved though. I suppose it's easier said than done."

"Yeah." Melanie reflected. "I remember doing my prac. I don't remember it being this hard. It was all so exciting back then."

"Yeah, I can imagine." Hayden agreed. "I can never believe how much the nurses do." He said earnestly. "I am always in awe of it." He tried to explain. "I mean for us, the doctors: We get to skip in. Fix up the patients. Save the day. Then skip out again. But you guys…" He said admiringly. "You have to take care of their endless needs, 24/7."

"Yeah." She nodded. "But, it can be interesting. You never know what to expect each day."

Hayden smiled back. "And you get to help people."

"Yeah." She smiled again. "We get to help them, and talk to them, and get to know them." She looked at him earnestly. "The doctor's don't have time to do that."

"No, not really." Hayden said, pensively.

Melanie had bleach blonde hair and bright red lipstick. She had an imprint of a tattoo from underneath her stockings.

Hayden knew that Melanie wasn't his type, even though she was such a nice girl

He didn't even know if he had a type. He just knew that she wasn't it. He didn't want to be rude to her, or seem like the signature snob, that some people thought he was.

"Hey Hayden?" She asked suddenly. "Do you go to many concerts?"

Hayden thought about it. "Not really. I took my little sister to see Bon Jovi last month."

She nodded impatiently. "It's just this band, 'The Strokes' are playing in the city this weekend. I really like them. Have you heard of them?"

"No" He said quickly. He tried to imagine where this was going. "Not really."

"Well they're really good. Maybe we could...."

Hayden was completely unprepared for this conversation. She was actually going to ask him out.

Then, circumstantially, she couldn't finish the sentence.

His phone was on the table and it started ringing.

Hayden shrugged apologetically. As if to indicate, he would be one second.

"Hello" he said, surprised.

"Hi." The voice on the other end paused. "This is Kara."

Hayden held his breath for a moment. She had actually called him.

"Oh... Kara." He said surprised. "Hi."

Hayden grimaced. "I'm sorry, I have to take this." He told Melanie, feeling like he was being rude, but he desperately wanted to take this call.

He smiled at her apologetically again, and got up, to walk into the hall, out of the lunch room.

"Oh, is this a bad time." Kara asked him tentatively. She sounded slightly nervous.

"Hi.... Kara, oh, no, it's no problem. How are you doing?" He tried to sound as if he barely remembered her. Like he hadn't been thinking about her every day since their last encounter.

"I'm good." She said softly. "You remember me right?"

Haden laughed to himself. "Yeah, of course I remember you."

"I was wondering if you're busy tonight."

"Tonight?" He asked surprised. She certainly moved fast. Hayden shrugged his shoulders. "No, no plans."

"I thought I could bring dinner or something, and we could talk. It's my shout, and I have to bring your mom's clothes back, anyway."

"Oh." Hayden said again. "Ok, yeah, sure. That would be good."

"Great, I'll see you tonight… about seven? Do you have any requests…for dinner?"

"No, you can surprise me." Hayden went along with the conversation.

"Ok, see you then." She hung up.

Hayden felt disorientated. He slowly walked back into the lunch room, and nodded. "Sorry."

"Who was that?" Melanie asked curiously.

"Just a girl." He shrugged, humbly. "She's coming over for dinner tonight."

Melanie looked confused. "I heard you didn't have a girlfriend."

Hayden shrugged. "No, I don't… But I like her." He smiled apologetically for a third time.

Melanie looked away. Hayden got up quickly. "I guess I have to get back to work." He told her. He tried to act blissfully ignorant about what was just about to happen.

He put his coffee cup in the bin, and walked back out into the halls of the emergency department. The patients were waiting anyway.

Chapter 7

Kara didn't know what to bring to Hayden's apartment. In the end, she just brought herself, a bottle of wine, and a few cartons of Chinese food.

As Hayden answered the door, he looked humble… and handsome.

He was wearing blue jeans, with a green Quicksilver t-shirt.

He had style, and casual good looks. He had no shoes on. His hair was slicked back, and there was even gel in it. He was wearing after shave, and it smelled really nice.

"Hi." He smiled warmly.

"Hi."

He wasn't sure what to do at first. He looked at her awkwardly. Then even more awkwardly, leaned over, and kissed her on the cheek.

She wasn't expecting that. It was like something your grandmother did.

None the less. She swooned. The sensation of his lips on her cheek, overpowered her for a moment.

"How are you?" He asked

Kara nodded. "I'm good." She smiled at him. "I hope you like Chinese." She said hopefully. She held out the food, so he could see it. She couldn't believe how nervous she was.

"I do." He replied quickly.

Hayden ushered her in. He put his hand on her back, then directed her to the dining table.

Kara felt something like lighting, go through her entire anatomy, when he touched her.

She sat down at the table, and it was already set, in a formal dinner type setting. She handed him the food, and he dished it out on the plates.

"How have you been?" He asked again. He pulled out his own chair and sat down.

Kara looked at him curiously.

Hayden always had a certain way about him. He looked at her like he was looking inside her. He asked her a question, but it was as if he already knew the answer.

Kara decided to eat the soup first, and picked up her spoon. "I've been good." She told him again, even though she had already answered the question.

Hayden poured the wine into two glasses on the table.

She picked up her second bag and handed it over to him. "Thank you for letting me borrow your mum's clothes."

Hayden grabbed hold of the bag, and put it behind his chair "You're welcome."

"Your mother must have style."

"She does." Hayden smiled. "She shops way above her pay grade."

Kara giggled.

"Did you go to work today?" He asked.

"No." She shook her head. "I worked last night."

"Do you work a lot of night shifts?"

"Well, I work at a nightclub." She told him, incredulously.

Hayden shook his head. "You didn't tell me where you worked. I asked, but you didn't tell me."

"Oh." Kara paused. "I'm sorry. I work at a night club." She paused again. "In the city."

"So you're like Kara54.

Kara laughed. "I get that reference. My friends call me Kara54. You know your history." She took a deep breath. "Have you ever been to New York?"

Hayden thought that was funny. "No. I've never been anywhere. I've never left the state." He changed the subject quickly. "So what club do you work at?"

"The Joker Club."

Hayden seemed caught off guard. "Wow." He said, amazed. "The Joker club. That's a pretty famous hot spot. I tried to get in there once, but the line was too long. We didn't think we would get in. So we split."

"We?" Kara asked quickly.

"A friend from Uni." Hayden replied shyly. "He used to be my roommate, but he moved in with his girlfriend."

"Oh, ok." Kara said softly. "I'll leave your name at the door next time." She suggested. "You can bring anyone you want. Just text me."

"That would be great…" Hayden said, but he looked doubtful.

"I hope I didn't interrupt you tonight."

Hayden lifted his head. "No." he answered softly. "I was just studying."

"So you study all the time then?" She asked him. Although suddenly it felt rude to ask.

"Yeah." He shrugged. "Med school isn't as much a walk in the park, as you might think."

Kara giggled. "You're being ironic."

"I kind of have to study." He clarified. "If I want to pass."

Kara nodded. "Good." She told him adamantly. "I suppose it's no use being a doctor, if you can't be the best."

Hayden smiled. "That's what I keep telling myself." He paused. "It was nice of you to bring dinner. Sometimes I start studying, and forget to eat."

Kara nodded and glanced at him. He did look a little thin. "Good." She said again. "I should do it more often."

Hayden was caught off guard. "Next time I'll pay." He said awkwardly.

"So are you studying for your exams?" She asked, remembering the argument he had with Randy.

"They start on Monday." He answered.

Kara continued to stare at him, so he kept talking.

"Then they're over, a week from Wednesday. I just have to get through them." He tried to explain.

"And I didn't distract you."

"No. I was starting to get brain freeze." He cried. "I'm glad you came over. I need a distraction." He told her adamantly.

"Well I'll be sure to distract you then." Kara giggled. She continued slurping up her soup. "I'll distract you with this food. Since I clearly brought too much."

Hayden shrugged. "That's the good thing about Chinese food. It tastes just as good when you heat it up."

Kara nodded. "Yeah, I agree, but that's not what I meant." She sighed to herself. "I was just thinking about all the starving people in the world."

Hayden laughed for a second. "Really."

"Yeah." She said honestly. "I've just been watching all that stuff on the news, about war torn countries, and refugees in Europe. It's kind of depressing. Makes me feel guilty sometimes."

"Yeah. It's pretty bad." He commented awkwardly. "But Refugees are suffering all over the world." He exclaimed. "It's not just Europe, and it's not just refugees either." He continued softly. "It IDP's as well: Internally displaced people."

"Yeah." Kara nodded uncertainly. Then she glanced again, at her big meal. "I give to charity sometimes, but I feel like I should do more."

Hayden was taken aback, for a moment. "I understand what you're saying Kara. But do not feel guilty."

"Why shouldn't I." She asked defensively.

He sighed. "Because people live by their circumstances." He started to answer. "And you have to remember Shakespeare: *'This above all, to thine own self be true.'*"

Kara watched him closely. "So I should just ignore everyone else's circumstances?"

"Kara." He said adamantly. "If you're talking about food security, and global inequality. Then you're talking about Geo Politics."

Kara grinned at him. "You look like someone who understands geo politics."

He shook his head. "Not if you're talking about the third world."

Kara kept glaring at him. "What does that third world mean?"

Hayden looked out the window. "What do you mean?"

"The first world, the second world, the third world." She pushed him again. "What does it mean?"

Hayden shook his head. He wasn't sure if she was being serious, but then he answered.

"I don't use the term correctly." He began slowly. "I quite arrogantly use it to describe poor nations, but that's not what it means. The first world was the capitalist world. The second world was the communist world, and the third world is all the decolonizing countries that tried to find a third way." He said emphatically. "The first world won out."

Kara thought about that for a moment. "How did they do that?"

Hayden shook his head again. "You're really interested in this? You don't want to talk about movies, or the last concert you went to."

"Fine." Kara battered her eyelids. "What concert did you last go to?"

Hayden shrugged. "Bon Jovi."

"Me too." Kara laughed. "Maybe we were at same concert. Now tell me... How did the first world win out?"

Hayden shrugged his shoulders, embarrassed.

Kara kept waiting, refusing to back down.

"Because capitalism is a natural state." He finally answered. "People want what's best for themselves, not what is best for the collective." He sighed. "And we always had the advantage anyway." He shrugged.

Kara finished the soup. It was good soup. "How did we have the advantage?"

Hayden took a deep breath in. "Because we had the money, and the power, and the weapons, and the communist world fell."

Kara chewed on her lip for a moment. "Isn't China a communist country? Aren't they are the new superpower?"

He paused. "You're pretty sharp Kara." He noted. "To some extent, China is Communist, but they allow a wealthy class.

As long as the wealthy, do not try to meddle, in politics." He paused again. "Basically communism fell."

Kara shrugged her shoulders. "It fell because it's not what people wanted?"

Hayden stared back, unflinchingly. "It fell for the same reasons that plagues the first world today – corruption, and mismanagement" He shrugged his shoulders. "But yes, it's not what the people wanted."

"I can understand that." She grinned at him.

"Well, so do I. I love capitalism." Hayden agreed. "But capitalism does have its draw backs."

"What draw backs?"

Hayden finished his own soup. Then cautiously moved on to the beef and black bean. "Are you serious?" He asked exasperated. "You really want to know about this."

"Yes." Kara told him bluntly.

Hayden nodded, and then shrugged. "Well, in a word… Greed." He told her. "And sometimes the greedy are controlling the playing field. Like what happened in the Global Financial Crisis."

"What do thcy control?" Kara askcd.

Hayden tried to hold back his answer. He must have felt like he was boring her, but she really wanted to know.

"Influence" He said finally. "The influence at The World Bank. The structural adjustment programs at the IMF. The veto rights at the United Nations. The tendencies at the credit rating agencies. The uneven bargaining power at the World Trade Organization. The first world forcing unfavorable conditions on the third world, while all the while, making itself a welfare state. Who do you think controls all that"

Now Kara was struggling to keep up. "So we have the influence in all those things."

Hayden sighed again. "Those who have an education, can learn to work the system. That comes down to intelligence and opportunity."

"I kind of get it." She told him softly, but she began to feel a little self-conscious.

Hayden glanced at her again. "You don't have to get it Kara. It's too complicated for anyone to understand. Least of all me." He shrugged. "It's not a lesson I cannot teach you, in one night."

She looked out the window, and something caught her eye. She thought she saw the reflection of lightning, on the window pain.

"I like that you try though."

There was silence for a moment. Kara ate her honey chicken. She finished as much of her meal as she could.

"This is really good meal." Hayden smiled.

"Yeah, it's my favorite restaurant." She said truthfully. She looked out the window again. "I think I just heard something." She told him. She looked around distracted. "I think I just heard thunder outside."

Hayden smiled meekly. "You did. It's going to storm tonight."

"Really?"

Hayden shook his head. "There has been a severe thunderstorm warning in place all day. Did you not here about it on the radio?" he asked.

"I didn't listen to the radio today." Kara shook her head. "I worked last night. So I slept late today."

Kara looked out the window again.

It felt strange being back, on the eleventh floor, with Hayden. On this floor, she was that much closer to the sky, and the sky was pitch black, with clouds.

Now there was a lightning and thunder outside. Just like the first night she met him.

Kara finished her meal and got up. She decided she would distract Hayden. Like she said she'd do.

"I'm really tired from work last night." She said suddenly. "You mind if we go lie down on your bed, and talk, and watch TV or something."

"What?" Hayden asked.

Kara sighed. She didn't wait for a reply. She just got up and walked to his bedroom.

Chapter 8

Kara hesitantly got under the covers of Hayden's bed. A place she had been before, and was eerily comfortable with.

She lay back against the pillows, and Hayden sat next to her. He tentatively lay beside her, but not too close.

Both of them were starring forwards, towards the wall mounted television, but it wasn't turned on.

Kara kept thinking about how nice this apartment was.

The building itself, was expensive and panache, but the furnishings in the apartment, were humble, and so was Hayden.

"So you're tired?" He asked her.

"I have a slight headache." Kara answered. She snuggled up cozily, on his down blanket. "I slept all day, but I am still tired."

"Your circadian rhythms are off?" He told her. Half question. Half statement. "Because you work at a night club."

"My sleeping pattern are always off."

"That's understandable." He agreed. "In life, you can't burn the candle at both ends, and I know you Kara. It seems like something you would do."

"You know me?" She asked.

"I know your type."

"I have a type?"

"You're one of those girls… Who thinks they can do it all."

"I *can* do it all."

"See, I told you."

Kara giggled. Hayden had no trouble speaking bluntly to her, but at the same time, he was cautious and unsure. He was still slightly nervous.

"It's kind of a cold night." She commented, griping the blanket closer.

"Yeah, spring has been cold this year." He mentioned. "I prefer the heat."

"Yeah, I wish I was somewhere warm now." She commented. "Like on the resort beaches of Maui."

"Must be nice to live in your imagination."

Kara giggled. "What were you talking about before?" She asked suddenly. Changing the topic back to where it had been at the table.

"What?" He asked again.

"About the world we live in." She reminded him.

"What?" He asked, shaking his head. "You want to talk about politics again?" He asked, confused.

"You were talking about the World Bank, and the IMF, and the all that stuff." She reminded him. "What is the IMF?"

Hayden shook his head. "I can't believe you want to know." He murmured. "It's the International Monetary Fund."

"Yeah, and what is that?" She smiled at him.

She was toying with him, in her own special way. "I do want to know." She continued. "I can't believe, you don't believe me."

Hayden shrugged.

"Tell me."

"Well." He began slowly. "There is context." He said be-grudgingly. "The IMF started at the end of colonization."

"Colonization?" Kara asked.

"The industrialized world in Europe, set out on their ships, to conquer the world, and obtain resources." He looked at her. "You might have heard of The First Fleet, in Australia."

"Yeah, I've heard of that."

"So, they sent ships all over the globe, and they conquered and colonized, and they were hugely successful at this."

"Ok." Kara nodded.

"Europe conquered The West Indies, The East Indies, the scramble for Africa, and the Caribbean. Even America, as well as Australia, were European outposts."

Kara chewed on lip while she listened.

"Once they got to these places, they set up plantations, and colonies, and farms. It was all about crops, spices, and raw materials."

"Ok." Kara said slowly.

"So much of the world, was all one big land grab."

Kara grinned. "Ok."

"So basically, Europe had their fingers in a lot of pies." Hayden smirked. "But the problem was… eventually… Colonies weren't all that economical to run, and coordinate. Then there were a lot of uprisings among the indigenous populations." He continued. "Over time, Europe was decimated by World War 1 and then World War 2. Then there was a new world order, in terms of money and trade. So the world *decolonized*."

"Right."

Hayden sighed to himself. "Decolonized countries were all supposed to have the same prospects for growth, and opportunity." He explained slowly. "The newly created World

Bank, and the International Monetary Fund, gave massive loans to all of those newly independent countries." He sighed again. "The money was supposed to help those countries invest in their infrastructure and development."

"Yeah." Kara said fascinated, nodding her head. She wished she was taking notes or something, so she could double check his answers later.

"But many countries didn't develop." Hayden exclaimed. "Many dictators around the world, misappropriated, mismanaged, or flat out stole the money. We didn't call them on it because of 'sovereignty'. Sovereignty is the policy of non-intervention." He told her. "In other words, we do not interfere in matters of state, in another country."

"Ok." Kara said again.

"So many countries didn't develop…For one reason or another. Often not of their own fault, and they couldn't pay back the money. So the IMF instituted structural adjustment programs on those countries. We forced strict, and unfair conditions on them."

"Conditions like what." Kara continued. She wasn't exactly following on, but she liked the rhythm of his voice.

"Things like lowing the price of raw materials. Selling off their public companies into private hands, and forcing them to devalue their currency. Just some of many."

Kara nodded.

"But the thing is." He tried to make a point. "We don't play by the same rules. When *we* get into trouble, the first thing we do. The first thing the first world does, is 'economic stimulus.' The very thing we stripped from the third world."

Kara tried to keep up. She listened attentively.

"So everything's changed, but it seems the corporations

have the power now." He stopped and grinned at her. "You look like you're bored." He said embarrassed. "I told you. I couldn't explain it one night. I don't want to put you into a coma."

Kara laughed. "I'm not bored. I'm fascinated. You know all this stuff."

"But I just freaked you out on our first date."

"Is this a date?" Kara asked casually.

Hayden flinched. "I don't know."

Kara took a deep breath in. "I wish I could date you, but I can't."

What?

Kara did a double take, at her own sentence structure. Those words seemed to fall out of her mouth, without her knowing it. She heard herself say them, but she couldn't stop herself. She didn't mean to say it. She didn't want to say it, but the words just came pouring out.

Hayden's smile dropped. "Oh." His voice faltered. "I didn't expect anything."

Kara continued breathlessly. "I don't want to distract you from your studies."

"You wouldn't." He tried desperately to tell her.

Kara shook her head. "You've been concentrating on your studies all this time. You only have one year left of medical school. I can't stand in the way of that. You don't want a girlfriend." She continued to hear herself say, out of nowhere.

"But I do." Hayden ran his fingers though his hair. "Who have you been talking to, about me?"

"Well for one, Randy." She answered him, amused. "He comes into the bar every second night. He tells me far more than I'm interested in hearing." She looked at him knowingly. "I don't think you have *time* for a girlfriend."

"You speak on my behalf. When you don't even know me?"

Kara nodded, and turned to him. She sat up on her elbow, so she could face him. "I don't want to hold you back."

"What if *I* wanted to go out with *you*?" He asked, confused.

"I couldn't. I wouldn't put you in that position."

"You would act on my behalf. Even if it's *not* what I want?" He looked away, upset. "I like you Kara."

"It's what you want *now*. Tomorrow, you would know it was for the best."

"What about carpe diem? Seize the day."

"You're not a carpe diem kind of guy."

"How do you know that?"

"Just by looking at you."

"Oh." He said softly.

"I think you're a med student, and you just told me how the world works, and you don't have time for a girlfriend."

"So you just want to be friends?"

"I just came over to talk." Kara said softly. She looked out the window and she was sure she saw lighting again, in the distance.

"Well I guess it's nice to have someone to talk to." Hayden practically whispered, disappointed.

"For me too." Kara told him sincerely.

She turned her head away. She didn't know what just happened.

She was forcing out the words, but they couldn't be more unplanned.

She couldn't be more interested in a guy like Hayden, but at the same time, she couldn't be with him either. She knew it in her gut. She would get in his way. Her doubts were taking over her.

Suddenly, a deep sound broke their stale mate. Thunder roared outside.

It started pouring down rain. The ferocious raindrops smashed on the windows. The teaming drops, cut the air like a knife. It was so chaotic, and blustery, and now the wind was blowing a gale.

"I love storms." Kara said, wistfully, like she was a little kid or something. "They're so exciting." She continued. Her eyes fixated on the lighting, and the wild conditions outside.

"Me too." He said thoughtfully.

Hayden lay beside her.

They were staring out the window, as the storm exploded over them. The lightning and thunder practically came in unison. It was loud and the thunder boomed, and the lightning streaked across the sky, and wind howled.

It was nice that they experienced it together. The storm seemed to last a long time.

Kara finally stopped looking outside, and stared at him.

"It's nice to be here with you now." She reflected." You can help me sleep tonight. I'm so tired." She said again.

Hayden stared into her eyes.

Kara moved over and snuggled into Hayden's embrace. She placed his arm across her body, so that he was spooning her.

He followed suit, probably because he didn't know what else to do. He was always so thoughtful, and attentive.

She felt his amazing warmth, and vibrations from his body. It was so beautiful.

Then she fell asleep. In her clothes. On top of the bed, under the covers. With Hayden so close. All of his warmth to protect her.

She woke up early though. She woke up and left. Before he woke up too.

He had his exams to concentrate on.

Chapter 9

Hayden was at work.

He put the novel 'Catching fire' down in his lap, and smiled at the girl in the hospital bed. She had a sweet oval face, and a button nose, although her head was completely bald.

She didn't look any worse for the dreary hospital conditions that she was stuck in, but then again, she was half asleep.

She stirred for a moment. Then looked at him accusingly. "Why did you stop reading?"

Hayden giggled at her. "I can't read you the book, if you're asleep." He explained. "There is a lot going on in the arena at the moment. I don't want you to miss it."

The young girl shook her head. "I wasn't asleep."

"You were drifting off." He argued.

"But I want to know what happens." She argued back. "I want to know if Katniss ends up with Peter or Gail."

"Well, that's what everyone wants to know!" He told her. "You have to go through the motions of reading the book first."

"Do you know?" She asked impatiently.

"No." Hayden shook his head. "I haven't see the final movie yet."

"Yeah, well" She shrugged. "I'm glad I'm reading the books, before I see the movie. Their keeping me entertained." She smiled at him. "I like it better when you read it to me, but I have to keep reading when you're not here, because it's three novels."

Hayden nodded. "Well, yeah. I'm sorry. I don't have time to read you all three books." He said sarcastically.

The girl nodded at him. "Well, fine, but I like it when you come though. It makes me feel happy."

Hayden nodded back.

This was the hard part of being a med student, or even an orderly, at the hospital. Seeing people sick, and in distress, was difficult.

It was nice when you got to help them, and make them feel better. It was hard when you had to see what they were going through.

The girl he was talking to, was brave and determined. Her name was Emily, and needless to say, she was a cancer patient.

Hayden met this girl a couple of weeks ago. He got to know her when he started wheeling her back from the oncology ward, every afternoon.

She was usually done with her chemotherapy sessions, right about the time that Hayden started work as an orderly. Every day he would wheel Emily back to her room, in the main hospital wards. Then help her back in to bed.

Her bright cheery face was always so inspiring. Even in the grip of such adversity, she was not going to let her condition bring her down.

Hayden liked talking to her, and reading to her. She was sweet, and fun, and thoughtful as well.

When he helped her into her bed, he could feel the dark, black hole, of her tumor, and it was quite disconcerting. He usually avoided any unnecessary contact with cancer patients.

When Hayden noticed that Emily was reading 'The Hunger Games' trilogy. He insisted he come back in his lunch break and read to her. Sometimes he'd read to her, in between jobs at the hospital. When it was a slow night.

Hayden picked up the draw string bag he had brought in with him, and reached inside. "I have something for you."

The girl's face lighted up. "You got it! Is it bright red?" She yelled cheerily.

He pulled out a bright red wig, and the girl instantly jolted forward, to grab hold of it.

"Yes. Bright red." He answered. "I still don't know why you insisted it be red."

"Red heads are more fiery." She told him. "I'm sick of being so polite and congenial all the time. It got me nowhere."

"Don't talk like that." He told her adamantly. "You're beautiful blonde hair will grow back when you leave here." He tried to convince her. "You can easily go back to being a dumb blonde. When all this is over." He joked.

Emily lightly punched him, but she laughed out loud. "You're so funny." She said sarcastically. "We can't all be brilliant med students like you."

"I'm not brilliant."

The girl shook her head, adamantly. "You calm people down, just by touching them." She cried. "You know all about medicine, and you actually explain it to people."

"How would you know?" He asked, dismissively. "I'm just your orderly."

Emily reached over and grabbed his hand. "When you touch me." She told him bluntly, and looked in his eyes. "I feel better." She squeezed his hand tighter, and widened her eyes, for affect. "I feel like I'm floating. I feel like that now."

Hayden shook his head, and took his hand away. "You're sicker than I thought. You're having delusions."

"No." She said desperately. "I've seen it in other patients! It's not just me! My roommate has the same look on her face, when you wheel her around, too."

Hayden glanced at Emily's 25 year old, sleeping, roommate, with the broken leg.

Hayden shook his head, slightly embarrassed. "I'm just super friendly, that's all." He said, scrambling, to cover up his telepathy.

Of course, this fourteen year old girl was the first one to inadvertently notice it. While she was also smart enough to know what she was seeing.

Emily grinned at him. "You have no idea."

Hayden shook his head again. "Are you going to put your wig on, or what?" He changed the subject quickly.

The girl sighed, at his evasiveness. Then placed the wig over her bald head, and smoothed it down. "What do you think?"

"Awesome." Hayden gleamed. "You actually do look good, as a red head." He finally admitted.

He looked at her curiously, with the cheap, bright red, polyester wig on. It actually brought out her features.

Hayden reached down and got out his phone. "Here." He told her. "I'll take your photo. So you can see what it looks like."

He carefully framed her in the shot, and then took the picture. He showed it to her, and she smiled with glee.

"I do look good." She shrieked.

Hayden smirked. "Here" He handed her the phone. "Why don't you send it to yourself?"

The girl grabbed the phone and started working the key pad, to send the photo to her email account. Hayden wasn't as good with technology, as most kids these days, so he let her do it.

"So…" She said mischievously. "I can be a red headed troublemaker, and be melodramatic, and give the doctors hell?"

"Because all red heads are bitches? Is that what you're trying to tell me?"

She giggled. "Maybe."

Hayden smirked to himself.

"What are you smiling about?" She demanded.

She seemed to notice everything. Hayden took a deep breath in, and smiled to himself. "The girl I have a crush on, has red hair." He said offhandedly.

"Really." Emily looked a little bit hurt. "Who is she?"

Hayden paused for a moment. He hadn't meant to start this conversation, or talk about his private life. He sighed. "Her name is Kara, and she's a bar maid." He said quickly. "Other than that, I don't know much about her."

"So how do you know her? Do you see her around? When you go out?"

"Something like that." Hayden lied.

He didn't want to ruin the illusion. He didn't want to tell Emily that he was shy, and he didn't go out that much.

"And you just have a crush on her?"

"Yeah."

"But you're not dating her."

"No I'm not." Hayden shrugged.

"And you've never kissed her." She teased him.

"I spooned her once." Hayden said, although he didn't mean to say that either.

"You spooned her?"

Hayden stayed quiet. Probably not the right setting for this conversation.

Emily didn't let up. "How did that happen?" She jumped to attention, and leaned forward.

"I don't know." Hayden shrugged. "She came over." He began, confused. "She didn't want to go home in the storm. So she stayed over. Do you even know what spooning is?"

"I'm fourteen years old. Of course I know." Emily said astutely. "This girl sounds like a head case to me."

Hayden sighed again. "We'll I don't know." He told her. "I don't know if I'll ever see her again."

"I'm sure you can do better than her." Emily rebutted.

"Not really." Hayden mumbled to himself. "You don't even know her." He said defensively.

"But she's not dating you."

Hayden shook his head. "No." He sighed again. "Sorry Emily. I'm shouldn't be dumping my problems on you." He explained. "I've been studying all day. I'm tired. I have an exam tomorrow."

"Yeah. I was going to ask you how your studying was going." She asked him, curiously.

"It's Ok. I think." Hayden suggested, then looked at his wrist watch. "Of shit, I'm late from my lunch break. I better go."

Emily looked up at him, longingly, as he got to his feet.

"I know you're an orderly now." She said softly. "But why don't you ever treat me? When you're in doctor mode?" She asked him quickly, before he could leave.

Hayden looked at her compassionately. "I'm in the E.R." He told her. "When I'm on work experience. I work in the E.R." He explained.

"Oh." She sighed. "Well it would be nice if you were *my* doctor."

Hayden nodded.

He didn't want to be an oncology doctor, but he didn't want to tell her that. He *did* have a lot of respect for them though.

Emily took the wig off. "It's scratchy." She explained, as she rubbed at her scalp.

She started speaking slowly. "If I get that bed in the children's hospital." She told him softly. "I'll be sad to leave. You treat me like I'm a competent adult. You're the only one who does."

"At the children's hospital you can make friends your own age. Who are going through the same thing you are." He explained to her. "You will like it there. Everyone's trying to pull some strings, to get you in."

"Well I think it worked. I think *I am* going there. My mum told me." She looked in his eyes again. "I'll miss you."

Hayden smiled at her. "Just try and get some rest. Don't stay up all night reading." He turned around quickly as he left. "I'll miss you too."

Hayden walked down the hall. He had to get back to work, but it was nice when he could help the patients sometimes.

Chapter 10

Hayden had specifically told Kara that today (Wednesday) was the last day of his exams. Today was also the day he was finished for the semester, and the year, at university.

It had been hard, avoiding him for those 12 whole days, but she managed to stay away.

She thought about him a lot, but she couldn't stay away forever.

Especially now that she was back at his front door again. Hoping she could see him, just one more time.

She was wondering what she would say, or why she cared so much. She couldn't put it into words, why she was simply, desperate to be near him.

She even brought a stupid bottle of wine with her.

She thought it would be nice to celebrate the end of exams. She hoped he would feel the same way.

So here she was, at his front door. Even after she rejected him. With nothing to approach him with. None the less, she figured 5pm, would be a good time.

The exam had probably finished by now. He would probably grab something to eat on his way home. Hopefully, after that, he would want to see her.

He could tell her about how stuff was going, and how his exams went, and all about the world again.

Kara took a few minutes to find the courage to knock. But then he didn't answer.

A wave of insecurity washed over her. Hayden wasn't home.

He was probably out with his *other* friends.

Maybe she was wrong about *all* of this. Maybe he didn't have time for her. He probably forgot all about her.

She was just assuming that he wanted her, and he liked her, but what if he didn't? What if he was just being kind?

In real life all he did was pick her up off the filthy ground. Take her into his apartment building, and let her sleep it off, in his apartment. *In real life* all he did was let her bring dinner over, and intrude on him, for one more night. *In real life* he was just be kind to her, and answered her stupid questions. *In real life* he was just being a gentleman.

Also, sometimes, there was a look on his face, and an edge to his words. He was quick to call her on it, when she was being arrogant.

Kara stood there for twenty minutes. She was intermittently knocking, but he wasn't home.

She just stood there for a long time, and she felt stupid. She was wearing a burgundy velvet dress, and make up, and black roc boots.

She desperately wanted to see him again. All she could think about was that night - When he held her in his arms. His touch had been *so* tender.

Kara felt so confused, and completely lost. She was just a lost, lonely girl, in a hallway. Then she turned her head.

The music was on in the apartment across the hall. She could hear it.

Kara's self-destructive impulses started to attack her. Randy was home. He would see her. He wasn't too good for her. In fact, he was way below her.

Randy was also quite good looking, and probably a bit of fun. He was probably a bit of everything. Probably *into* a bit of everything. Just like the other trust fund babies, with the good sense, not to get addicted, to any one thing.

She found herself steadily walking to his door step. Even worse, she knocked.

What the hell was she doing?

"Well, what do we have here?" Randy asked, grinning as he answered the door. "You bought wine."

Randy answered the door in a faster time than it took her to turn around and run away. She should have run away, if she had any sense at all (which she quite often didn't.)

"Is penny here?" Kara asked flatly.

"What do you know about Penny?"

Kara instinctively got irritated. "I see her at the club sometimes." She said exasperated. "I'm very smart Randy. I know what's going on with half the people in this town."

Randy took the grin off his face. "Ok." He shrugged. "So what if she's not here?"

"Then I might come in" Kara stared at him blankly.

He nodded. "She's not here."

Kara thought about it. She didn't handle rejection well.

She never actually had to handle rejection before. For crying out loud she used to be an uptown girl. She still had the attitude for it. She deserved to have her fun, and besides that, she didn't have to work tonight. What else was she going to do?

She looked closely at Randy.

He looked good. He looked like he was getting ready to go out. He was wearing a red shirt, with black chinos, and expensive leather shoes.

It occurred to Kara suddenly: How could she ever think she knew Hayden? Hayden wasn't from uptown. He dressed nicely, but he didn't exactly wear Giorgio Armani. He looked good, but he didn't have the G.Q. pose that her boyfriend's always had. He looked like someone who struggled, rather than someone who walked along the yellow brick road, paved with Gold. Not like most of her friends.

He certainly wasn't rich, and he didn't have money. She could tell by the furniture in his apartment.

He was probably waiting for the girl, from the little house on the prairie. He was waiting for someone sweet, who was *actually* good enough for him.

It was a devastating thought. Randy was waiting for her to say something, or make some kind of move.

The choices weren't good. She could go in, or she could go back to her own house, and watch TV all night.

"Ok." She went in.

Kara looked around, the apartment was surprisingly clean. He must have had a maid on the payroll.

"So what's on the playlist?" She said referring to the semi-loud music.

"You are." He grinned.

Kara shook her head. "On your IPod" She said irritably.

Randy saw she was serious, and flicked through the playlist. "Do you want me to change it to soft rock? A bunch of Bryan Adams and Roxette songs, that Penny downloaded on here"

"Sounds good." Kara said absentmindedly.

"So what changed your mind?" Randy asked, as he fiddled with the music.

Kara didn't feel the need to explain herself. She put the bottle of wine on the coffee table, and then sat down on the couch.

"Who said I changed my mind?"

He sat down next to her. "Did you give up on Hayden?"

"Far out Randy, just pour the wine, ok. Don't talk about Hayden. He's the nicest guy I've ever met." She yelled.

Randy was caught off guard. He didn't know what to think.

He went out to the kitchen and poured the wine into two actual wine glasses, and then brought them back to the table.

Kara sipped her glass slowly. She wondered again, what she was doing here. The music was good though. Penny had good taste.

"So how is the landscaping going?" She finally asked.

Randy shrugged. "It's ok." He answered slowly. "But a little slow." He admitted. "I'm getting into concreting, and sculpting, and retainer walls. People's yards can look so good, when they have good ideas. Or they let me talk them into some."

"So you do a lot of design?" She asked curiously.

"Design, excavation, landscaping. Land clearing, paving." Randy informed her. "It's a lot of work."

"I bet it is." Kara glanced over his muscled body.

She was surprised that Randy actually took pride in his work. Was it possible he was a good guy? She saw the human side of him… but just as quickly the obnoxious side returned.

"How's the club going?"

"It's going good." She said blandly.

He wasn't really interested in the answer anyway.

He put the wine down on the coffee table. Then he took that specific moment, to put his arms around her, and start making out with her.

Kara didn't move. He started caressing her, but she stayed numb because she wasn't supposed to be here!

If only Hayden had been home.

Randy started kissing her mouth. She kissed him back. Sort of half moving her jaw around. Then suddenly he had his hand up her back.

He continued getting even closer. Even though, for all intents and purposes, she was only half conscious. She just let him do it.

When his hands moved south, she jumped back on the couch.

"What the hell are you doing?"

"What's the matter?" he asked incredulously.

"I came over because Hayden wasn't home. I'm taking advantage of you."

"Are you serious?"

"Ok." She acknowledged. "You're taking advantage of me." She shook her head. "I'm just not in the mood for this." She ran her fingers through her hair. "I'm sorry I disturbed you. I just didn't know you were going to move that fast."

"Sorry, I thought that's what you wanted." he whined.

"Well it wasn't." She said adamantly.

Randy stared at her. "Ok, fine."

He sat up. Then ran his fingers through his own hair. "We can just hang out." He told her earnestly. "We can just listen to music."

"Can we?"

Randy moved back and nodded at her. "I'm sorry. What else do you want me to say" He asked her.

She nodded back feebly.

He was being quite nice about the whole thing actually. Even though he went from zero to sixty, in the space of about twenty seconds. One minute she sat down on the couch. The next minute he was all over her.

Kara sighed. "Why? What else is on the set list?" She asked distracted.

"Westlife! And lots of them."

"I love Westlife! '*When you're looking like that.*'" She said quoting a Westlife song.

She found herself smiling again, but she also felt puzzled. Randy was being sensitive, and she didn't think he had it in him.

Kara decided to hang around. She sat back on the couch, and then suddenly Randy started singing.

He actually started singing the words to the songs. He was leaning back on the couch with her, making fun of himself, as he sang.

Randy knew the words. He obviously liked soft rock. The music choices probably had nothing to do with Penny. He knew the songs off by heart.

With every song, his voice would get louder and more satirical.

Kara jumped in and joined him. It was fun. She knew all the songs off by heart as well.

Kara couldn't believe she was having fun.

The music went on for an hour or two. Randy tried to outdo her, with both loudness and lyric expertise, as they sat together on the couch.

When the playlist ended. She got up and smiled at Randy. "Thanks for the Karaoke." She said sarcastically.

"No problem. It's been fun" He nodded at her again. "You don't have to go, you know?"

There was a soft tone in his voice. Randy actually *liked* her. She could tell.

His touch may have been gruesome, but to him, it was tender. He seemed a little bit upset that she didn't want to be with him.

Kara was taken aback for a second. As she got up she saw something on the table. She hadn't noticed it before. A cylinder of white power, behind a book. It was half empty, and there was a smattering of powder still on the table.

It wasn't a surprise that he did that stuff, but at the same time, it was a complete surprise.

Interesting. Kara thought to herself, *Was he high right now?*

"I should go." She told him softly, as she backed off. She turned around and headed to the door.

He followed her, and stopped her at the doorway.

"It's been real." She told him.

She looked in his eyes, and he *was* high. She couldn't believe she hadn't figured that out sooner.

He kissed her on the cheek.

Kara just looked at him, confounded.

"I'm always here for you." He said obnoxiously. Then he pinched her on the butt, showing his true colors.

Kara shook her head and giggled. "You're such a tool." She said, brushing him off.

She turned around, towards the elevator.

That's when she saw Hayden.

It was exactly that moment that he showed up. Coming down the hall. He was looking at her desolately, like he had just been punched in the stomach.

He had just seen everything that had transpired. He saw the kiss on the cheek, and the giggle, and the pinch on the butt.

Anyone walking past, would have assumed that she just had sex with Randy, but Hayden looked like he was turning a pale shade of white. Kara's stomach tied itself in knots.

He looked shocked, and in disbelief, at first. Then, as he came closer. He looked like someone who was on the verge of tears.

He looked wounded and hurt, like a wounded animal.

As he walked towards her, it was like he was going to throw up, or maybe that was just her.

When he got to his door, he paused with the key in the lock. He looked around awkwardly, like he didn't know what to do.

It would have been rude not to acknowledge them, but at the same time, he was still in shock.

Hayden paused at his door, trying to look casual. He was trying to get his mouth to work. "Hey." He said softly as if he was short of breath.

Randy saw him and nodded. "Hey Hayden." He nodded at Kara and smiled deviously.

Kara looked around disorientated. Her mouth was hanging open. She watched Randy disappear inside his apartment, and close the door.

Hayden, was also trying to get inside, as fast as he could. He had nearly accomplished his task, but she stopped him.

"Hayden."

He stopped, and turned, very slowly. He stood still, and stayed firm. He was so firm, Kara wasn't sure if he was still breathing.

"Congratulations on finishing your exams."

"How did you know about that?"

"You told me."

"Yeah, but how did you know it was today?"

"You mentioned it."

"And you remembered that?"

"Yeah."

"Oh." He gave her a compassionate look. Kara melted on the spot. "Thanks." He whispered.

"I'm sure you did great." She tried to encourage him, but he wasn't interested in hearing her talk.

"Thanks." He mumbled. "I think I hear the phone ringing." He told her quickly. "I have to get inside."

Then he was gone. The door was closed.

Kara wondered why she was constantly sabotaging her own life.

The last thing she ever wanted to do was hurt Hayden. It was probably the only thing she had done for him, since she met him.

Chapter 11

Hayden felt sick to his stomach.

He didn't want to be melodramatic, because he hardly even knew Kara, but he finally convinced himself that he had a shot at love, and now it turned out, he was wrong.

Of all people that Kara could have been with, she chose Randy. It was inconceivable the amount of pain he was in.

It was inconceivable how many times he had played *Every Rose has its Thorn* by 'Poison', on his IPod.

Kara was not his girl. She did not love him. She did not care for him. Whatever relationship they had, was purely in his head.

Like all his other hopes and dreams that took years to fruition. There was no girlfriend on the horizon.

He felt so optimistic that morning too. He was thoroughly prepared for his exams, and he thought he did well on them.

It turned out all of the hours he spent studying, had paid off. When he finished the exam, he was sure he passed, if not aced it.

Kara was right. He had needed time to himself, with and no distractions. Getting a good grade would make it all worth it.

Now he had three months off school, and he hoped he could call upon Kara in that three month period. He thought he could win her over. He thought they could be together, but her heart was a little colder than he anticipated.

Kara had just ripped out *his* own heart, and crushed it.

The sad thing was, he had been planning on calling her the second he got home.

He was going to ask her out to some fancy restaurant. She could have help him celebrate one more completed semester of university. Then he would offer to give her one more life lesson. Maybe on some contemporary topic, like finance, or economics.

But Kara had been humoring him the whole time. Probably, especially, as he went on about 'Global history and uneven development.'

She must have conferred with Randy about what a nerd he was. They probably said the nastiest things, and howled with laugher, at his inexperience and naivety.

He was such a daydreamer.

It only he didn't like her so much.

There was a softer side to her as well, but she had completely misrepresented herself. The problem was, for him - it didn't seem real. It didn't make any sense. Why would she hurt him like that?

The night that he held her, he had stayed awake for hours.

The experience was too wonderful to miss. Her body was soft and warm. Her movements were subtle. Her dreams were peaceful. Or at least they seemed to be. He could sense them, being so close to her.

His intuition didn't put up *any* fights about being with her.

She was the right one, and that had never happened before.

He knew the right girl would bring him to his knees, and that's what Kara did.

He didn't just feel like he was holding Kara in bed. He felt like he was protecting her. Protecting her from a cold world.

Hayden buried his head in his hands. He sat in his chair and stared into space for an hour, feeling so gutted, before he went to bed.

Hayden didn't want to deal with it. So he didn't. He just hauled up in bed, with his IPod.

He never expected the knock at the door the next morning. As he drearily woke up.

"Hi Penny." Hayden said, surprised.

He suddenly felt even sicker that Randy's 'girlfriend' was standing in front of him.

He looked at her curiously. Penny was a thoughtful, and beautiful, but he never knew what her game was.

She had a blonde hair that came just past her shoulders. She had floorless white skin, and a wide mouth, but she had a perfect set of teeth to show it off. She had blue eyes that were big and deep. Maybe her nose was a little too big but it gave her character. She dressed a little bit like she was from the seventies, with lots of colors and patterns, but her dress sense was her only drawback.

Kara was also right about Penny, she looked eternally hopeful.

"Hey." She bit her lip and stared at him. "Would you mind if I come in?"

Hayden looked down at his pajama pants and grey t shirt. "Sure." He said.

He showed Penny in to his apartment, and ushered her to his couch.

His apartment was a bit of a mess, but she didn't appear to notice. Neither had Kara "What's up?" He asked, as they both sat down.

"I wanted to ask you about something."

"About what?"

"About Randy."

Hayden rolled his eyes, but tried not to let her see it. "What about him?"

"Randy's doing drugs."

"I know."

"No, he doing coke." She explained. "More than he normally would do something stupid like that."

Hayden put his hand to his head, and rubbed his temples. He wasn't all together prepared for this.

"When you say coke, you mean cocaine right?" He said, verifying for the record.

Penny rolled her eyes at him.

He took a deep breath in, and tried to ground himself inside the cushions of the couch. So he could avoid this conversation.

"Yes." Penny answered finally. "He's doing cocaine."

"And that's not usually what he does?"

"No." Penny mumbled. "I mean yes, but he's always just trying to look cool. It's different this time." She said adamantly. "I'm worried about him."

Hayden fell back on the couch. He felt tired all of a sudden. "How often?"

"I have seen him do it twice in a month." Penny said carefully.

Hayden shook his head. "I thought his libido was his drug of choice." He mumbled to himself. "Isn't he just experimenting Penny?" He asked finally. "I certainly don't condone it, but twice isn't exactly off the chart."

Penny shook her head. "That's only twice in *my* presence." She exclaimed. "I know he's doing it more." She looked him, desperately, in the eyes. "It just feels wrong this time. It feels dangerous."

"It's always dangerous." Hayden told her. "Cocaine is dangerous, right from the moment it leaves Columbia, or Guatemala, or wherever the hell he got if from. He's not playing a game Penny. This could get bad. You're right to be concerned."

"Yeah I know. That's what I mean." She told him.

"And why now?" Hayden asked. "Is something wrong?"

There was usually an underlying reason for these things, Hayden was curious to get to it.

Penny shrugged and nodded as if he correct. "Two of his clients let him go lately." She answered softly. "They thought he was doing a good job, but they couldn't afford his services anymore. Randy is finding it hard to solicit new business. He's been kind of depressed about it."

Hayden nodded. "Yeah, ok, I get it."

"It's really scary out there."

"Yeah."

"Jobs seem to be disappearing all the time. I heard on the news last week that an airline announced they are cutting five thousand jobs, and before that, the car industry announced it was closing in Australia."

"Well…Australia has trouble competing in a globalized market place." Hayden said awkwardly.

"What does that mean?" She asked, confused.

"If our wages are too high, and our working conditions are too stringent. If we refuse to compromise." Hayden shrugged. "I mean, In Asia, people work six days a week. Twelve hours a day, in an electronics factory, but they'll never be able to afford the electronics, that they spend all day making."

"So what are you saying?"

"I'm saying we *can* afford electronics." Hayden scratched his head. "I'm not sure what I'm saying. The economy has worried me for a while now." He admitted.

Hayden realized that he wasn't going anywhere with this conversation. He was supposed to be lifting her up, not dragging her down. He really *did* feel tired now.

"You think Australians take too much for granted?"

"I don't know." Hayden said softly. "I know how lucky I am to live in Australia, and be free, and have good working conditions. I know how lucky I am to have a job and make my own money, but it's not for me to say who takes what for granted."

"So what has this got to do with Randy?" She asked confused.

Hayden looked in the direction of his kitchen. He needed another hot coffee. This conversation was going well off track

"We'll it's all interconnected, but really nothing." He told her.

Hayden didn't want to explain the economy. She wasn't interested anyway.

"So what can I do to give him confidence?" She asked, confused.

"Be supportive. Help him with his advertising. If that doesn't work, tell him that Australia is protected by a resources boom, and we always bounce back." Hayden said ironically.

"Would you talk to him?" Penny asked being optimistic.

Hayden ran his fingers through his hair. "I don't know Penny. I don't know why you came to *me*. I don't know what I can do for the guy. He's never taken much notice of me."

"He thinks the world of you Hayden."

"He makes fun of me Penny."

"He's always talking about his friend the doctor."

"I'm not a doctor, and I'm not his friend." Hayden said.

"Yeah but you're going to be a doctor."

"I have to pass my board exams first."

"You're the smartest person I know Hayden. That's why I came to you." She pleaded with him. "I mean what if he overdosed or something? What would I do?"

Hayden shrugged. "Call 000."

"What would a doctor do, if he overdosed?"

"A shot of adrenalin to the heart, and a whole lot CPR." He sighed. "You should just pray."

"I am already doing that."

"Penny, this sounds pretty bad. Have you ever thought about leaving him? I've seen where this can lead."

"I'm not abandoning him Hayden." She said annoyed.

"But what about *you*?" Hayden pleaded with her. "Do you ever try cocaine with him?"

Penny sharply shook her head from side to side. "How could you ask me that? No! I never tried it." She scolded him.

"It's called peer pressure Penny." Hayden tried to explain to her. "Since you know he cheats on you, and you stay with him. I'm guessing you're not as resilient as you think you are."

"We are not exclusive, and that's none of your business! I don't do drugs." She said, hurt.

"Ok." Hayden patted her on the back. He was careful not to touch her skin. The last thing he needed was to get any kind of medical, or emotional reading from her. He was too tired and exhausted to try and block it out.

"I'll try to talk to him." He said finally. Swallowing every ounce of pride in his body.

"Thank you. Hayden." She said sincerely.

"I might not be straight away, but I'll try."

Penny nodded. "Thank you Hayden. You're always the good guy."

"Yeah, and good guys always come last."

Penny looked him in the eyes.

Then she did something *un*surprising. She leaned over and kissed him on the lips. She held it for a moment.

"Why do you do that?" He asked her.

Penny grinned to herself. "I don't know." She smiled at him coyly. "Every time I'm around you, I have this feeling...I feel like I'm a fly, trapped in your net." She shrugged. "I want to kiss you."

"And I'm the spider in this scenario?"

"Yeah."

Hayden fell back on the couch. "Ok." He said confused. "Just don't tell your boyfriend. Ok." He mumbled.

"Just don't tell your girlfriend." She countered.

"You know I don't have a girlfriend."

"You should." She told him.

"I wish I had a girlfriend." He said, slightly embarrassed.

Penny nodded. "I don't know what's holding you back." She smiled at him again, and then kissed him on the cheek, before she got up to leave. "I'll see you later"

Hayden scratched his head. He never quite knew what was going on around here.

Chapter 12

Hayden had just swam 40 laps at the pool He had just walked home from the aquatic center, and he was running a towel through his hair, when Kara showed up at his bathroom door.

Apparently, she just let herself in, without knocking.

He sighed. He wasn't in the mood for visitors today.

He was in the process of moving on, and in doing so, he was ready to watch his fifth consecutive *Die Hard* movie. He was also taking pride in wallowing, with ice cream and chocolate topping, on the couch.

His brain needed rest. Especially after his exams, and then the humiliating episode with Kara. However, now she was standing right in front of him.

"I knocked on your door but you mustn't have heard me." She practically whispered.

Hayden thought about Kara being with Randy again, and all the hurt came rushing back to him. He thought about the two of them being together, and the things they would have said about him, behind his back.

Hayden looked upon her. Her face was all red, and there was something not right with her. She was upset.

Not that he had the patience for her, or her state of mind.

"Is this Halloween?" He asked, mumbling.

Kara was seriously in a ballerina outfit.

She was in tights, a skirt, and a leotard. She had fresh makeup on, and white ballet slippers, laced all the way up her ankles.

He had been thinking of her lately, as public enemy number one, but looking at her now. She was just a young girl, with red hair. She had a cute, confused, look on her face, and she was in a ballerina costume.

"No." she said exasperated.

"What's going on?" He asked, confused, and distracted. He looked again, at her outfit.

"I was wondering… if you could…. would you help me?"

Hayden looked at her confused. "Help you with what?"

"With my friend." Kara told him quickly. "We were practicing for her ballet recital." She said slowly. "We had some wine, and then we were being stupid. Then she fell over, and hit herself pretty hard on the coffee table."

Hayden was taken aback. "What." He wiped at his chlorine affected eyes.

Hayden touched Kara's hand, to calm her, and he got a flash. She was suffering an enormous amount of anxiety about something.

"I rushed right over" Kara continued. "But I need your help. I think she's hurt." She breathed in deeply. "I really need you to come with me…please?"

"How bad was it? Was there blood?"

"No. Maybe. I don't know. I don't think so." She stammered.

"And it just happened?" Hayden asked, trying to refocus.

"Yes. Just now." Kara affirmed. "I ran straight out, to come get you." She told him, desperately.

"And you said she fell over?" Hayden clarified.

"Yeah." Kara nodded her head. "She's a ballet dancer. She was practicing her routine for the showcase, and she tripped over the furniture or something. The coffee table. You have to help her... Would you help her?"

"What apartment number is it?"

"14C." Kara said softly.

Hayden grabbed his make shift, medical bag, from the cabinet, and threw some shoes on. He didn't really have time to stop and think on this one.

He closed his door and started walking towards the elevator.

He immediately put his hand on Kara's back. He was trying to gently nudge her forward because she was shaken, and slow to move.

As he got to the elevator he pressed the button. He practically had to push Kara in, because she was tightening up, and ridged.

"Is the apartment unlocked?" He asked her softly.

"Yeah." Kara mumbled. "It's just three floors up." She informed him.

The elevator made it quickly up to the fourteenth floor. Then they ran to Lucy's door, and Kara threw it open.

The apartment was in disarray. All the furniture had been moved back, against the wall, to create a dance space.

The phone, and some books, were on the ground. The coffee table was at an angle. Then he saw Lucy.

The girl was on the floor. She was a very thin, and agile, young girl.

Lucy had blonde hair, and she looked so delicate.

Her hair was so blonde it was practically white. She also had the whitest skin he had ever seen. Her eyes were narrow but closed. Her hair was thin and soft. Her forehead was broad, but she had a small nose, and her lips had, bright pink lipstick, on them.

She had the most petite frame, and she was wearing a leotard, and tights, as well.

The girl was out cold.

Hayden rushed towards her. He got down on his knees, and bent down over her. He looked upon her desolately.

"You didn't tell me she was unconscious." Hayden complained.

"She wasn't. Not when I left." Kara moaned. "She was talking to me. I swear."

Hayden *had* seen this girl before. Everything started to make sense. It made sense that she was friends with Kara.

Hayden surveyed the scene, assessed her body position, and then put his hands on her shoulders. He closed his eyes.

She had a lot of bruises, but you couldn't see them yet. They would form tomorrow, when the blood rushed towards them.

Her body was disrupted. Her organs seemed to be intact... but wait, no, there were two broken ribs. One of them was non-displaced, the other one, *fuck*... Hayden pulled down Lucy's Leotard, so he could see her chest.

Her belly was distended. She had internal bleeding. There was a sickening yellow mark around her left ribs.

Hayden grabbed a blanket, from the couch behind him, and covered the girl with it.

He jumped up and called 000 on the nearest working phone.

It was a mobile on the coffee table. He called the police and told them that there was a girl here. She had fallen, and she needed an ambulance.

He told the operator the address, and the apartment number, and told them to hurry. Then he hung up.

"She's got two broken ribs." Hayden told Kara.

This time *his* voice was shaking. "Lucy's lung hasn't collapsed, but it's her bottom rib that's the problem. It has gone into her belly." He explained further.

"How do you know that?"

"Because I know." He said annoyed.

Hayden quickly got down besides Lucy again.

The First time he touched Lucy, there was too much adrenalin. He didn't feel her pain, but this time, he did feel it. The girl was in a lot of pain. She even had a hairline skull fracture.

Lucy had hit her head, but luckily there was no serious head laceration. It was just her ribs that had taken the brunt of the fall.

Luckily there was no swelling in the brain. Also, just as lucky, there was no real damage to her spinal cord. It was just the internal bleeding, and that was serious.

He started talking. More to himself, than to Kara, but he couldn't help but say it.

"Do you know how much force it takes to break a rib? She must have fallen with some velocity?"

Hayden grabbed Lucy's arm, and tried to feel the extent of her injuries. He wanted to see if there was anything he was missing, but he wasn't missing anything.

The main problem was still clear. A broken rib, stabbing into her stomach.

Kara grimaced as she watched him. She didn't know what to do with herself. She just stood there, staring at him.

Hayden was doing little more than mentally examining her friend. Hayden finally broke away and looked up at Kara.

At that point, Lucy's pain was hardly bearable. It was exhausting, just to hold on to her, as long as he did. There was nothing anyone could do for internal bleeding, except a surgeon, and they would have to operate on her.

The ambulance sounded down on the street. Luckily they lived in the heart of the city. It came incredibly quickly.

Hayden waited over the girl's tiny body.

He held her hand, and he was focusing all of his energy *into* her. Then the paramedics rushed in.

It was surreal. They put her on a back board. Asked a few questions. Then took her away.

When Hayden answered the questions, he kept emphasizing her broken ribs, and distended belly. Hopefully they would diagnose the problem as quickly as possible.

Then they left without him. Kara didn't demand to go with them either. She just stood there. Staring out, at what was going on around her.

Hayden looked at her. She was in a mild case of shock. Hayden put his arms around her, and hugged her tightly.

"It's going to be ok." He told her.

"I swear I didn't know she was unconscious." Kara cried, looking at him desperately. "Lucy was talking." She proclaimed. "She said she was hurt, but I would have called an ambulance earlier, if I thought it was more serious. I swear, I would have!" she tried to persuade him. "I didn't know that it was this bad."

"It's ok Kara." Hayden tried to reassure her. He kissed her on the forehead. "She'll going to be fine. The ambulance came really quickly."

"But I should have called earlier." She sobbed again, resting her head on his shoulder.

"It's going to be fine. We can go see her. We can go see for ourselves, that she's going to be fine."

Hayden tightened his grip around her. He felt her body pressed right up against him. She gripped him back, like a vice clamp. She held him so tightly, and wouldn't let go.

Finally, after some time, she pulled back, and stepped away.

"Well go now." He told her. "She'll be ok." He assured her.

Kara smiled at him wearily, but she kept giving him a funny look. She knew something didn't add up here.

Hayden was showing his cards, but he had to do that, if he was going to diagnose her friend that quickly.

Chapter 13

The admittance desk at the hospital was not busy at this time of night.

Hayden had gone swimming late today. So it was already eight o clock, by the time, he and Kara, got to the hospital.

Hayden used his employee, inside information, to seek out, what was going on with Lucy. One of the nurses who's name was Rita, had been in the trauma room, when Lucy arrived.

She explained what had occurred. The doctors had immediately diagnosed Lucy's displaced rip fracture. They had stabilized her, given her some medicine, and then sent her to the operating room.

The doctors up on *that* floor, had been working on Lucy for half an hour. All signs were good, so far.

Hayden checked his watch again, as he went back to Kara.

Kara was invariably hanging off him. In fact, he was practically holding her up. News of Lucy's condition made her even more disconcerted.

She actually needed his steady grip to stay vertical.

Hayden knew there were some people around, who *couldn't* handle the sight of blood at all. Nor could they even hear about it. Kara seemed to be one of those people. She was squeamish, and she wasn't coping.

Eventually he helped Kara to the waiting room. She was so weak. She practically fell into the chair. She rested her head on his shoulder.

Hayden waited next to her, as he was holding on to her.

He wasn't feeling his best either. Eventually he got up, and got her a can of soda, and a chocolate bar, from the vending machine.

She didn't touch them at first. She just sat there, on the waiting room chairs, staring into space.

Finally Kara turned to him. She looked at him with her delicate, wide, and red eyes. "Thanks for coming to the hospital with me."

"I'm glad to be here." Hayden replied. He took her hand and squeezed it.

"Lucy was doing an arabesque when it happened." She told him feebly. "I can't believe I let her get drunk."

Hayden shook his head. "No one ever wants to end up here, Kara." He told her formidably. "Things go wrong, and this is where people end up."

"This is the world you live in."

Hayden shrugged. "I'm on the other side of the waiting room."

Kara sat in silence for a long time.

Hayden just sat there, resting against the back of the chair. Occasionally he would close his eyes. Occasionally he would rub Kara's back, and she seemed to like it.

He whispered to her. "They will have to double check everything, but I know your friend will be ok." He paused. "I know we got to her, in time." He explained to her.

"I'm so sorry Hayden." She said suddenly. She looked up desperately into his eyes. "I'm so sorry."

"What?" He asked confused. "What do you mean? You have nothing to be sorry about." He told her earnestly.

Hayden had already decided to forgive Kara, from the last few days. When he hated her. Her regret and despair was shimmering right through her.

Kara whimpered helplessly. "Yes I do!" She told him adamantly. "I kissed Randy." She said bluntly. Then dazedly tried to explain. "I was waiting for you to come home that day. I wanted to see how your exams had gone" she told him. "But you weren't home." She recalled. "I was waiting for so long, but you weren't there. So I went over to Randy's instead. I kissed him. I didn't want to. He started kissing me, and slobbering all over me."

She hesitated. "I mean... I let him at first, but then I cut him off, before anything happened. I didn't want to be with him. I wanted to be with you!"

Kara started crying. She rubbed at her eyes and buried her head into his shoulder. "I screwed up your friendship, and I screwed up Penny's friendship, and I screw up everything." She meandered. "I don't know what to do. I'm so sorry Hayden. Why would you ever talk to me again?"

She looked up at him with bleary eyes. "Not to mention, every time you see me, I'm drinking alcohol, and usually I don't even drink that much." She cried.

"It's ok." Hayden felt slightly reprieved by the explanation. He snuggled in closer to Kara, considering, he already had his arm around her, anyway. "It's ok."

"But what if it's not." She sobbed. "It was stupid of us to dance when we were drunk."

Hayden finally let her go. "It's ok Kara. You didn't screw up anything. I'm your friend. Our friendship is fine. Lucy is going to be fine as well."

Kara nodded, and sobbed, before she fell back into his arms.

She was silent for another length of time. Then she started talking again. "Tell me about something."

"What?"

"Tell me more about the world… the way you did on our first date."

"I thought it wasn't a date?"

Kara nodded again. "It was always a date. Tell me."

"Tell you about what?"

Kara looked into space for a moment. "I don't know… History."

"That's a pretty broad theme."

"The cold war." She said simply. "You said something about the Cold War."

"It's complicated." Hayden said confused. She was baiting him again.

"Tell me." She pleaded with him, giving him no direction at all.

"The Korean War. The Vietnam War. The Cuban missile crisis. America versus the Soviet Union. Capitalism and communism, and the nuclear threat. I wouldn't know where to start Kara."

"I need you to distract me." She asked him feebly. "And you explained some of it already." She told him. "The world was divided into certain camps: Capitalist, communist, and the third world." She reminded him. "But, as you said, capitalism is a natural state. People like it, when it's every man for themselves."

Hayden shook his head. "That's not what I said." He laughed at her. "It's a little too callous. People like it, when they can control their own destiny."

Kara nodded. "Just talk… please." She mumbled. She remained collapsed on his shoulder.

Hayden cleared his throat. He turned his head, and kissed her on the cheek. Then he went along with it.

He started talking, but it was only what he believed to be true.

"America was the first country to have a nuclear war head." Hayden began slowly. "But Russia was able to replicate it. By that time. After World War 2 ended. Russia had well and truly established itself as a communist state. And America was staunchly liberal and capitalist. Both superpowers wanted to rule the world, according to their appointed, political, ideologies."

Kara nodded and wiped her tears away.

Hayden shrugged. "All around the world, the ideologies spread. The different global nations, asserted themselves based on their allegiances." He articulated. "But Asia had parties in both camps. They were torn by different factions, and Asia was always in contention." He explained slowly. "Many Asian states got torn to shreds, in the tug of war, between the two superpowers."

"OK." Kara commented.

She was simply hanging on his words. Like the last time he gave her a lecture.

Hayden continued. "The Korean and Vietnam War were pretty heinous exercises, and generally, pointless ones too." He commented, using his own opinion. "They were mostly directed by China and America." He explained. "China was a big player in those wars. They thought that they were *more* communist than communist Russia. So they took matters into their own hands."

"Really." Kara asked surprised.

"Well America didn't like that, at all." He proclaimed adamantly. "America thought there would be a communist domino effect; all over Eurasia. So they defended their capitalist position in the region, to stop communism from spreading." He explained. "The hot wars rolled on for decades in Asia. While Russia watched on with a Cold War stare."

"But why would Russia think Communism was so great?" Kara murmured. She sounded like she was speaking more to herself than to Hayden.

"Well…." Hayden began. "Stalin was a stubborn Jackass. He did a lot of horrible things trying to eliminate the bourgeoisie, and the upper middle class. He killed a lot of people…" Hayden grimaced. "But he did take a broken, outdated country, and built it up with communist labour superpower. He did it the only way he knew how."

"Yeah. He was a dictator." Kara said flatly.

"Yeah, your right, which was terrible for a lot of people." Hayden exclaimed. "But as a matter of fact… Russia did modernize, and industrialize, very quickly."

"Ok." Kara said unconvinced. "So what about the Cuban Missile crisis?"

"I'll get to that." Hayden told her. "I have to flip the script a little bit. I like to think of the Cold War in a different way. I think there was some divine intervention involved in the whole situation."

Kara looked up startled. She finally cracked her can of coke. She took a sip and offered some to Hayden. Hayden took a sip too. "How is that possible?"

"It *was* possible." Hayden told her. "Something took the pressure off. I think God stepped in."

Kara blinked twice. "How did he do that?"

Hayden inhaled. "The Space Race."

"What?"

"The space race." Hayden said again. "You know… The race to put a man in space, and successfully bring him back alive. The race to put a satellite in space! The race to put a man on the moon. Ring any bells?"

"Well, yeah, of course, but was that part of the Cold War?"

"Yes, Kara, of course it was." He nudged her. "It was a time in history when the world turned their eyes from the horrors of war, and potential nuclear disaster, and looked to the heavens to find inspiration in the stars."

"Sounds poetic."

"It was." He told her. "Have you ever looked through a telescope? All of space is poetic."

Kara nodded.

"You have to understand." Hayden tried to persuade her. "Both America and Soviet Union already had nuclear technology. That was the problem. They kept building bigger and bigger bombs, to potentially outdo each other, in terms of destruction."

"Really?" Kara asked again.

"Yeah." Hayden nodded vigorously. "Both countries were looking at how to deliver it. Both countries were looking to missiles. They were both looking to expand on Hitler's V2 rocket, but they only had short, to medium range technology, at the time. Russia was the first to perfect the long range intercontinental ballistic missile, but then, amazingly, the order came down from Russia leadership that changed the world."

"What order?"

"Well it came down to a decision." Hayden tried to explain. "Russia had to decide: Allow their chief rocket scientist, Sergei Korelov, to pursue his dream of space exploration. Or force him to keep building intercontinental, ballistic missiles for the nuclear program." Hayden paused. "Russia allowed the dream. They allowed inspiration to dawn on the Soviet Union, and the world. The preoccupation allowed the Cold War to stay cold."

"So what are you saying? Russia wasn't so bad?" Kara asked, unsure.

"I don't know about that." Hayden said dismissively. "The cold war, and the arms race, were all initiated by Stalin, and as I said: Stalin killed a lot of people. You'd have to be Russian to answer that. All I'm saying is, that Russia blinked first."

Hayden turned to Kara and tried to explain his theory.

"If the world had stayed fixated on long range ballistic missiles, rather than space rockets. We could have destroyed ourselves ten times over by now. But no. Instead we were blessed with inspiration, as we have always been. We looked to the heavens and the heavens answered."

"And you think that was God."

"Yes" Hayden said eagerly. "The thing was Kara." He started to explain again. "Russia had to stay strong on in the face of such a Cold War onslaught. For that, they needed money, and defensive weapons, and technology. They cost of a space program was enormous." He told her resolutely. "Stalin, and Russian leadership, had to divert a lot of funds into the space program, which made them vulnerable. They took a big chance focusing on space, instead of war."

"So they blinked first." Kara said, repeating Hayden.

Hayden thought about it for a moment. "Yeah. I mean their goal might have been to put a satellite in space, to spy on America. But the ultimate goal turned out to be a scientific mission to put a man on the moon, and that's inspiration. I think God certainly shined through in that decision." He told her, but he continued quickly. "Really it was just good sense." He explained. "Russia put the first satellite into space. Satellites were, and still are, at the forefront of technological advancement."

Hayden looked around. Everyone left in the waiting room was listening to his space story.

"So, anyway." Hayden continued. "Because of satellites and new technology, long range ballistic missiles could be suddenly detected." He sighed. "That would create time for a warning signal, a second strike, or for a missile to be shot down. Hence the Cuban missile crisis." He explained. "Russia was building a rocket launcher on Cuba to get their medium range missiles closer to America." He told her. "So less warning time. Russia and America had to stare each other down, and negotiate a way out."

Kara was fully absorbed. "How do you know all of *that*?" she asked exasperated.

"The BBC did a documentary on it."

"Sounds interesting." Kara started chewing on her chocolate bar.

She snapped off a portion at the end, and gave it to Hayden. He ate it quickly, and then watched her, as she put her head, back on his shoulder.

"It's quite a complicated web." she said pensively, contemplating the story.

"Yeah. Just remember. There is always hope." Hayden told her.

Kara smiled.

Hayden looked around the room. It was quiet, and ominous, at this time of the night. It was now almost eleven o clock. Suddenly Rita the nurse was coming towards him.

She looked him over as she stepped up. She looked over at Kara. Then she looked back at Hayden.

"Lucy is out of surgery" She told them, reassuringly. "She is going to be Ok. She is in the recovery room." She nodded at him. "You won't be able to see her for a while, but the doctors repaired all the damage." She assured him. "She is expected to make a full recovery. You might want to go home, and get some shut eye."

Rita was speaking to Hayden, but her eyes kept wondering to the ballerina, beside him.

"Thanks Rita." Hayden said sincerely.

She tapped him on the arm. "I hope your friend's ok."

Hayden smiled at her, and then she walked away.

Hayden looked awkwardly at Kara. "You can come back to my place, if you want." He offered. "For a few hours of sleep." He shrugged. "You know it's closer. So it might be more convenient."

Kara, tiredly, nodded her head. "Thanks Hayden." She smiled at him. "Take me home."

Chapter 14

As they came back from the hospital, Hayden offered Kara some left over chicken and salad for dinner, but Kara didn't eat anything. She said she was tired again, so she went straight to his bedroom, without asking.

Hayden joined her in his bedroom, after he had something to eat, and washed up.

He laid beside her awkwardly, but she just smiled. She grabbed his arm, and pulled it over her body, so she was in his embrace again.

This time, Hayden turned on the television for a bit of distraction, but Kara fell asleep pretty quickly.

She just lay against him, as she slept, and he held her tight.

It was late when they woke up the next day. It was about 9:20 AM. Hayden woke up first, but Kara was still out. He just let her sleep, and he watched her as she did it.

The problem was, last night, he had been under the covers with her.

Unlike the last time this happened. She didn't have her jacket, and jeans, and all her clothes on. She was just wearing a flimsy t-shirt that she had stole from his closet

He had been rubbing up against her for over seven hours now. Which would have been fantasy otherwise. Except his empathy and powers kicked in, and he felt what Kara was feeling.

He felt exactly what was going on in her body, and it was a mad scene. Her digestive system was a mess. There were ulcers in her esophagus. She had low levels of gastric acid in her stomach, which was causing her constant acid reflux.

When she ate the chocolate last night, she was eating lactose, and her body couldn't digest it. It left her bloated, and she had stomach cramps.

Recently Kara had bread too, and the gluten intolerance was worse than the lactose. It was causing her bowel to become inflamed.

Hayden had been dealing with it all night.

He felt guilty that he had been the one to buy her the chocolate bar. He forgot at first, but now he certainly remembered.

Hayden let go of Kara's sleeping body, and slowly climbed out of bed.

He checked his watch, got his track clothes on, and jogged down to the supermarket.

He searched the store for some coeliac friendly breakfast supplies. He got some soy milk, gluten free bread, and cereal, and other gluten free products.

As he carried them back up to his apartment, he wondered why she never figured out she was sick. All this time, she just put up with it. Her body was under a lot of stress.

It was slightly cold outside, and a pretty windy day. Hayden had nothing to do until his orderly shift started at 6pm tonight.

As he waited for Kara to get up. He made himself a relaxing hot coffee, and flicked on the TV in the lounge room.

"Good morning." She said sheepishly, as she finally got up.

"Good morning." He nodded at her.

"Are you busy? She asked quickly. "Am I interrupting anything today?"

"Nothing." Hayden shrugged.

"But, you've got all your track clothes on." She enquired.

"I went for a jog."

"How early did you get up?"

Hayden jumped off the couch, and headed for the kitchen. "I was going to make you breakfast."

Kara looked at him for a long time, and then smiled. "I just don't want to distract you today." She told him softly.

"You're not."

Hayden went out to the kitchen and set up his frying pan. He grabbed the gluten free pancake shake bottle, then added water, and shook it.

Kara had realistically been distracting him, all night. Specifically with her inflictions, but Hayden was also distracted by the smell of her shampoo, and the warmth of her body, and the softness of her skin.

He was pretty sure he might be in love with her.

Kara walked out in his mom's blue trousers. The same ones she had borrowed before, and brought back since. Now she was wearing them again. As well as his shirt.

Hayden grabbed the butter and the raspberry jam out of the fridge. He started setting up the breakfast table, and flipped the pancakes, as they became ready.

Kara cautiously sat down at the table. She sat with her left leg hitched up, underneath her body.

Hayden put the plate down in front of her. He watched her as she took a pancake off the pile.

"I hope you don't mind, but these are gluten free pancakes." He told her casually.

Kara spread the jam on the pancake and took a bite. She shrugged her shoulders. "They taste good to me."

"Yeah. You can hardly tell the difference, hey?"

"Are you allergic to gluten?" She asked carelessly.

"No, I'm not" He told her. "But intolerant, is a better word than allergic."

"Oh." Kara said, disinterested.

"I have this friend…" He began to telling her. "She always felt exhausted. With no energy. She always had heartburn, and reflux, and sometimes she found it hard to swallow her food." He let the words sink in.

Kara battered her eyelids. Her head spiked up, as he finally got her attention.

"Well." He continued. "It turns out…the girl had this thing called coeliac disease."

"Yeah?" Kara asked, mesmerized.

"Yeah." He answered. "So she just stopped eating foods that were bad for her like gluten, and lactose, and she learned to embrace a new diet." He explained. "Then, she had so much more energy." He looked directly in Kara's eyes. "It was really rewarding too, because it caused her *other* problems, and now she doesn't have them anymore."

Kara's mouth dropped wide open. She stared at him, as if he had just came up with the theory of relativity. "What other problems."

"It caused her severe period pain." Hayden said sheepishly.

Kara's eyelids fluttered. She sat there for several moments digesting his words. "Did you diagnose this girl?" She asked, stunned.

Hayden nodded. "Yes."

"And she felt full all the time?"

Hayden nodded. "Yeah."

"And she had stomach cramps?"

"Yeah."

"How did you know to diagnose it?"

"I have studied it." He said casually. "I tried some of the gluten free food with her. I kind of liked it. So I buy it sometimes too. That's why I have it here."

"Who is this girl?" Kara asked curiously.

"Just a girl I met in the building." He said evasively.

Kara nodded, and tried to downplay her fascination. She nodded carelessly as if it didn't affect her, but she continued to look at him curiously. Then she curiously looked into space.

She hardly said anything more for a while.

She ate her next few pancakes, and then wiped her face with a napkin.

"Are you working today?" She asked him suddenly.

"Yeah." Hayden answered.

He saw the look of emotional turmoil on her face. She was coming to terms with his stark revelation. She was finally realizing that there was a diagnosis to her lifelong condition.

"Are you?" he asked softly.

"Yeah." She nodded, and smiled humbly. "I should get back to the hospital soon." She continued softly. "Lucy's parents texted me."

"I don't think I can come with you today." Hayden told her quickly. "I have a lot of chores to do."

Kara looked off into space. "That's ok. You have done enough." She nodded at him earnestly. "Thank you for everything." She started to leave. Then she came over and kissed him on the cheek. "I'm glad you're my friend."

Chapter 15

Kara leaned over the sink, in the back of the bar, and dried up the cups that they had used for tonight's trade.

She had her hair tied back in a bun, and she mindlessly did her work, while thinking about everything that had happened, in the last few weeks.

"So have you got any other gossip from tonight?" Her boss, Corey, asked her.

Kara smiled, and shook her head.

"Come on Kara." He insisted. "There is always something happening on a Friday night."

"Well" Kara mumbled. "David Jenkinson left the bar with Carly Simmons."

"What?" Corey mused.

"I don't know what happened." Kara giggled. "He was drunk, and somehow she got her claws into him." She shrugged her shoulders. "I actually had to refuse him his last drink, he was so drunk."

David Jenkinson was a regular who was 'extremely' popular because he was a professional football player. Tonight he had left the bar with a girl, who was, at best, an opportunist.

"I smell a paternity suit coming on." She added.

"Or a penicillin shot." Corey smirked. "Didn't he know who she was?"

"He didn't seem to care that much." Kara sniggered. "She was probably giving him vodka, and telling him it was beer."

Kara laughed easily. She liked to gossip with her boss, as the night wore down.

The two of them were on clean up duty tonight, so they were the only two people left, in the whole club.

Corey, her boss, was a really good guy. He was also really good looking as well.

He had almond hair and green eyes. He was average height. Just a little taller than her. He had a good physique, and he was a good person. He was always dressed well, and he was always well spoken.

Corey was strong, fit and handsome. Many girls hit on him, from the other side of the bar, but he was faithful to his wife. So far.

He just had eyes for two girls. His wife and Kara.

Kara started to clean down the bar.

"She'll be back tonight." Corey said referring to Carly Simmons. "Find someone who'll talk to her, and get the low down."

"I'll see if her BFF Shannon comes in tonight." Kara hesitated. "She can fill me in."

"Anything else happen."

Kara shrugged her shoulders. "No, not really."

"Not that you would know." He commented.

"What does that mean?" Kara asked, surprised.

"Your mind was somewhere else tonight." He said bluntly.

Kara shook her head. "It was busy tonight. I was swamped. I was just trying to keep up." She explained. "It Christmas holidays, for crying out loud."

"We were *all* swamped tonight. That's not what I'm talking about."

Kara thought about that for a moment. "What *are* you talking about?"

Corey stopped what he was doing. He walked over to her. Then he looked squarely into her face.

"You seem different lately."

"Is that a bad thing?"

"No, I like the softer side of you. I just hope there is nothing wrong."

Kara averted her eyes from his. "I don't know." She mumbled.

"Is there a *guy* involved in your new attitude?"

Kara smiled. "Sort of." She admitted.

"It's not that guy, Randy, is it?"

Kara laughed. "No, it's not Randy. It's a really smart guy, but I don't know if he likes me." She whimpered. "Even if he did, he probably doesn't anymore. I kind of gave him the brush off… but at the time, I thought it was for his own good."

"Well, that sounds complicated."

"It would be less complicated if he actually took my phone calls. I've been ringing him for two weeks."

"You've been ringing someone, for two weeks?" Corey rolled his eyes at her.

Kara looked at him. "This guy is kind of sensitive. I'm not even sure he knows how to work a phone properly."

"So, now you like guys who don't even know how to use modern technology?"

"Well he is in med school."

Corey shook his head. "Fucking med school." He mumbled. "I should have known that's who you'd fall for." He laughed at her. "Well, it will be fun, to see where this takes you."

"Probably nowhere."

"If he doesn't like you, then he's an idiot." Corey commented. "It's such a shame. I have to see you with such idiots." He told her. "I would treat you so good Kara."

"Yeah, tell that to your wife." She mocked him.

Corey had his hands on her shoulders, but then he let go of her. He picked up his rag and continued cleaning down the bar. "I wish you'd stop throwing that in my face." He sighed.

Kara giggled again. "You know there is such thing as sexual harassment laws, right?"

"You know I've loved you." He said, incredulously. "Ever since you turned up for that interview. With your pig tales, and your freckles. You looked like Pippi Longstocking."

"Well, that's direct." She said sheepishly. "But thank you. Thanks for asking about me. It's true I haven't been quite myself lately." She grinned to herself, for a moment. "Who the hell is Pippi Longstocking?"

"You know I worry about you Kara." He said, dismissing her last comment.

Kara shook her head. "Why did you marry so young for? She asked, genuinely interested. "Didn't it occur to you that once you settled down, you get bored? Working at this bar is not doing you any favors."

"You don't understand Kara. When you find the right one. You know it."

"You seem to indicate that I'm the right one too?"

Corey was caught off guard by her frankness. "Well… I found *two* right ones." He murmured. "But I'm not hitting on you. I'm just joking around." He assured her.

"Really?"

"I am." He argued with her. Then he looked up at her, concerned. "I'm sorry Kara. You don't take it seriously right?"

"No." Kara shook her head. "I like the flirting" She whispered. "I like it a little too much actually. I'm just trying to figure it out."

"Figure what out?" He enquired, still concerned.

"I don't know." Kara laughed at him. "Guys in general." She shrugged. "And your fantasy."

Corey gave her a funny look. "I never should have told you about that fantasy." He said slightly embarrassed. "It's a comrade thing. We share the field of battle. My wife has never worked here, so she wouldn't understand." He shook his head. "Let's just get back to work."

Kara watched him fill up two mop buckets. Then he handed one to her.

She walked out on to the floor, and mindlessly started picking up bar stools. She put them down again, upside down, on top of the bar. Corey flicked the radio on, and of course it was a slow sultry song.

Kara felt like something was coming over her.

She grabbed the mop, and started mopping up her section of the club. Corey mopped up his section.

Tonight, specifically, her adrenalin had kicked in a while ago, because it was a busy night. Now she was feeling all sorts of funny. All of her emotions were welling up like a time bomb. Somehow they needed to explode.

It didn't help that it was such a hot night in the club. Sweat was glistening on Corey's, hardworking, body.

Kara tried to shake it off. It had been busy tonight. She was all sweaty too.

She finally finished mopping the floor. Corey grabbed her bucket and emptied it. He stowed it away, in the cupboard. Then they were finished cleaning.

Corey wandered into his office, to finish up.

Kara waited for him. He always gave her a lift home on Saturday mornings.

"Well let's go." He said, as he meandered out of the office.

"The thing is…" Kara stopped him, sheepishly.

"What?"

"Well, this guy has done something to me."

"What?" Corey asked distracted.

"Ever since he touched me, I feel like my nerve endings are on fire, or something. Is that how you felt? When you met your wife?"

"What on earth?" Corey asked. He locked the door to the office, and looked at her incredulously. "We were pretty hot and heavy when we first met. If that's what you mean." He explained.

"No, that's not what I mean. Did she add nitrous oxide to your sex drive?"

"What?"

"I just feel funny." She mumbled.

Corey shook his head at her. "I've never seen you like this. You must really like him." He commented, but then he changed the subject again. "Thanks for your help tonight. I'll drive you home now."

Kara shook her head. She walked close to Corey. Then she did something that surprised even *her*. She suddenly, teasingly, turned around. She put her hands on the bar. Then she jumped up on the bar. Then she laid down on it.

Corey did a double take. "What are you doing Kara?"

Kara closed her eyes. "The fantasy."

Corey shook his head. "You're just messing with me?"

"You always wanted to." She exclaimed. "Just do it Corey. We've both been so good. We deserve this, and I can't take it anymore."

"But you have to know. I never thought it would really happen."

"Stop being contrite Corey. We both know you *wanted* it to happen."

Corey looked in her eyes, but she didn't back down.

"This could change things between us."

"I don't care." Kara put her head back on the wooden bar and closed her eyes.

"What is wrong with you?" He asked her desperately.

Kara shook her head. "If only I knew."

Corey thought about that for a moment, but a look of desire crossed his face. She could see it.

He moved around her, and hesitantly started undoing the buttons on her shirt. Then he opened it up. Then he undressed her further.

He rested a slice of lemon between her lips. He sprinkled the salt over mischievous place of her body. Then he grabbed the tequila bottle and poured the alcohol down the middle of her stomach. Then leaned over again, to lick it up.

Kara closed her eyes and felt every sensation he had to offer.

Corey hesitated for a moment. Then his passions overcame him. He basically flicked off his shirt. Then he jumped up on the bar with her. Then he was on top of her.

She let him consume her. It was exactly what she needed right now, and he certainly left it all on the playing field.

She certainly gave, as good as she got.

Kara was still the same spoilt brat she used to be.

This was why she wasn't good enough for Hayden.

Chapter 16

Hayden just got in the door to his apartment. It was late on a Thursday night, and he dumped his suitcase, backpack, and guitar case on the lounge room floor.

He just got home, from being at his mum's house, for the last two weeks.

As he walked home from the train station, he had his stuff clobbered all over him. He was exhausted. The first thing he did, when he got through the door, was order a pizza.

He grabbed his IPad, scrolled the menu, and ordered a hot margarita pizza, and lava cake, via the dominos website.

Eating all that junk food was his version of being sinful.

When there was a knock at the door, he didn't expect anyone, except the pizza delivery guy. Which was confusing. He had only ordered, ten minutes ago.

The girl at the door was *not* carrying a pizza.

His visitor was just a young girl. She had a petite figure, ash blonde hair, and bright pink lipstick on.

She was standing on her own, but she looked very curiously at him.

"Lucy."

She was taken aback for a moment. "You recognize me."

Hayden blinked twice. He had never officially met her before. "I do." He said smiling.

She smiled back at him. "You practically ignore me in this building. Then Kara points you my way, and you practically save my life."

"I just called the ambulance. I didn't do anything." He replied, modestly.

The drama of that night came flooding back to him.

"I'm sorry we haven't met, before now."

"I see you in the elevator sometimes." She said softly. "With your push bike, and your books. I always wanted to introduce myself." She told him. "I know we go to the same university, but I guess now, is *not* the ideal situation, to say hello."

Hayden shook his head. "No. This is fine. I'm glad you came by. I would like to meet you too." He assured her.

He stood aside and ushered her in. She was wearing a light blue skirt, with a pink t-shirt. Her feet were covered in black sandals.

She also still had a bandage around her ribs. Hayden could see the imprint of the bandage, from beneath her shirt.

Hayden sat on the couch. "How are you doing?"

Lucy exhaled. "Better than I thought I would." She nodded. "The doctors say I'm healing, almost miraculously quickly."

Hayden nodded discreetly. "Well that's a good thing."

"Yeah, it is."

He hesitated. "How about with your ballet? Was it an important recital?" He asked, trying to remember the details of that night.

Lucy looked into space for a moment. "No. Not really." She recalled. "I wasn't getting graded on it, or anything, but it would have been fun though." She looked around awkwardly. "Thanks for asking me. I hope I'm not distracting you tonight?'

"No. I just got home from my mom's house." He told her. "I just got off the train."

"You stayed for the holidays?"

"Yeah."

"That's really good." Lucy shook her head. "I mean… when I see you around. You always look kind of… alone…. I'm glad you have a family to go home to." She fumbled her words

"Yeah." Hayden shrugged, at her blunt statement." My mum's really great." He told her.

"Well, to be honest. That's kind of why I came to see you." She admitted. "I was looking out the window, and I saw you walking up the street. With a guitar case, and your suitcase, in your hand." She grinned at him. "Kara didn't tell me that you played guitar."

"She doesn't know." Hayden said frankly. He chewed on his lip for a moment. "So, Kara is your best friend?" He asked curiously.

"Yeah, she is." Lucy looked down, and changed her tact. "You shouldn't give up on her. She'd love to hear from you."

"What do you mean? I haven't." Hayden said defensively.

"Am I the reason you won't take her calls?" She asked innocently. "Kara said she rang you a few times, but you haven't replied."

"No." Hayden said quickly. He glanced at his mobile phone, on the coffee table. It was still on the charger.

"Honestly, I didn't have my phone." He admitted. "When I left for my mum's house. Two weeks ago. I forgot to take it with me."

Lucy gasped. "You've been without your mobile phone, for two whole weeks?" She shrieked. "I think I'd go crazy."

"Yeah, I've been a little out of touch." He shrugged. "I don't usually get that many phone calls anyway."

He wished he had never said that.

"Oh." Lucy looked at him. "Well, you are in med school." She acknowledged. "Kara says you're always studying. I can only imagine how time consuming that would be." She said diplomatically. "But you should call Kara." she reminded him. "I know she's complicated, but it's just that Kara has trouble showing her emotions. She'd love to hear from you."

"Really." Hayden asked.

Lucy continued. "I don't think Kara know what she wants." She explained further. "Kara used to have rich parents, like mine, but now they are struggling. She's sort of jealous of us, that we live in this apartment building, and have fancy cars."

"She's jealous?" Hayden confirmed.

"Yeah." Lucy nodded. "But she's so independent." She proclaimed adamantly. "For a while now. Kara has moved on to her new friends at the club. I never see her as much as I used to." She said sorely. "But I wish I did. She's a good friend."

"I'm sure she is." Hayden smiled at the girl again. "I know she cares about you, a lot."

"Well, yeah. She saved me that night, with you…."

Hayden shook his head. "All I did was call an ambulance." He said again.

"Yeah, but you knew exactly what was wrong with me." She reminded him. "I didn't know at first. I was still awake and talking, when Kara left, to find you."

Lucy leaned forward, towards him. "I hurt myself, in ballet, all the time." She proclaimed. "I know it doesn't seem like a physical sport, but it is. It's so demanding, and grueling to the body." She told him, persuasively. "Kara will tell you. She used to do it with me. She still practices with me, but she doesn't go to lessons anymore."

Hayden smiled. "I've seen a lot of sports injuries. I do know what you mean." He agreed with her. "But I'm glad you were with Kara. It could have been a lot worse, if you were by yourself."

"Kara's a good friend." Lucy said again. "If she still had the time and money. She would still be doing ballet with me. She still loves to practice." Lucy shrugged, and looked around the apartment. "So how was it? At your mum's house?"

"It was good." Hayden told her, briefly. He couldn't decide if this girl was being friendly or nosy, but he continued.

"We caught up with everything, and did all the usual Christmas stuff." He explained casually. "We put the Christmas tree up. Made Christmas dinner. I did a bit of swimming and exercise, while I was there. She lives by the beach, so…." He didn't finish the sentence.

"That sounds really good." Lucy nodded. "You look athletic."

"Thanks." Hayden said awkwardly.

She shrugged, and then glanced again at the guitar case. "How well do you play guitar?"

"Not that well?" Hayden answered.

"Honestly." Lucy reflected. "I didn't see you as someone who owned a guitar." She grinned at him. "You don't exactly look like the rock star type."

"I'm more the ballad type." He blushed.

Then, suddenly, for some unknown reason, he felt like talking. He suddenly felt like opening up, and telling her everything.

"When I was fourteen." He began slowly. "It seemed like everyone had a guitar." He exclaimed. "It was the cool thing to do, and I was always so into music."

Hayden sighed. "I wanted something for myself. So I asked my mum, and she got me a guitar. We didn't have much money, at the time. I worked at a coffee shop, washing up dishes. So we went halves, in a half way decent guitar."

"You had a job when you were fourteen?" Lucy enquired, interrupting him.

"I've always had a job." Hayden answered truthfully. "I've always *had* to have a job." He mumbled to himself. "So I got a few lessons." He told her. "My mum always knew I was the sensitive type. So she thought it was good for me. She thought I'd be able to write my own songs, or something."

"And do you?"

"I've written a few." Hayden blushed again. He had never talked about this before.

"Sing one to me."

"What." Hayden asked stunned. He didn't even know this girl.

She kept staring at him.

"No I can't." Hayden didn't know what to do.

"Please." She persisted.

Hayden kept shaking his head, but she wouldn't seem to take no for an answer.

He found himself getting up. He got his guitar, out of the guitar case. He brought it back to the lounge, and placed it in his lap. Then he started strumming it.

"I'll sing a song" He said softly. "But please don't make me sing my own." He pleaded with her.

"Ok fine." She answered. "Sing whatever you want."

Hayden wasn't sure why a Nickleback song came to his head.

They were his favourite band, and somehow it felt natural to sing it. He sung the song in front of Lucy, but it was really meant for Kara.

As he finished, he blushed once more. "That's a great song." He told her. "I hope I didn't ruin it too much." He exclaimed, as he went completely red. "I never had enough money, to the get the guitar lessons that I needed, to be *really* good."

"You were awesome." Lucy told him, excitedly.

Hayden blushed again, but luckily a knock at the door, disrupted the awkward moment. Hayden went to get his pizza.

He put it down on the table, and opened the lid. He left the lid open, so Lucy could take a piece, if she so desired.

Lucy glanced at the pizza. "That was beautiful." She said, referring back to the song. "You're a really good singer."

"Not really." Hayden mumbled. "But thanks." Hayden dug into his lava cake with enthusiasm.

He always ate the lava cake first, so he could eat it, while it was hot and steaming.

He was also trying to act distracted, so he could escape his embarrassment, about singing.

"I should go" She said slowly, and distractedly.

She declined the pizza by not taking any.

"But I should ask." She said suddenly. "Do you want Kara to call you again?" she shrugged. "Because you can't keep calling a guy, without looking pathetic, at some point."

Hayden laughed. He thought that was funny. "Yes." He said, enthusiastically. "Tell her to call me. We're friends." He clarified. "I'd like to hear from her. Just tell her I misplaced my phone."

"Oh, ok." Lucy asked curiously. "Just friends?"

"Just friends." Hayden answered, almost sadly.

Lucy nodded. "We should be friends too."

"I'd like that."

Lucy nodded, and touched his arm. "I have already got your number off Kara. I'll call you." She grinned. "We could go out for an ice cream, or something."

Hayden nodded, confused. He wasn't expecting... ice cream. "That would be fun."

Lucy giggled to herself. "When we were in high school, Kara and I would go out for ice cream, nearly every Friday night." She said enthusiastically. "Then, recently, Kara got diagnosed with some food allergy." She exclaimed. "She says she can't eat ice cream anymore because it's got like.... Lactose, or something, in it."

"Really?" Hayden said, pretending to be surprised.

"Yeah." Lucy nodded. "It explains a lot though. When we were in high school, she would get sick sometimes."

Hayden looked her over. "Yeah. It must have been hard for her."

"Yeah, well, she might need your help... To explain it." Lucy suggested. "You're a med student. So you probably know what's going on in her body."

"Probably." Hayden nodded. He smiled at Lucy. "It looks like *you're* bouncing back from your injury, pretty quickly." He tried to change the subject.

"Yeah, well... I don't have time to be sick" Lucy said mischievously. "I should go." She smiled at him warmly. "I just wanted to introduce myself, but I'll call you." She got up and turned to leave.

"Of course, if you need some medical advice, for the pain, or rehabilitation." He offered

"I will do that. Thank you." She turned around.

"See you later." She said, as she walked out the door. Her face was brimming with a bright smile.

Hayden smiled too. She was a nice girl.

Chapter 17

Hayden was standing in his apartment, looking in the mirror. It was his friend's big engagement party tonight. At ball room, in a fancy hotel, in the city.

Hayden's friend from anatomy, and biology class, was getting married.

Hayden was looking in the mirror, trying to decide if he looked good enough. He was wearing his dark grey, formal, long sleeve shirt, with collar, black trousers, and black buffed up shoes.

He thought he looked good, but he wanted to look really good. He had been looking forward to this engagement party, for a long time.

As he was getting ready, his phone started ringing, and that caught off guard. The display said it was Lucy calling. She had called him three times in the last week.

Hayden was always a little anxious, when she called. He never quite knew what to say to her. He was always afraid of coming off boring, but luckily Lucy steered the conversation toward herself, most of the time. She would always, happily take over. So the conversation came surprisingly easily.

Notably, it was a little one sided.

She loved talking about any topic he brought up. Movies, music, her dance classes, her studies at university.

Lucy wasn't *just* a ballerina, she did rhythmic gymnastics as well. She was very good at it. She won competitions.

When Lucy was in primary school, she played the trumpet. Her parents were millionaires. Nothing was too good for their little angel.

Kara, on the other hand, had *also* called him twice this week, but he hadn't called her back yet.

Every time Kara called, for some reason, he was always busy doing something. He was busy with extra shift at work, or going the gym, or swimming. But, when Lucy called him. She knew exactly when to dial.

He was always within arm's reach of his phone, when Lucy called.

Hayden was still refreshing his brain, from studying. That's why he hadn't called Kara back. He just needed time, to get some perspective. He was actually planning on calling her tomorrow. After the engagement party. When he, at least, had something to talk about.

"Hi Lucy." He said cheerfully answering the phone.

"Hey Hayden." She said softly.

"What's going on?" Hayden asked suspiciously. There was a tone in Lucy's voice. "Is everything Ok."

"No I'm fine." Lucy mumbled. "It's just…I'm kind of torn about something actually."

Hayden was suddenly nervous. "Why? About what?"

"It's Kara." Lucy began. "She's done something stupid."

"What does that mean?" Hayden enquired.

"Well, she has been kind of upset about something lately." Lucy explained. "I don't know what it is, but she has been a little out of character." Lucy huffed. "Anyway, she went out with our old friend Trish tonight."

Lucy seemed to adjust the phone in her hand. "Trish is bad news, and always has been." She informed him. "She thinks she's little miss rebel heart. Even though her parents are just as rich as mine." She said vapidly. "Anyway, she's out spreading her bad influence, with Kara." Lucy hesitated. "Trish had ecstasy, and they went out to a rave."

Hayden was caught off guard again. "Is everyone doing drugs these days?" He asked annoyed. "I didn't think Kara would do that."

"She never has before."

Hayden thought about it for a moment. "But Kara's an adult." He exclaimed. "Isn't she around this kind of thing, all the time, at the club? Surly she could handle herself."

"Not the way she's been acting." Lucy commented. "I mean usually, with her, I would just live and let live. But I owe her." Lucy sighed. "I think she's out of her depth tonight."

"Well." Hayden said, reflecting on his ER experience. "At every rave, there is almost always, a bad drug circulating." He paused. "Kara would know her limits wouldn't she?"

"She has her moments." Lucy said bluntly.

"A lot of people go to raves. I'm not sure you should press the panic button on her." Hayden tried to sound positive.

"Have you ever been to a rave?" Lucy asked him.

Hayden looked at the floor, embarrassed. "No. I haven't."

"I don't like raves." Lucy said bluntly. "They're always in some seedy warehouse, or deserted office building, with no windows and few exits. Everyone is crammed in like sardines.

Trying to outdo themselves, with the latest designer drug. It's just one big mosh pit."

Lucy paused for a moment. "Hayden" She said suddenly. The tone in her voice changed to a more serious pitch. "After what happened to me… I just have this bad feeling."

Hayden thought about it. He had a bad feeling too, and that bothered him.

For some reason, he just knew, that he was supposed to protect Kara.

"Hayden." She said suddenly. "I was thinking of recruiting you to go get her. I can't do it myself because I'm still on pain medication." Lucy paused. "Also… she won't come home with me. But she will, with you."

"Oh" Hayden shrugged his shoulders. He had never been to a rave before. He didn't know the protocol. "Of course." He continued, unsure of himself. "Where is it?"

"It's at…" Lucy hesitated. "Well, come and get me. We'll take my car."

That was a new development, Hayden thought to himself. He had his license, but he hadn't been behind the wheel of a car, in over two years. Or at least not on Sydney streets.

"Ok." He said cautiously.

He heard Lucy take a deep breath in. "Actually Hayden meet me in the parking garage. I'll see you down there." She hung up.

Apparently she meant right now, this second. It was just past 8 o clock, on a Thursday night, after all.

Hayden put his engagement party plans on hold. He grabbed his wallet, and raced downstairs, to the basement garage.

It was dingy down there, with all the cars. The sensor lights came on, and the place lighted up. Hayden had never really been in the basement before. He had no reason to.

There were a lot of nice cars down here.

Lucy came down, ten minutes later. She kissed him hello.

Just a peck on the cheek, and a touch of her hand. Hayden got a quick visual, of her healing body.

She looked nice though. She had make up on, and nice clothes. She had jeans on, and a purple coat.

"How are you feeling?" He asked.

"I'm ok." She nodded. "I've been at my parent's house, for a couple of days. Everything's good." She said honestly.

She instinctively took his hand. She led him past a few cars in the lot, towards her car.

Hayden was almost bowled over when she stopped in front of the high performance, red, BMW convertible.

It was one of the nicest cars Hayden had ever seen in real life. It was sleek, it was sporty, and it looked like she had just driven it off the lot. The car was in mint condition.

Lucy had no intentions of driving it. She threw him the keys.

Hayden had to take a breath for a moment. It was too momentous. He opened Lucy's door, and she got in. He waited till she was settled in the passenger seat, before he closed it again.

He looked the car over, one more time. Admiring it, as he circled round and jumped into the driver's seat.

As he sat down, in the leather seats, he tried to get his bearing for a moment.

It was intimidating to be in a car, worth almost more than his mom's house. Especially since he hadn't driven in so long. He usually walked everywhere, or rode his bike.

He tried not to let it show, that he was so clueless. Lucy really was this rich.

Hayden turned to her. She nodded, as if to say it was ok, before he turned over the ignition.

"So where is this place? Do you have a street directory?" he asked, anxiously.

Lucy laughed at him.

She pressed a button on the front panel of the car, and a screen popped up. She effortlessly set the directions into the satellite navigation system, which was programed into the car.

It was awesome, and so was everything about the entire car. Hayden had to pinch himself.

He had never felt more alive, in his life, than driving this car.

He put the car in gear and drove out of the building's parking lot. The car was a manual. He worked the gears one by one, as he sped off down the street.

The journey became exponentially easier with the talking satnav program. The car told him where to go, and he just followed its directions.

Hayden silently thanked God for modern technology.

The ride was so smooth. Cruising around the streets. Late at night. In a beamer, with a beautiful girl by his side. Hayden felt like he had just won the lottery.

"I think Kara is in love with someone that is not interested in her." Lucy said out of nowhere. "I've never seen her mope around like this before." She told him.

Hayden glanced at her, surprised.

Lucy hugged her big jacket close around her body. She was clearly still sensitive, about her mending ribs.

"Really."

"I don't know who it is." Lucy said. "I mean, I don't know who she talks to anymore. I never even knew she was friends with you." She exclaimed. "I don't know many of her friends from the club."

Lucy played with the radio, trying to get a better station. "I mean, Kara *always* gets the man she's after. She never usually has to try."

"Oh."

Lucy continued. "Once Kara starts at Uni, she might be on track, but I think she's deferring for another year." She annouced. "I'm just worried about her. I'm not sure she's making the right choices." Lucy sighed again. "But she's been so good to me lately. She has been taking such good care of me. For the last couple of weeks. While I get better."

"Yeah, you mentioned that on the phone." Hayden said.

He changed gears and let the car roar, as it flew down the street. "She's a pretty good friend. I would think." Hayden hesitated… "So Kara has been in the building, a lot?"

"Yeah, like every second day." Lucy conferred. "At least when I'm not at my parent's house. She is my *best* friend."

Hayden nodded, as he pulled up at a traffic light. "She seems very attentive, and thoughtful." He mumbled.

"She cares about me, but also you, too." Lucy told him. "She's always talking about you."

"She is?"

Lucy ignored him. "Wait." She said suddenly.

Hayden slowed down.

"This is it. The warehouse is over there." Lucy pointed in the direction of a large brick building. The place had two bouncer like officials, standing at the front door.

Hayden circled around the block and finally found a park.

Lucy pointed again.

"The rave is in the closed furniture warehouse. I can see the bouncer from here." She told him. "Just give him twenty bucks, and he'll let you in."

It helped that she explained these things.

Hayden took off his seat belt. "Sit tight, Lucy. I won't be long... hopefully."

He jumped out of the slick car.

He cautiously walked up the street, and up to the warehouse steps.

The bouncer took Hayden's twenty dollar note, and he walked in to the abyss.

Chapter 18

As Hayden walked in to the warehouse. The place was jamming with bodies.

There was a makeshift bar, and makeshift strobe lights, and a whole lot of music. It was going to take him awhile to find Kara.

Even if he did find her, he didn't know, what kind of reception she'd give him.

Basically, he didn't know if they were even friends? He hadn't called her back yet, and despite everything that had happened. They barely even knew each other.

Except for the strobe lights, the place was dark. He was looking around for a long time. It took him over six minutes, of making his way around the entire crammed floor, before he found her.

He thought the only reason that he did find her successfully, was his intuition. It was drawing him *to* her.

She was dancing pretty hardily, amongst the crowd.

"Kara." He yelled. He reached out, and put his hand on her shoulder.

Kara stopped dancing and stared at him, slightly disorientated. "Hayden?" She asked confounded. "Is that you?"

Hayden nodded, and tried to yell above the roar of the music. "Yeah it's me."

She looked him, stunned. "Oh my gosh!" She yelled ecstatically.

She moved forward, and threw herself on him. She gave him the biggest hug.

She held on to him, with a closeness and longing that he didn't expect. She did it for a long time, and didn't let go.

"You look so handsome." She told him, as she finally stepped back.

She looked down at his formal, engagement party clothes. "I'm so glad you're here" She told him, incredulously. "I can't believe you're here."

Hayden looked her up and down, then looked into her eyes. She didn't seem to be high on drugs, or at least, he didn't think she was.

She did, however, seem to be extremely drunk. Hayden tried to yell over the music. "I came to find you."

"What." Kara yelled at him. "Why."

"Lucy is in the car. She wanted me to come get you."

"Why?"

"She's worried about you. She thinks you're in trouble here."

"I don't understand." Kara told him. "What's wrong with here?" She shrugged carelessly. "And since when does Lucy ever worry about anything." She concluded. "Why tonight?"

"She thinks you took a drug." Hayden explained to her. "She thinks you're putting yourself in danger."

Kara shook her head. "Well, she should stop worrying." She said adamantly. "Look around. It's not dangerous. Live a little." She grabbed his arm, and put it around her body. "Dance with me Hayden." She said looking in his eyes. Taunting him.

Hayden wasn't sure what to do at first. He wasn't that bad at dancing, but he wasn't that good at it either.

Kara pressed her hips up against his. She put her bent leg, up on his hip. Then her head fell backwards. She arched her back around in circle, then lifted it again, to straighten up.

She looked in his eyes, as her head reared up. It was a stylish dance move, and an intimate one.

Kara stayed pressed up against him. Her leg still up on his hip. Her eyes still piercing into his.

Finally she put her leg down, but she continued dancing, while taking the lead with him. She coerced him, into moving his body, in rhythm with hers.

Hayden closed his eyes.

He let the thumping, electronic dance music, into his brain.

He started moving his hips, and then his arms, and started swaying and jolting his body, in rhythm to the music.

Then they were dancing, together, bumping into each other every few seconds. Kara was letting loose, and she was clearly a very good, trained, dancer.

People were staring at them.

Kara would occasionally take his arms and pull them around herself. Then she would dance in his grip. She continually led him to reciprocate, as she threw in some salsa/ballerina/jazz moves.

Hayden liked it.

It was somehow exhilarating.

He threw caution to the wind, and let himself go with the music.

He danced for a while, and it was chaotic, but it was also so exciting.

He continued, at least until he started to worry about Lucy in the car, again.

"Have you taken any pills tonight?" He yelled at Kara, after a while of dancing breathlessly.

Kara moved in, and pressed herself, up against him. She put her arms around his neck, and started slow dancing, in a provocative way.

Hayden held her. He could feel her body, pulsing up against his.

He looked around distracted. Everything was very distracting in here.

He didn't know what was going on with her, but he didn't want to take advantage of her.

He still couldn't sense any drugs in her system, but he confirmed she was drunk just from her breath.

She moved her leg up against his waist again, and moved his hand underneath her thigh, so he was holding it up. They moved slowly and close. Kara continued looking in his eyes. Hayden followed her lead.

"No I didn't do any drugs." She said finally. "I didn't take them, because of what *you* would think of me." She pouted at him. "I had a few drinks though." She admitted. "I think they're starting to wear off."

"Not from where I'm standing." Hayden mumbled to himself.

He said that softly. He wanted to gain her trust, so she would come with him. The girl was practically all over him.

If he let her continue down this path, he would be *definitely* taking advantage of her.

"You look pretty tonight." He told her.

Kara nodded. Then she finally pushed back. She pulled herself out of his grasp. Then she spun around.

He looked at what she was wearing, and she had certainly dressed the part.

She had black high heeled boots on. A short, black, leather skirt. With a purple, sleeveless, canvas top, which showed her midriff.

She played every bit the rave goer. As the strobe lights caught her, every now and then, she looked sexy in mid movement.

"Thank you Hayden." She said, energetically. She took his hand again.

This time she danced more haphazardly, sort of jumping up and down. She was putting her hands in the air, and all over the place.

Hayden looked around distractedly. He could feel menacing vibrations around him.

There were definitely drug circulating around him. Money was being exchanged for little plastic baggies.

One enthusiastic dealer was bumping into people with a hand gesture that Hayden had never seen before.

Hayden thought that the three fingers, the dealer was showing off, were in the shape of an E for Ecstasy.

The electronic dance music continued to thump in Hayden's ears.

Even Hayden had to admit, that his adrenalin was pumping. People were everywhere, it was crazy. People were bumping up against him, in every direction.

"Go get a drink Hayden." She twirled around again. "Let yourself have fun." She tried to persuade him.

"No thanks." He grabbed her waist again, so she would stand still. "Did I tell you Lucy is in the car? I have to get back to her. If you don't want to come with me. Then I should go. I think you should come though. It's getting a bit intense in here."

At this point it wasn't clear where her friend Trish was. Kara seemed to be on her own, but too drunk to care.

"Oh Lucy." Kara mumbled. "Is she your girlfriend now?"

"What do you mean?" Hayden asked.

"Did she drive here, in her little red corvette?"

"Her BMW?" Hayden corrected her. "I drove."

"Yeah." Kara shook her head. "I can't compete with that." She looked at him incredulously. "You know Lucy wants to ask you out, right?" Kara slurred her words. "She's the one that wants to ask you out, and *I'm* the one who's in love with you."

"Kara, you're drunk."

"So what." Kara yelled back. "What do I have to do, to make you be with me, instead?" She asked him. "Or make you ring me back? Or not go out with my best friend. Why can't you serenade *me* with your stupid guitar?"

"Kara, please, let's talk about this later. We should go. You don't know what you're saying."

"I *do* know what I'm saying." She said defensively. "Is Lucy in the car?"

"Yeah, Lucy is in the car."

"I don't want to go. I want to stay here. Trish said she was going to get another E, and one for me too. That was a while ago."

"That's a bad idea Kara."

"But you should get a drink Hayden! And not be so serious all the time."

"I don't want to drink Kara." He told her. "I'm sorry that I'm so serious." He backed off a little. "I should go. You don't want to come?"

"No." She said to him, annoyed.

Hayden stared at her, defeated, for a moment. He turned around.

"Wait Hayden." She yelled, changing her mind. "Don't go." She said groggily. "I don't want you to leave me."

"Kara, I like dancing, but Lucy's waiting. You have to come with me now" He practically begged her.

She nodded slightly.

Hayden grabbed Kara's arm, and led her though the hoard of bodies, to the entrance. As they were walking out someone screamed, but the music was so loud that most people didn't hear it.

Hayden stopped. He felt something pulling on him.

Something was drawing him over to a certain side of the room. "Stay here." He tightened his hold and Kara's wrist, and looked her in the eye. "Don't move." He told her.

Hayden left Kara, then went to investigate the kafuffle.

Someone had slid to the ground.

They were in very real danger of being trampled on. Hayden didn't want to cause a stampede. He quickly picked up the young kid, probably about seventeen, and carried her out through the crowd, to the entrance, towards Kara.

He found Kara again, and pushed her out, with him. He had the young girl over his shoulder. Finally they got clear. He put the kid on the ground, clear of the entrance.

He checked the pulse, breathing and air way. "Call triple 0" He told Kara, since she had her phone on her.

Kara was sobering up, just enough, to gage the situation.

The young, strawberry blonde haired girl, had vomit in her mouth. He used his finger to try to clear the airway. He pushed her head back to begin resuscitation.

Meanwhile he could hear Kara stagnantly dial the emergency number and talk to the operator.

"Damn it. "The girl had no pulse.

Hayden started to do mouth to mouth, and compressions.

Then the place erupted. Everyone started screaming and running out.

The front entrance was wide enough. People were not exactly running over the top of each other, but it was a dangerous procession. There must have been another overdose inside.

"Just stay where you are." He told Kara. Together they were on the grass, well to the side of the entrance. People streamed out, around them.

She nodded and stayed close. Hayden visualized his breath, going through the girl, as he did another set of breathing and compressions.

Then the girl started coughing and wheezing.

This could have been bad. Very bad.

Hayden rolled the girl on her side.

He waited beside Kara. Then, before long, he could hear both an ambulance, and police siren.

He looked at Kara. She was starting at him.

When the ambulance arrived, Hayden identified himself as a med student.

He told the ambulance officer that girl was ok, but there was probably someone worse off, inside.

When the second ambulance arrived moments later, he let the paramedics take over.

When they were satisfied. He grabbed Kara's arm, and ran with her.

The police were dealing with whatever was going on inside the warehouse. Kara had been in there too. He didn't want her to get in trouble.

He ran up the street, holding Kara's hand.

As Lucy saw them running, she leaned over, and turned on the ignition of the car.

Hayden watched Kara jump in the back. Then he jumped in the driver's seat, and took off. It was the strangest night ever.

Chapter 19

Hayden *did* end up going to the engagement party, after the rave.

When Lucy found out that she was delaying him from his party, she was in a shame spiral about ruining his night.

He told her that he didn't mind, and he insisted he would drive them both home, but Lucy would have none of that. She overruled him. She insisted that he drive himself, straight to his event.

He really wanted to drop Lucy and Kara off, at the apartment building, to make sure they got in ok, but he was driving Lucy's car. It was her rules, and she said not to bother.

Hayden was still hesitant. He wanted to be a gentlemen, and he was worried about how bombed Kara was in the back, but he finally agreed. He drove straight to the hotel entrance, and got out.

Lucy got out of the passenger seat, and gave him a quick hug and kiss, as she walked around the car.

Hayden held open the car door for her. Then she got in, and drove off.

After that, Hayden was a really good mood.

The adrenalin of the night, manifested itself, and Hayden actually felt confident at the party.

Not to mention, he was instantly popular, because a few people noticed that he turned up in a BMW, with a couple of pretty girls in tow. Finally he had something to talk about.

He also got a few drinks into him. So the night turned into a raging success.

The next day, Hayden groggily called Lucy, to thank her, and make sure Kara was ok.

He talked to for a while, then out of nowhere, she blindsided him, and asked him out on a date.

A double date with Kara, but none the less, a date.

Hayden said yes, for whatever reason. He had nothing else to do.

So, now, here he was, at a club, with both girls, on the following Saturday night.

Lucy had asked him out, specifically as *her* date. Kara was supposed to find her own.

Apparently Kara *did* find one, but he *didn't* show up. The guy had cancelled, at the last minute.

Hayden suspected that Kara had never invited anyone in the first place, but it was hard to tell. She was hard to read sometimes.

At the moment Kara was playing it cool. She didn't want to go to the club where she worked, so they went to one of her competitors.

It was a cool place. Authentic, wooden panels on the ceiling. A large wooden bar. A large stage. A bit of boot scooting. Kind of a cowboy bar. He liked the music, he liked the crowds, and he liked the atmosphere.

Lucy giggled. "I can't wait to get you on the dance floor!" She tapped him on his shoulder, and smiled at him. "You can't say no either" She warned him. "I want to see your moves!" She grinned. "Kara said that you were a good dancer at the rave, and I didn't get to see it!"

"I can bust a grove." Hayden said trying to be charismatic.

Of course she was right. Hayden had done some very interesting dancing, at the rave. With Kara draped all over him.

Lucy laughed, and got up. "Well." She said. "We'll hit the dance floor when I get back. I'm just going to the bathroom."

"Yeah, of course." Hayden said. He moved out of the way, so Lucy could slide out of the booth.

"I swear alcohol goes straight through me." She said giggling, as brushed past him.

Lucy ran her fingers across the back of Hayden's shoulder blades, as she left. Hayden got a tingling sensation down his spine. Lucy disappeared towards the ladies toilets.

Kara looked at him from across the booth. "She's right you know." She informed him. "Alcohol does go straight through her. She will have to go to the toilet, about twenty times tonight."

Hayden nodded. "That's a good thing. She's has about 2% body fat. She needs to purge it from her system" He said being sarcastic, but also serious at the same time.

He knew that the girl, the ballerina, was tiny. Hayden didn't think she should be drinking much at all.

He looked around the club. It was a place called 'The Houston Bar', and he was actually having a really good time. He had been here a few times before, but Hayden didn't go out much. He really appreciated it, when he did go out.

He looked at Kara again. He had been watching her closely, since they came in.

Kara may have been alone, but she was still in demand. Hayden watched how carelessly confident, and popular she was.

Half the people who walked past the table said hello to her. They recognized her from The Joker Club, and she seemed to be part of the late night, fabric of society, around here.

Obviously, night club revelers, tended to bar hop from one club to another. Kara's club was just up the road, so everyone seemed to know the girl, with long red hair, and provocative freckles. She was definitely in the 'in' crowd.

She could have picked up one of the guys who walked past, and invited them to join her at the table. Yet, she chose not to. She was watching Hayden

Hayden tapped his foot, and bounced slightly in his seat, to the rhythm of the dance music. He looked around, and it looked pretty crowded around the bar, on the dancefloor. Generally the place was pretty packed. He tried to take it all in; the hustle and bustle.

The club was well designed too. The dance floor, stage, and the theatre screen were up front in the middle. The Bar was to the left. Rolling back in waves were the booths and tables, for people to sit at. To the right, there was a pool table. Beyond that, there was a place where people could congregate, on open seating, to watch the pool tournaments.

"You know she is on the rebound right?" Kara said looking slightly irritated at him.

"Yeah." Hayden began cautiously. "She told me about her ex-boyfriend." He explained. "It was one of many things she has told me, on the phone, lately." He explained.

"Yeah. It's nice that you take her phone calls." Kara said, irritably.

"She insisted that we all go out tonight." Hayden continued. "She would not take no for an answer. It was supposed to be a fun, double date. She said it was a friend's thing."

"Yeah but you know she wants more."

Hayden sighed. "Yeah, I know." He shrugged. "Is that a bad thing?"

"Well, do you like her?"

Hayden was usually so congenial and polite, but something about that question annoyed him. "Is that any of your business?"

"I'm sorry." Kara said quickly. She sat back, and looked slightly wounded.

Hayden shook his head. "I don't know if I like her." He began. "She's really sweet."

Suddenly Hayden took a deep breath in. If he was going to speak the truth; it was now or never. "I mean, there is another girl I like, but she keeps giving me the run around."

He looked in Kara's eyes, and she looked back in his. A moment passed. No one looked away.

"Well Lucy is pretty." Kara started to say slowly. "And she's also rich. You drove her car the other night, and she lives in your apartment building. I guess you guys could easily hook up. "She shrugged her shoulders. "You would treat her well, and she's kind of in your league." She shrugged again. "It's not the worst idea I've ever heard."

"I could definitely get to know her." He agreed.

Kara looked slightly deflated. "Yeah, you could." She answered. "I mean she deserves someone nice. It's not like you have to marry her. You should have some fun."

Hayden shook his head. "She wouldn't see it as fun though. She would see it as a relationship."

"Yeah, that's true." Kara looked in his eyes again. "And you would too. You're not that kind of guy."

"You keep saying that." Hayden said annoyed. "I don't know what kind of guy I am. I didn't expect this."

Kara nodded. She looked at him again, and he could feel her eyes burning with a strange contempt.

"You know…" She began sheepishly. "Whatever I said in that warehouse…I was drunk." She explained clearly.

"I know."

"I mean…I was so out it. I didn't know what was happening."

"I know Kara."

"But you knew." She told him sternly. "You knew what was going on. You walked straight up to that girl, and saved her." Kara glared at him suspiciously. "You were really brave that night."

"I'm a trained doctor, Kara. I'm trained to help people."

"Yeah. I just thought you would be overwhelmed. I thought your plate would be full of 'training'. I thought you should wait till you graduate, before you start dating."

She stopped and looked into space for a moment. "Lucy is kind of high maintenance."

"I don't want to wait Kara." Hayden said, annoyed again. "I don't want my whole life, to pass me by."

"Yeah well. I was confused too." Kara murmured. "I thought we could hang out over the uni break. I thought we could have had fun, but you didn't take my calls. I guess Lucy is a better fit."

Hayden didn't have a chance to reply. He could see Lucy coming back from the bathroom. She was smiling to herself.

For Lucy, the world was back in balance. Her ribs were almost mended. Her schedule was back on track, and her only problem was sobering up in time, for ballet lesson tomorrow morning.

As she came to the table, she giggled again. "The dance floor" she ordered him. "You promised."

Hayden smiled. He took Lucy's hand, and they left Kara behind, as they headed straight down to the dance floor.

As they started dancing, the beat wasn't hard to find. During each song, the spot lights were going wild over the crowd.

There were certainly no love songs, or slow songs. Hayden found himself, getting up close and personal with Lucy, as she danced half ballet, half salsa.

Lucy was hard to keep up with, but much like Kara, she tried to lead, and he tried to keep up.

When the *good* dance songs came on. Lucy got so excited. A song like 'Nut bush city limits' sent her into a frenzy. She danced like someone was shooting at her heals.

Hayden found himself just as enthusiastic during Tupac's 'California Love'. Which was still a favourite among DJs, after all this time.

Tupac actually got Lucy dancing so closely, and provocatively, that Hayden lost himself in the moment. He lost himself in the music. The alcohol swirled in his brain. He kissed her. He kissed her on the mouth, on the dance floor.

He started heavily making out with her. In between all the other people on the floor. It was fun!

When they broke apart, Lucy gave him a big grin and then went on dancing, like it was completely normal.

He guessed it was normal. This was what *normal* couples did. It was how young people were supposed to behave. Life was *supposed* to be this fun.

None the less, at that point, Lucy probably just became his girlfriend.

Fifteen minutes later as they continued dancing, Lucy wiped the sweat of her brow and motioned back to the tables. She put her arm around his back, and started moving, back to their table.

As they returned to the booth, Lucy sat next to him. As they slid in together, she turned her head, and briefly kissed him on the lips again. Hayden went along with it. Kara looked completely confounded.

"Should we get another drink?" Lucy asked

Hayden looked at Kara. She looked back at him.

Kara was silently asking him; if he knew what he was getting into. When he nodded in the affirmative, he could feel her silently backing off.

It was amazing. He had only known Kara for a short time, but it seemed like they could speak, without using words.

"No, I've had enough." Kara said decisively. "I'm going catch a cab and get out of here. You two should stay."

Kara got up and made a move for the exit.

Hayden jumped slightly "But we only just got here an hour ago."

"Yeah, I'm tired." she said irritated. "You should stay. Enjoy your life."

Then she stormed off.

Lucy looked at him. "Kara gets in a mood sometimes. You just have to let her go" She shrugged. "I can't believe *anyone* would stand her up."

Hayden nodded. "I guess." He said confused.

He had no idea what his next play was. For the first time in his life, it was out of control.

"I'll go get another drink?" He asked Lucy.

Lucy nodded.

Hayden tried to let himself go, and enjoy the rest of his night. However, now, apparently, he had a girlfriend.

He had to try and figure out; what having fun looked like.

Chapter 20

Hayden spent most of the night, last night, at the club with Lucy.

Tonight his orderly shift, at the hospital, finished at midnight. He couldn't have measured the fatigue he was feeling. He didn't *ever* remember, feeling so tired.

He finally got to his building lobby at about 12:30am, and sluggishly got his mail, out of the mail box.

He ripped open four letters during his time in the elevator. His letters incorporated two bills, his credit card statement, and a letter from *Animals Asia*, which was his favorite charity.

Hayden groggily got out of the elevator and made his way to his apartment. All he could see, as we walked down the hall, was a young girl sitting in the hallway, next to his front door. She had red hair and freckles.

It was Kara.

"Hi." He said awkwardly, as he came towards her.

"Hi." She said softly.

"Is anything wrong?" He asked, worried.

Kara looked up. Her red hair was up in a loose, messy bun. Her features were a little fatigued.

Kara smiled at him warmly. Then she slowly held up her left hand. It had something shiny in it. "I stole your keys."

"What?" He asked, stunned.

"You're keys." She told him again, holding them out.

"There they are!" He said, bewildered. "I've been going crazy, looking for those keys. I couldn't find them anywhere." He hesitated. "When did you steal my keys?"

"At the club. Last night." She told him, bluntly. "You left them sitting on the table. So I put them in my bag, for safe keeping. Then I forgot to give them back to you."

"I thought I lost those!" He said earnestly. "I had to get Randy to let me in last night." Hayden grinned. "And he wasn't impressed."

Kara laughed. "Good." She muttered. "He finally got a taste of his own medicine."

Hayden continued to stare at her. "I had to go to the hardware store, and get another key cut."

"I'm sorry." She told him, softly. "I should have let you know. I should have texted you."

"That's fine." He said. "You can bring them back now. In the middle of the night."

"Yeah well." Kara shrugged. "I only worked half the night, tonight. I just got here, a few minutes ago." She paused. "Looks like we worked the same shift." Then she added softly. "But I wouldn't have just barged in… if I thought… I mean I knew Lucy wouldn't be here tonight. She's at her parent's house."

Kara's seemed despondent. Her voice was soft and raspy, and she looked somehow, defeated.

"We haven't got that far yet." He said, honestly, since he had only been dating for two days.

"Yeah. I know." She said softly.

"Well." He shrugged. "Do you want to come in?"

Kara nodded.

Hayden let himself in his apartment, with his *new* keys. Then grabbed the old ones out of her hands, as he walked past.

He walked in and flicked on the TV, out of habit.

"Oh great, the news is on." He mumbled to himself.

"What?" Kara asked curious.

"The news." Hayden smirked. "If you can call it that." His voice went into a mumble again.

Kara grinned at him, because she had caught what he said. "Why couldn't you call the news, the news?" She asked, amused.

"No reason." Hayden shrugged.

"Tell me about the news." She insisted.

"No, it's nothing." He tried to brush her off.

"Tell me." She yelled at him.

"Come on Kara." He sighed to himself.

He looked in her eyes, and she continued staring at him, intently.

"It's trivial and shallow." Hayden finally said, beginning to answer her question. "Commercially sponsored entertainment."

"Why?" Kara asked.

"It doesn't matter. I'm not going to drag you into a global affairs lecture again. Not like this." He responded.

"I want the global affairs lecture."

Hayden smiled. "No you don't."

"Yes I do." She argued.

Hayden shook his head. "It's rarely newsworthy." He tried to explain. "It's irresponsible. It stirs up the left, versus the right. With no responsibility about educating the public about the issues."

"Really." She nodded. "Is it that bad?" She asked, stirring him up.

She fell down on his couch, and Hayden did the same.

"It's not that bad, but it's not that good either." Hayden nodded. "They do try. You get about eight minutes of news in a one hour broadcast, but most of it has no depth. Most of it is irrelevant, or repetitive, and anything of any substance gets pulled straight of Al Jazeera." He shrugged. "SBS world news is ok."

Kara nodded, confused. "What could they do to give it depth?" She nudged him, and lightly kicked at his foot, with her foot.

Hayden smiled gleefully. "Are you sure you want to know?" Girls your own age don't usually care about this stuff?"

"I care." She said defensively.

Hayden sighed, and shook his head at her. "Well, for a start: What is really going on in the world?" He asked her. "What's going on with Africa, or central Asia? What's going on with peak oil? What going on with the environment, or rising sea levels, or growing food insecurity. What going on with humanitarian relief? What going on with the overfishing of the oceans? What's going on with international poaching of endangered animals, or international human rights? What's going on with the suicide rate of returned soldiers? What's going on with the privatization of the military? What going on with corporate greed? Where is the investigative side to investigative journalism?"

Kara grinned at him. "So you're passionate about this then?"

Hayden nodded his head. "You know I am." He sighed. "The media sponsor every monotonous issue that is cheap to produce, and won't piss off their advertisers." He shrugged. "Occasionally they get it right."

Kara raised her eyebrows, and smiled to herself. Then she ran her fingers through her hair.

"So they should widen their scope?"

Hayden laughed again. "You're an intelligent girl Kara." He looked into her turquoise eyes and smiled again. "Don't worry about any of that now."

Kara smiled, but she stayed quiet for a while. "I know your political convictions, but I don't know much about *you*."

"My life is boring." He said flatly.

"No." She disagreed. "Tell me something." She kicked his foot again.

"But you haven't told me anything about *you*, yet." He protested.

"I asked first."

Hayden shrugged, hesitantly. "What do you want to know?"

"Anything you want to tell me."

Hayden chewed on his lip for a moment. He always felt very uncomfortable, opening up.

"I work as an orderly, at the same hospital, that I intern at, as a medical student." He said finally. "All I ever wanted to do was work at the hospital… But now I wish I worked somewhere else."

Kara looked at him confused.

"I would have liked to experience something different." He confided in her. "It would have been nice to work somewhere else. At least while I was at med school." He paused. "There is a whole other life out there, away from medicine, and I don't know anything about it."

"I get that." Kara nodded.

"I keep saying I should look for another job." He continued. "I mean, I still have the holidays. Maybe I should start looking."

"You could easily get another job." Kara told him sympathetically. "But, I'm the one who's jealous. You're in med school, and I deferred university for the second time this year. I want to go, but I have to earn some money first." Her voice got even softer. "It's so hard when you have to do it all on your own."

"Yeah it is." Hayden agreed. "But I must say I'm jealous of you. *Your* job sounds really exciting."

"Yeah sometimes." She raised her eyebrows. "Night clubs always have something going on. But I'm sure, being a doctor, would be much more rewarding."

"I'm not a doctor yet." Hayden commented.

"You will be though." She said adamantly.

"Maybe exciting beats rewarding." He gestured.

"In the short term." She shrugged. "Certainly not the long term."

Hayden looked at her wistfully. "It's nice that you came over."

"I wanted to see you." She said slowly. "I was rude to you last night, and all you've ever done is be good to me." She sighed. "You were so good to me that night. When you found me."

"I am a trained medical student. I was just doing what I could."

"But it seemed like fate, that you found me." She said suddenly.

"Do you believe in fate?"

Kara shook her head. "I don't know." She looked in his eyes again.

Kara looked away, and started talking suddenly. She started opening up, out of nowhere.

"My family lost all their money in a failed business venture. When I was seventeen." She told him softly. "I got pulled out of my private education, and my dance lessons stopped. I got shoved into public school for my final year of high school."

"Really." Hayden asked her.

"Yeah." Kara nodded. "It was tough. Then as soon as I turned 18, I found the job at the club. I finished my HSC. Then my boyfriend left me, to join the air force." She smiled. "So, I've been working at the club ever since." She shrugged again. "I casually dated, but with no one I really liked. Then I met you."

Hayden looked at her for a long time. "So it wasn't easy for you?"

"Not so much." Kara looked around awkwardly. "Everything got turned upside down, and I never knew what was going to happen." She shrugged. "My parents fought a lot, back then." She sighed. "Every time they did. I'd go outside, and take my dog for a walk. I think *he* was the one who got me through it."

Hayden gestured to her. "Your trials only make you stronger." He told her wearily. "They test your fortitude."

"I was a spoilt little princess for most of my life." She informed him. "Then it all came crashing down. Now I'm terrified of taking anything for granted, in case it happens again."

"Yeah, but you're independent now. You know what you're doing. You can control it."

Kara laughed. "You're always so nice, Hayden." She shrugged. "I only hope I know what I'm doing?"

"You do." He told her.

"So do you." She assured him.

Hayden smiled at her.

Kara smiled back at him, but then she looked into space for a moment. "I should go." She said suddenly.

She got up quickly, and got ready to leave. "Thanks for talking to me Hayden." She said sincerely. "I'll see you later." Then she was half way out the door.

"Thanks for bringing my keys back." He called out to her. Although she was already gone.

Chapter 21

One of the Sydney newspapers wanted to do a story on Hayden, and the girl he saved at the rave.

Initially, Hayden refused the request, but his colleagues at the hospital wanted him to do it.

The ambulance officers were being interviewed as well, and they said the story was worth it. They said it would highlight the endemic problems in society, about drugs, kids, and peer pressure.

Hayden had done the interview last week, and it had been awkward to say the least. Trying not to give anything away, was difficult. Trying to understate his part in it, was also difficult. Especially when Annabeth, the interviewer, wanted to write about a hero.

Hayden wasn't a hero. He was just a slave to his instincts.

The truth was, he was drawn to that girl. He went straight to her.

It turned out the girl was only seventeen, and she needed saving, so he saved her. He knew she was there.

After the story came out, he got quite a few brownie points at work. Firstly for saving some random, young, girl. Secondly, for bringing her back to life. Then, thirdly, for being at the illicit rave in the first place.

He told the story, about the rave, a few times. By the time he got to the interviewer, he felt like, he was getting good at it. Good enough to leave out, anything about healing hands, or his overzealous intuition. Annabeth didn't exactly believe he went to the rave to pick up a friend, but she agreed to write it that way, anyway.

Luckily, the article had a lot of elements in it. It wasn't just about Hayden. It was about drugs, and worried parents. It was also about overworked ambulance officers, who faced horrendous dangers in their everyday jobs.

The girl he saved that night. She had a chance to tell her story, as well, and Hayden was interested to hear, what she had to say.

The truth was, he had never visited the girl at the hospital. He never even knew if she pulled through, or what her name was. Not until Annabeth, the reporter, told him. Her name was Emma.

Hayden was thinking about what the article would be like, when suddenly, Lucy snapped him back to reality.

"What's the matter Hayden?" She asked suddenly.

She took her hand off his waist, and looked at him, from the opposite pillow.

Hayden turned towards her, and sighed.

They were lying on his bed. He was previously kissing her, but he must have got distracted.

Of course it was nice to kiss someone, and keep kissing them, while putting your hands where ever you wanted. But something was holding him back. He was half into it, and half out of it. His couldn't focus.

He had been 'dating' Lucy for about three weeks now. This was their fourth make out session, not including the one at the club. They hadn't gone any further though.

Lucy thought that was her decision. She wasn't ready. Not after what had happened with her ex-boyfriend, which was a whole another story.

The thing was, Lucy was so outgoing.

Hayden had to shift gears to keep up with her. She loved, nothing more, than to go out to fancy restaurants. Or go out dancing. Or go to her friend's house, for a party.

She had so much energy. They hardly had time for physical intimacy anyway. She partied till she dropped

Lucy was a little immature, and Kara was right; a little high maintenance. She was always asking him to do things for her. Can you pick this up? Can you circle the date in your calendar for that event? Can you massage my shoulders where I hurt them in ballet today? Can you meet here, at this time?

She was also quick to get upset, when things didn't go her way. She was also a little judgmental sometimes, but then again, she was daddy's little rich girl. It wasn't surprising.

If Hayden wasn't in love with someone else, he probably could have handled all that.

Shifting gears, for him, was long overdue.

It's not like *he* was perfect anyway. He was, maybe, slowing her down, more than she was speeding him up. He just wasn't sure if *this* was what he wanted.

"Come on Hayden, What's the matter?" Lucy asked again, stroking his hair with her fingers. The two of them were kind of intertwined. One of her legs, was up over his hip, as they lay facing each other.

Hayden looked at her. She had a sweet, but accusing expression on her face. He never knew what she was going to say, because sometimes she was blunt, and imprudent, as well.

Hayden was focusing on something different though. He was in the midst, not only trying to sort out his feeling for her, but also figuring out, how to block out his empathy towards her.

He hated to say it, but Lucy was acting as his guinea pig.

Every day, when he touched her. He would work on blocking out everything that she was feeling from her mind, and inside of her body.

His intuition and empathy was such a problem.

He needed to practice on someone, so he could figure it out. He needed to figure out exactly how to block it all out, and keep his feelings separate from hers, and anyone else's.

He was constantly working on being neutral. He tested himself more every day, and he was getting better at it.

He successfully doing it, now. With his hand on Lucy's back; he didn't feel anything. Not the last twinges of pain, from her mending rib bones, or her constant confusion about her ex-boyfriend.

If her mood changed quickly, or there was a stab of pain, he would get a flash of it. But for now, he was successfully blocking it all out.

"The article came out today." Hayden said softly.

"What article."

Hayden looked at Lucy again curiously. She could be kind of self-centred when she wanted to be. "The article about the girl, at the rave. The one who almost died."

"Oh, that kid, wow. That is so freaky." Lucy began. "Who could have known?" She contemplated. "You'd go in to for Kara, and come out with someone else? I sent you in there, and you changed history."

"Yeah it was kind of a trip."

"But you just pulled her out, and called the ambulance, didn't you? The article is really about the ambulance drivers. Didn't you tell me that?"

"Well technically, Kara called the ambulance."

"Kara did?" Lucy asked suspiciously. "What were you doing?"

"Doing resuscitation." Hayden said softly.

"You resuscitated her?" Lucy shrieked. "You didn't tell me that."

"I didn't want to make a big deal about it." Hayden started to explain. "I don't know exactly what happed." He said, distracted. "It all happened so quickly."

He suddenly felt disorientated. He felt like a soldier, who couldn't talk about their war time experiences. He couldn't talk to Lucy about this, because she wouldn't understand.

"You should go to the newsagency and get it." She said excitedly. "We could read it together."

Hayden changed tact. He suddenly felt claustrophobic in his own bedroom. He couldn't be here right now. He had to read the newspaper article on his own, and think it through. He need to contemplate the story, and how it affected the rest of his life, like he always did.

He had to get out of here.

"Actually, I just remembered" He said suddenly" I have to go." He tried to explain. "I was supposed to meet a friend of mine. I have to discuss a project that we are working on at university." He continued, lying.

He slowly untangled himself from Lucy. "I'm sorry. I have to go." He said, disorientated.

Lucy pursed her lips. She looked at him doubtfully. "You have to go now?"

Hayden got up. "I'm really sorry Lucy. I forgot all about it. I don't want to keep this guy waiting. It's a really important."

"But Uni is not even in session?" She queried him.

"Med school is different. You never stop doing projects." Hayden said quickly. "And I have to do the first weeks readings ahead of class." He mumbled. Which was also true.

He jumped up suddenly, before she could ask any more questions.

He looked in the mirror, and then quickly collected his shoes and socks, and mashed them on to his feet.

He looked at Lucy one more then, then he grabbed his keys and wallet.

He kissed her on the lips. "Stay here as long as you want." He told her. "I'm not sure how long I'll be."

"I'm staying at my parent's tonight." She said softly.

"Well then I'll call you." He touched her arm. "I'll see you later, ok."

Hayden walked out of his apartment. He started walking down to the newsagency, but suddenly, he felt the need to check his mobile phone.

He was right. There was something surprising on there. Kara had left him a message:

Hi Hayden, I was wondering if we could talk, some time. I wanted to ask you something. Text me, if you want to meet up.

Hayden put the newspaper article on hold.

He didn't text Kara back. He did something better. He grabbed a cab, and went to her house.

Chapter 22

Kara's house was a small, box type, brick house, in the close suburbs to Sydney city. The house was one story. It had a small porch, and a grey tiled roof. It didn't look like anything special, but then again, neither did the neighbourhood.

The lady who answered the door must have been Kara's mum, because she looked exactly like her. She had red hair and a few freckles.

Hayden's first impression was that the woman seemed friendly, and she had a nice smile. There were some worn wrinkles around the woman's eyes. She had obviously been through some hard times.

"Hi. Mrs Cooper is it?" He asked tentatively. "My name is Hayden. I'm a friend of Kara's. I was wondering if she was home." He asked quickly and nervously.

"Oh." The lady nodded. "So you're Hayden." She looked him over tentatively. "It's good to meet you." She told him. "Yes Kara's home. She's in her room."

There was a look of surprise on her face. Her daughter wasn't dating anyone at the moment, so she probably didn't expect him.

She looked him up and down, for a moment. Deciding whether he was good enough for Kara. Then she smiled. He must have passed the first inspection.

"Come in." She said, quickly. She ushered him in. Then she led him down the hall, towards a bedroom door.

The lady knocked, a couple of times, and then called out. "Kara, you've got a friend here to see you."

"What friend?" Kara mumbled from inside the door. Hayden heard some shuffling around, and then a chair being moved.

Kara opened her bedroom door. She jumped slightly, when she saw Hayden. She looked at him spellbound for a minute. "Come in. Thanks mum."

She nodded at her mum. Her mum nodded back, then disappeared back down the hall.

Kara looked around her room, and did a quick tidy.

"What are you doing here?" She asked stunned.

"I read your text. You wanted to see me."

"Yeah, but not here?" She said incredulously. "How did you get this address?"

"Lucy's IPod address book."

"Of course you did."

Hayden moved towards her. "I thought I'd surprise you."

He looked around the room. It was a cosy room. Kara did not have a closet, but she had a couple of clothing racks, and some seagrass draws. She had a few movie posters, on her walls.

Her bed was a double bed, with a white quilt, and white pillow cases. The sun was shining through the window.

However, the first thing Hayden noticed, was the dog lying on Kara's bed. It looked like a husky, but not a Siberian husky.

Obviously the dog didn't have a thick coat of fur. Not in this climate.

The dog looked up immediately, and raised its head. It glared at Hayden suspiciously.

Hayden looked back, apprehensively.

"That's Jack." Kara said, motioning to the dog. She walked over to the extremely alert animal, and gave him a scratch behind the ear. The dog seemed to like it.

"If you give him a pat." Kara told him. "He'll stop glaring at you."

Hayden nervously, walked over to the dog, and gave him a pat on the head. The dog watched him for a moment longer. Then he seemed to relax, and started panting. He looked at Kara, happily, with his tongue hanging out of his mouth.

Kara smacked her thigh, and the dog jumped out. "Out Jack." She told him.

She held the door open, and the dog jumped off the bed. He gave one more suspicious look at Hayden, and then slowly and apprehensively left the room. Apparently he was pretty well trained.

Kara smiled to herself. "Lucy thinks she's my best friend, but really Jack is." She told him, giggling.

Hayden smiled, and laughed to himself.

He looked at Kara, and she was just wearing a black knitted top, with a bright yellow skirt. She looked pleasant, and her room was a pleasant room.

"I thought you would actually *be* with Lucy." Kara commented dryly.

"I just left Lucy. She's at my apartment."

"Oh." Kara shrugged her shoulders. She sat down exasperated on her bed. She looked at the notebook, on her desk. It looked like her diary, and she had just been writing in it.

"I can't believe you came." She sighed. "I didn't think you'd come here. I didn't really want you to come here." She told him flatly.

"Why?"

"I didn't want you see where I lived." She said softly.

"What." Hayden asked stunned. "What's wrong with where you live?"

"Look around."

"I am. This is a really nice room. In a nice house!" He said adamantly.

"Yeah. Sure. For a shoe box." She grumbled.

Hayden nodded. "Ok, it's not the biggest house. But this is a nice room."

"Yeah, well. It's about the quarter of the size of my old room, but…it I suppose it's my sanctuary." She smiled at him. "It's nice of you to make your way down here… From up town I mean." She fell back on her bed and stared at the ceiling. "Something I always wanted to ask you Hayden..."

Hayden looked at her doubtfully. "Yeah?"

"How do you afford to live in that apartment building?" She asked bluntly. She sat up, and looked at him curiously. "It's a building in the city! It's a big apartment, and you don't look like Richie Rich. You certainly don't act like it."

Hayden sighed again. "It's a long story."

"Well you came over. You must want to talk about something." She commented.

"My father." He told her ominously.

He sat down next to her on the bed. Even though Kara had flopped over again, on her back.

"My mum was my dad's secretary. They had an affair. Then she had me. Obviously they had a falling out. My mum refused to acknowledge him for a really long time. He offered money, but mum wouldn't take it. She hates him."

Hayden looked at Kara to see if she was listening. She was, so he continued.

"She gave me the option of getting to know him, but I didn't have any interest in it, so we rarely met." Hayden explained. "For a really long time we were estranged. Then, when I was old enough. I finally did get to meet him." Hayden shrugged. "He was good to me, and he really wasn't so bad." Hayden took a deep breath in. "He found out that I wanted to go to med school, and that's when he really became interested. I'm pretty sure he wanted to brag to his friends about his son the doctor, because he's a doctor too."

Kara suddenly grabbed Hayden's arm. She pulled him down on the bed, so they were both lying on their back.

"Really." She asked softly.

"Yeah." Hayden nodded, and then continued. "I got to know him better, and learn about him, and his profession. It was a surprisingly good experience." Hayden said pleasantly. "He's a good guy." Hayden admitted. "Then, when I was in my second year of my undergraduate degree. He bought the apartment near the university, for me to live in...He was looking for another investment property anyway. He already had two. This was his third, and he lets me stay there rent free."

Kara nodded, immersed in the conversation. "What kind of person is he?"

Hayden laughed. "He's intelligent. He's driven. He doesn't play games with people. He's not too bad, actually. I guess I like him."

"Sounds like he played at least one game, with your mum." Kara suggested.

"My mum's emotional. She takes things too personally." Hayden explained. "She probably came on to him. I love her, but she gets carried away sometimes." Hayden shrugged. "I'm sure my dad would have been good to her. If she let him." Hayden shook his head. "It's a shame. I only found out a few years ago that I had a sister."

"That would have been a nice surprise."

"Yeah it was." Hayden moved his hand, across the bed, so that it touched Kara's hand. He wasn't sure what he was doing, at first, but it felt natural.

Kara laid still for a moment. She slowly took hold of his hand. Then they were holding hands.

Hayden flinched. He suddenly got a flash. Kara had had sex with someone recently. It was still on her mind. Hayden didn't expect that. It hurt him actually. He thought she wasn't dating anyone. He took his hand back, and sat up.

That surprised her. She sat up next to him.

"I read your article this morning." She said suddenly.

"What." Hayden asked, stunned. "Already?"

Kara nodded. "I got up early, and went for a jog to the newsagency." She explained, and took a deep breath in. "It was a really important article. It was really convincing, and *you* played an amazing role."

She grinned at him, ironically. "The sober medical student, who was just in harm's way, to pick up his trashed friend." She sighed. "I put you in that position."

"You didn't put me in any position. I wanted to be there." He told her adamantly, but then he recanted. "Ok, maybe, you *did* put me in that position. But if you didn't: A girl might be dead." He continued. "Besides, I was glad to go get you."

"But you were supposed to be at your friend's engagement party that night." Kara cried. "And how much drama can I force into your life?" She asked incredulously. "You were just a quiet humble guy, trying to finish his studies. Now you've dating Lucy Meyers, and you're busy saving everybody."

"Can you hear yourself? I'm a doctor. I'm supposed to save people."

"But I'm distracting you, and my friends are distracting you, and that's exactly what I tried to avoid."

"It's ok Kara. Uni is not in session. I need the distraction. I was going crazy without it."

"But just let me apologize. I'm sorry Hayden."

"For what?" He asked desperately.

"For making you my designated rescuer."

"I was dancing at that rave too. I was having fun."

Kara let her guard down and smiled for a moment. "Thanks for saying that." She shrugged her shoulder. Then she smiled at him, and took his hand back. Hayden let her.

"So the girl you saved" She began. "She came out looking like quite the victim in the story. It's not like, she didn't make her own decision. When she took that drug."

Hayden raised his eyebrows. "So you don't have any sympathy for her? She was only seventeen."

"I had to stand on my own two feet when I was seventeen." Kara told him. "Why shouldn't he?" She argued, slightly resentfully. "Besides she didn't need my sympathy, she needed you, and she got you." Kara nodded at him. "She doesn't know how lucky he is."

Hayden blushed slightly, and looked away.

"So." She began, a slight sadness in her voice. "Did you come here, to tell me how you're relationship with Lucy is going?"

"You texted me." Hayden said defensively

"So I did." She nodded and her face changed to a sombre expression. "I wanted to ask you something."

"What." Hayden asked, curious.

"I was wondering…" Kara took a deep breath in. "I was wondering if you wanted a job… at the club where I work"

"What?" Hayden asked again. He wasn't expecting that.

Kara looked at him sheepishly. "You said that you wanted another job. Outside of the hospital. You said you wanted another experience. Well I'm offering you one."

"Shouldn't your boss do that?"

"He is. Via me." She said bluntly. "I talked to him about it last night."

"You asked him to hire me?"

"You would be doing us a favour." She began, trying to explain. "You're a good guy, and hard worker, and you're smart. You have medical training, and that would be invaluable for us. Especially if a fight breaks out or something." She shrugged. "I mean, it's getting bad. Alcohol fuelled violence is on the rise. Fights break out all the time."

"But do you really think I could be a bar tender?"

"What's wrong with being a bar tender?" Kara asked hurt.

"Nothing." Hayden said, surprised. He lowered his voice. "I'm not sure I'm trendy enough."

"You're plenty trendy." Kara grinned at him. "I think you could hold your own behind a bar."

"What if I'm not any good at it?"

"I'll teach you." Kara got up suddenly. She walked across the room, and picked up something off her desk. She came back and handed him a small, A5 sized, information booklet. It was a book of different cocktails, and how to make them.

Hayden flicked through it. "You're really serious about this."

"I'll be serious about it if you are." She told him.

"I know I said I wanted a job, but I never thought I would get one. Not like this."

Kara closed her eyes for a moment. "I would like it if you worked there." She told him earnestly. "I'd like it, if you worked with me. Besides…" She added. "You can see how people start out there, and end up in your emergency room…You said you wanted to know; what is out there in the world. This job is an all access pass."

"You're right on the front lines, huh?"

Kara laughed to herself. "You have no idea."

"Can I think about it?"

"For as long as you like." She fell back onto the bed and looked into space for a moment. "I could have taken that drug." She said softly, out of nowhere. "I was drunk, and I didn't know what I was doing. If you didn't show up. That could have been me. I'm so glad you were there."

Hayden laid down next to her again. "So am I."

He put his arm over her. He held her close. She nestled into his embrace one more time, so he was spooning her, yet again.

Kara took a deep breath in. "Do you want to stay? We can take a nap." She asked delicately. "My alarm will go off in a few hours. I start work at seven tonight." She said restlessly.

Hayden nodded. "Ok." He went along with it. He couldn't think of a reason not to, nor did he want to move away. "I'll stay with you." He told her softly.

Kara nodded, and closed her eyes. "Thanks Hayden." She breathed in deeply, and then sighed. "You're so good to me."

Hayden put his hand under her shirt. On her flat stomach.

She flinched a little. She didn't expect that, but she didn't mind it either. In fact she relaxed a notch. She seemed to like it.

Hayden had direct contact with the skin. He took in all of his senses, for a moment.

Kara was healthy. Her heartbeat was regular. She was nice and relaxed. Blood was moving through her body smoothly. Even, if not especially; her digestion had improved.

Hayden saw these things briefly. Then he used his concentration, to block them out. It worked. He was getting better at this. He felt nothing except her skin.

He kissed her on the cheek, and she smiled.

Soon she fell asleep, and then he fell asleep too. Next to her. Holding her.

Chapter 23

It was 9 o clock on Saturday morning. The Joker Club was closed, but Hayden was allowed in, with Kara. So she could teach him the ropes.

This was Hayden's second day of training. Yesterday, Kara had spent a few hours teaching him the rules and procedures of the club.

She gave him a tour of the whole club. In both the public and private areas. She showed him the cocktail list. What each of their ingredients were, and where to find them on the bar. She showed him the cash register, and how it worked. Then she explained to him, generally, what to expect from the customers.

Hayden didn't know the first thing about alcohol, but Kara was patient.

She started from the basics. Beer was first. It was the most popular. Not spilling it, was quite a task.

Second were the spirits, and there were seven main ones. Bourbon, Scotch, Vodka, Gin, Rum, Brandy and Tequila. Once you familiarized yourself with the different types of alcohol. Then you could figure out the cocktails.

Hayden got the lay of the land with the; 'Screwdriver', 'Bloody Mary', 'Margarita', 'Mai Tai', 'White Russian', 'Whiskey Sour', 'Manhattan', 'Martini', 'Cosmopolitan', 'Singapore Sling', 'Mojito', 'Pina Colado', 'Sea Breeze' and 'Cuba Libre'.

Basically, at his disposal, he had lemon and lime juice. Tomato juice for the Bloody Mary. Pineapple juice for the Pina colada. Cranberry for the cosmopolitan, and a whole list of others. Then there was also soft drinks, on tap.

Hayden had spent all night last night, studying each different cocktail, and how to make it. He even had to memorize the garnish it was served with. The drinks were even more complicated than they looked.

Most of the drinks were exotic, and making one was an art form. The white Russian even had cream in it, and that was interesting, trying to put it together.

Yesterday, it had been completely cosy. Just the two of them. The club had been empty, and it felt like another world.

Kara was teaching him, and she was a natural. She was good at both the job, and at teaching it. She instinctively based her training on the fact that he, literally, knew nothing, and she didn't embarrass him for it.

Today, Kara was trying something different. The club was still closed, but she invited some *honorary* customers along. These were people that Hayden knew. People who could easily put the screws to him, but who could also afford the drinks they ordered.

These particular customers, had volunteered to get a little tipsy, at nine o clock in the morning.

If Hayden was nervous yesterday. He was practically shaking today. On the business end of the bar, he stood with Kara. She was smiling at him graciously, and patiently.

On the other side of bar, there were four people, sitting on stools, along the counter. They were: His girlfriend Lucy. Lucy's roommate Bianca (who had just got back from a Europe a few days ago.) Hayden's neighbour Randy, and Randy's girlfriend, Penny Lane.

Hayden was self-conscious, in front of these people, as it was. Now they expected him, to serve them a drink.

He wasn't *practically* shaking, he *was* shaking. Kara had insisted that if he could serve his friends, he could serve anyone.

Kara had set up this little shin dig, and he felt like an idiot already.

Kara looked closely at each of her friends. She slapped Hayden on the back, and went around to the other side of the bar. She went and stood with the others.

"You order first Bianca" She said decisively.

Hayden looked at Bianca. She was a tall and slim girl who had broad facial features and shoulder length brown hair. She had brown eyes, and a subtle mouth. She was a pretty girl, but she knew she was pretty, and she had an astute look on her face.

Kara continued talking to Bianca. "You don't know Hayden" She said, boldly. "So give him a chance to make small talk."

Kara turned to Hayden. "Hayden you check the bar." She reminded him again. "Make sure all your glasses, garnishes, and juices are in order. Make sure there is plenty of ice."

Hayden looked up and down the length of the bar, and double checked all those things. "They look in order to me." he said, trying to sound confident.

"Ok, grab a cloth, and wipe down the bar. Give her a friendly greeting." She explained.

Hayden did as he was told. He wiped down the bar. "Good morning Miss, how are you today?"

"Miss?" Bianca laughed. "I'm good."

"What can I get for you?"

"I'll have a Martini." Bianca ordered.

"One martini coming up." Hayden tried to jog his memory.

"You could have ordered something more difficult." Kara said, irritated.

"I like Martini's." Bianca defended herself.

Hayden grabbed one of the funny looking triangle glasses on a stand. He poured his approximate portions of gin, and dry vermouth, and added an olive. He cautiously handed it to Bianca.

Kara was right. It was an easy drink. He went to the cash register and pressed the martini button. "That will be $9.50 thanks."

Bianca handed him a $20 bill. Hayden made the transaction, and gave her the change.

"Who's next?"

"No, wait." Kara interrupted. "Unfortunately, when it's *this* quiet." She looked down the bar at the four customers. "They expect a bit of chit chat. Talk to her."

Hayden gulped down the lump in his throat. "So, Miss, I heard you were in Europe for a few months. How was your trip?"

Bianca sipped her Martini. "Skiing in Europe was a dream." She looked at him accusingly. "It was just when I got back, that everything was turned upside down."

Bianca looked deep in Hayden's eyes. "I found out my roommate was previously in hospital, with a broken rib. Then

I found out she's got a new boyfriend. She landed the only guy in the apartment building, who doesn't talk to anyone, and now he's a bartender, at the hottest club in Sydney." She grinned. "Colour me surprised."

"I can't believe it either." Randy piped in.

"Keep your dogs on a leash Bianca." Kara yelled at her. "Hayden is the best thing that ever happened to Lucy."

"Don't be so defensive, Kara." She argued back. "He asked me a question, and I was answering it."

"Don't fight you two." Lucy said, upset.

Hayden exhaled. Kara obviously had issues with her friends. She was taking the pressure off him.

Kara turned to Hayden. "Wipe down the bar again, and take Randy's order." She told him.

She turned to Randy. "Randy you order for yourself, and for Penny as well. Make it harder this time." She ordered him.

"No" Penny jumped in. I'll order for both of us." She demanded. "Randy is not sophisticated enough to order anything more than a shot of Whiskey, or a boring beer."

Randy smiled at his girlfriend, and slapped her on the thigh. "Order away." He encouraged her.

Penny thought about it for a moment. "I'll have a Pina Colada, and Randy will have a cosmopolitan."

Everyone started laughing. "Very funny" Randy mumbled.

Hayden quickly laughed too, but he started making the orders. They were two difficult cases.

The Pina colada had white rum, coconut cream, and pineapple juice. It was served with a segment of pineapple.

The Cosmopolitan had Lime, pink grapefruit, and cranberry juice. It also had something called Cointreau, which all mixed in with the Vodka.

Hayden made the two drinks nervously, trying to get the proportions right. He finally put both drinks down on the counter. He went to the cash register, pressed the buttons, and came up with the total.

"That will be $21.50" he told Randy.

"Penny ordered. *She* can get the check." Randy said smugly.

Penny gave Randy a face, and rolled her eyes.

Hayden shook his head. "I didn't ask Penny. I asked you. Cough it up." He clarified, trying to sound tough.

"That's the ticket." Kara told him quickly. "Don't take his shit, and besides, I can't believe you remembered all that. Most people *don't* order all that stuff, and for the ones that do. I *still* have to look it up sometimes."

Hayden smiled modestly.

Randy stuck his hand in his pocket, and handed the money over. Then he practically gulped down the drink in one go. Hayden put his change down on the counter.

"You have to hand them the change." Kara said softly. "Otherwise they'll leave it on the bar, while they're getting their drinks organized."

Hayden picked up the change and put it directly into Randy's hand.

This was the *same* Randy, he was supposed to chastise, for using cocaine. He hadn't done it yet.

"And for you mam?" He said talking to Lucy, his 'girlfriend.'

He felt awkward trying to talk to Lucy, with all these eyes on him. He still wasn't sure how he felt about her. It was a complete new experience with Lucy, so he was just learning, as he went.

Lucy gave him a big smile. "I'll have a bloody Mary."

"Are you sure you don't want a screwdriver?" Randy asked obnoxiously. "I'm sure you could use one." He laughed.

Hayden felt his cheeks flush red. He turned around quickly to get the ice.

Kara shook her head. "I'm sure Hayden's drink is more the sea breeze than the screwdriver. Girls like making love. Not getting nailed." She yelled at Randy.

Randy couldn't find a comeback. He opened his mouth a few times, but didn't say anything.

"I think Randy's drink is more the Singapore sling." Penny said, in between sips of her Pena colada.

Everyone laughed. Even Hayden laughed again. He was grateful that Kara and Penny had saved him from the comments.

Hayden made the bloody Mary with tomato juice, vodka, a dash of Worcestershire sauce. The drink had a celery stick in it.

Hayden wondered who came up with these recipes. Lucy accepted her drink graciously. She started to pay, but Hayden wouldn't let her. He waved her off.

He got the money out of his own pocket, and paid at the register.

"Now there's an interesting piece of history." He started to say, as he put the money in the till. "The catholic queen of England, who killed off half of England's protestant population." He turned around, and everyone was looking at him strangely. "I mean bloody Mary."

They continued to look him strangely, except Kara, who was smiling meekly at him. She reached over and touched his arm. "You'll have to tell me about that later."

Hayden nodded. His nerd roots were starting to show.

Lucy looked at Kara suspiciously, but Kara was watching Hayden. Kara was closely monitoring all of his interaction with Lucy, like Lucy was monitoring all his interaction with Kara.

"My turn." Bianca jumped in, ready and rearing for her next drink. "Where is the salt? I'll have a margarita."

Hayden remembered the instructions he was given. He had to clean down the bar after every drink. He got the cloth and wiped it over.

Then he started the next drink. Bianca went on talking to him, as he did it.

"So, Hayden" Bianca started to say. "Lucy tells me that you're one of the smart ones." She said enquiringly. "I mean Lucy said, that Kara said, you've been telling her how the world works"

Hayden glanced at Kara.

Kara cautiously handed the salt to Bianca. She was clearly unsure, of where Bianca was going with this.

"We talk about global affairs sometimes." Hayden said hesitantly, as he grabbed the Tequila bottle.

Bianca nodded. "Can you tell me what the European Sovereign debt crisis is?" she sighed. "All they ever talked about in Europe these days is the debt crisis. It was downright depressing. They are all in a tizzy over it. *They* say it wasn't even coming out of Europe, it was coming out of America, and Europe was just the victim of it."

Hayden finished making the drink and handed it to her. She put the money on the bar. Hayden took it, and gave her the change.

"A lot of European investment banks, and institutions, got stung buying up American collateralized debt obligations." Hayden said wistfully. "CDO's included subprime mortgages bonds that weren't worth the paper they were written on."

Hayden knew that Bianca wouldn't quite understand, but he kept answering anyway, because she asked.

"So many people defaulted on their mortgages in America that the system collapsed everywhere." Hayden shook his head. "But Europe got into their own trouble with sovereign debt. Especially Greece, and Iceland, and a few other countries."

"Ok." Bianca said confused.

Hayden redirected. "But the European sovereign debt crisis, is just debt, in any language." He said simply. "It's just debt that rich nations encounter, to finance their welfare systems, and high standard of living." He continued. "Those debt levels are getting out of control."

Bianca stared at him, fascinated.

"Europe is incorporated, so many of the nation states, can stabilize each other, but now, some are starting to wobble."

"So their trying to stabilize each other, because some countries are in trouble?" Bianca asked simply.

"It's simple." He shrugged. "It's just like anyone who uses a credit card. Some countries have spent more money than they are making. They can't reap enough money back in income, trading, and taxes. So the go into debt."

Hayden didn't explain it particularly well, but Bianca seemed to be following on. "Now those countries have to keep borrowing more, and more money, to finance their operations, utilities, welfare, and high interest payments." He sighed. "You're right. Some countries are doing better than others." He grimaced. "Some countries invested better than others, which was another big problem."

Bianca shook her head distracted. "So what you said before? What is this subprime mortgage?" She asked concerned.

Hayden chewed on his lip. That was an incredibly complicated question, and he was never sure how *interested* people were, in actually hearing the answer to it.

Hayden paused for a moment. "Ok." He said awkwardly. He started *trying* to answer the question.

"The mortgage market was so legitimately big in America." He started to explain cautiously. "Home loans were issued at banks, and mortgage lending institutions. Then those same mortgage contracts, were sold off to bigger institutions, like the ones on Wall Street... This was very profitable." Hayden clarified.

He continued. "Wall Street combined thousands of these mortgages together, and then sold them off to investors, all over the world. They sold them off as something called collateralised debt obligations or CDOs." Hayden paused again for effect. "So, Wall Street was making a lot of money off this institution, and the American dream was being realised, by families getting their own homes."

Hayden paused again. "However... Wall Street was making so much money off these mortgages, they wanted the industry to be bigger and bigger, and they started buying up *any* mortgage they could get their hands on, regardless of the quality of it."

Hayden checked to see that Bianca was keeping up. She nodded at him to continue, so he did.

"So sleazy mortgage lenders, who cared little for the original loan, as long as they could sell it off to someone else, started to take advantage of Wall Street's greed."

"Ok." Bianca nodded again. Everyone else was listening on eagerly. Hayden continued again.

"So they started offering up loans with less regulation. They actually encouraged people to sign loans they couldn't afford to pay for. Or they urged people to take out investment properties, on top of their existing loan. Or they encouraged clueless immigrant to buy loans." Hayden stopped to explain. "Immigrants were targeted because they had no existing credit rating. Therefore had no *bad* credit rating, which made the loans look more legitimate. They offered up these loans through subprime lending." He exclaimed.

"What's that?" Bianca asked, fascinated.

"Subprime mortgages had an adjustable rate, with a honeymoon period." Hayden explained. "The banks signed up people at an incredibly low rate of interest. With no money down. I mean, it was so prolific, they practically encouraged people to lie on their loan applications! They didn't even check their references. They called them 'no doc' home loans."

Hayden paused again. "So the honey moon rate was adjusted after two years, to the *real* interest rate, which was very high." He paused again, to let it sink in. "People knew they couldn't afford the *actual* rate, but after two years came and went. There was a sinister, implied, promise that the banks would refinance the loan." Hayden took a deep breath in. "But they could *only* do that if the price of the house went up." He looked Bianca in the eyes, and she looked back astounded. "And house prices historically always went up. Just like they are in Australia."

Bianca nodded, again.

"But they went down! People started defaulting in record numbers, so basically the system collapsed. Then that caused so many flow on effects."

"That sounds so stupid."

"It is stupid." Hayden looked around.

Everyone, especially Kara, was listening closely. Even Randy was all ears. He had a trustee, to manage his money.

Kara put her hand on Hayden's arm. "Can you make me a Mai Tai, while you're explaining this to Bianca?" She whispered.

Hayden nodded.

"How did they let it get that bad?" Lucy asked, confused.

"Good question Lucy." He smiled at his 'girlfriend.'

He started making the Mai Tai, and assertively answered the question.

"There were all sort of tricks. Using multi layered tranches, of asset backed securities, in one mortgage bond. Which just means that they put legitimate loans, and bad loans together, so the good loans would pay off first, and hide the losses." He paused for affect again.

"There were also shady dealings with the credit rating agencies, who rated the bonds, according to dodgy credit scores, that could be manipulated. Then there were people who were deliberately shorting the market."

"What does that mean?" Kara asked, curious.

Hayden shrugged. "They call it a credit default swap." He said wistfully. "It was like buying insurance policies on a CDO, in case they failed, which they did."

Hayden shook his head. "I know you just got lost in that last part, but I hope you got the gist of what I was saying, so far."

"It all sounds pretty dodgy to me." Kara grumbled.

Hayden finished making her drink, and handed it to her. He even remembered the cherry. He felt like he was doing a pretty good job, on this side of the bar.

Kara reached into the pocket of her jeans, and gave him the money.

Hayden stared at the currency, in his hand, for a moment. He didn't want to let Kara pay. He wanted to pay for her, but Lucy was watching, and Kara wasn't his girlfriend.

Besides, Kara was very independent. He put the money in the cash register, then continued with his story.

"It *was* dodgy, because they never in million years imagined that house prices would go down, but they did go down. In some areas they plummeted. The whole show went up in flames." Hayden bit his lip. "So the banks started to go under. That made even the good loans turn risky."

"Far out." Bianca said, consumed.

"All loans were under attack anyway because the economy was crashing, but there was something else about the good loans."

"What." Randy asked mystified.

"Well, let's just say you bought a six hundred thousand dollar house. Then the neighbourhood slumped. Suddenly, all the other nice houses, in the neighbourhood, are only worth three hundred thousand dollars. What are you going to do?"

"What can you do?"

"In America you can walk away." Hayden answered. "Stop paying your mortgage. Walk away and buy a cheaper house." Hayden shrugged. "Like I said, all loans were under attack. The system crashed, all because of greed. But some hedge funds knew it was going to happen."

"Ok." Bianca said again.

"It wasn't only greed. It was tactic. Some hedge funds used these credit default swap insurance policy, to hedge the risk. When they defaulted… That brought down the biggest insurance company in the world. Leaving the government to pay the huge bill, and clean up the enormous mess."

"Wow." Penny said, exasperated. "Can that happen here? Sydney prices are astronomical."

"I don't know." Hayden shrugged. "We have less banks. Our banks are far stronger. Far more powerful. Far more regulated.

I don't know if it can happen. Depends if we follow America down that road of greed." Hayden sighed. "We have other problems. A limited amount of houses. The houses we do have, are being bought up by wealthy Asians. Not that I have anything against Asians, but they have the money, and they are driving up Australian house prices, very quickly. The government is in a mess because generation X, Y Z, can't afford to buy their own homes."

"Maybe I should explain all this to my dad." Bianca said. "Who knows what he invests in?"

"People should walk into investments with their eyes open." Hayden assured her. "The government *won't* always have your back." He explained. "George W Bush didn't have anyone's back, except the uber-wealthy, and America voted for him twice. Not to mention the credit rating agencies."

"Wait a minute. Isn't that what you told me" Kara started to say "That we have power over credit rating agencies, so we can manipulate the system?"

"You catch on quickly Kara, but it's a complicated business, and I don't pretend to understand it." He exclaimed. "There is so much at stake with these ratings! You have to assume that most of the ratings are right."

"Why do I have to assume that?" Kara asked, sipping her Mai Tai.

"Because that's the way it works." Hayden said bluntly. "I just hope I answered your question Bianca."

"You did." Bianca nudged Lucy. "I like your boyfriend Lucy. He knows stuff."

Hayden grinned. Kara smiled at him

Randy sat up straight, on his bar stool. "It's my turn. Can you get a tequila sunrise, Hayden" He turned his head "And don't give me shit Kara. I don't feel like one of your fancy drinks."

"Whatever." Kara rolled her eyes.

Hayden started making the more simple drink of tequila, orange juice, and grenadine.

Lucy grinned. "I'll have a Mai Tai, like Kara's."

Penny giggled to herself. "I'll have a sea breeze."

"Fuck off." Randy swore. He shook his head. Everyone laughed again.

"Why don't we play some drinking games?" Bianca said enthusiastically.

Hayden smiled to himself. Maybe this job was going to be ok after all. He was having fun, and his patrons were really listening to him. He *could* be a good bar tender.

Chapter 24

Today was Hayden's sixth shift, working at the club.
He was still a bit slow, but Kara was right. Most people
didn't order fancy cocktails. They ordered a beer, or a shot of
whiskey, or a rum and coke.

Half of the time, he simply had to pop the top off a bottle.

When he poured the beers, he had to make sure he didn't
spill them, but it's not like the customers cared. They didn't
even care, if he poured the wrong drink. As long as it was liquid,
and it would get them drunk faster, they didn't mind.

During the nights, the club was always pumping. The music
was always going. Some of the girls were behaving badly. Some
of the guys were either complete gentlemen, or complete arse
holes. They would either, make sure the pretty girl at the bar, got
her drink first. Or they would push in haphazardly, trying to get
their beer quicker.

Hayden, subtly, liked to do some people watching as he did
his job. He liked to catch a glimpse of all the people he was

serving. Most of the customers were young and energetic, and dressed up. They were mostly fun, and they were generally all there, for a good time.

That was *so* different, from his hospital job.

Right now, he took a deep breath, then looked up and down the bar. It was the busiest night of the week tonight.

Having fifty people, pinned against the bar. Trying to give him their order, at the same time, on a Saturday night, above the roar of the music, was a little *trying* on his nerves.

His next customer ordered 2 coronas. That was easy enough. This guy had at least spoken clearly, so Hayden could hear him.

Luckily the bar, and the dance floor, were on opposite ends of the club. The music wasn't too overwhelming, but his ears *did* get a regular pounding.

Sometimes he would have other duties as the busboy. He would leave the bar, and go collect all the empty bottles around the club. That job always took him close to the music, and close to all the action. Every night was an adventure so far.

Hayden's served the next customer, a rum and coke, and 2 beers.

Hayden made them halfway quickly. He didn't even spill them this time. He was getting better at this.

He had to admit, there was a certain amount of power being behind a bar. He could flirt with the pretty girls. Chat with the other guys. He was the gatekeeper to what the customers wanted, and they had to be nice to him, to get it.

He had the right of refusal, and the law was on his side. Theoretically.

Working beside Kara, was comforting too. She would bump into him, on purpose sometimes, to make him smile.

It was funny when they both went to grab the same bottle. Or they both wanted to use the cash register, at the same time.

Even though the club had two cash registers. Kara went out of her way, to be at the same one that Hayden was using. Then she would playfully hassle him, about getting in her way. It would make him laugh.

Hayden smiled, as he served another order. He could definitely see the fun in this. Not to mention, Kara kept grinning at him, every now and then.

He served the next customer, but it made him pause.

He served a middy of beer, to some middle aged guy.

The guy seemed kind of seedy looking, with lots of facial hair, and a beer gut. He was slurring his words. He couldn't stand still. He was erratic and when Hayden touched the guy's hand. He could feel both the intoxication, and the blood alcohol level, were embarrassingly high.

Hayden shook his head. He could feel his own heart start to pound wildly. He knew he had to handle this situation, and basically cause a scene.

He didn't like confrontation, but he could not *legally* serve this man.

The guy didn't look like too much of a problem. He didn't look a mean, or cunning drunk. He looked like a funny drunk.

Hayden could feel the unsound vibrations, running through the guy's digestive system.

When he touched the man's hand, to get the money. The man had liver issues, and he was a borderline alcoholic. The amount of alcohol consumed, made Hayden's *own* legs feel unsteady.

This guy was definitely over the limit, and rules were rules.

Hayden assessed the situation, and the guy looked stubborn.

If Hayden refused to sell the drink that was already sitting on the counter. The guy might try to take it anyway, or smash it on the ground, or throw it at someone.

As Hayden started to take the money, he quickly hooked the offending drink, with his arm, and swished it backwards. It fell *into* the bar, and smashed on the floor.

Everyone stopped and stared.

Kara made eye contact with Hayden, but then she, and the other girls, went back to work, as if nothing had happened.

Hayden looked up, disorientated. He grabbed the guys arm, and leaned forward to talk to him.

"I'm sorry sir. I can't serve you. You're too intoxicated." He started to explain. "Your judgment seems to be impaired. I have to cut you off." He said, giving the official speech, and the official explanation, for his refusal of service.

"What's do you mean?" The guy asked confused. "What are you talking about?"

"I have to cut you off, Sir. I'm sorry." Hayden said again, trying to gain some authority in his voice.

The guy looked around Confused. "Why are you doing that for? Why am I anymore drunk than anyone else?" He demanded

"I believe you are sir. I can't serve you. It's against the law." Hayden tried to clarify.

"What law?"

"The responsible service of alcohol law." Hayden said, for lack of better words.

It was a course he had to do, before he could start work here.

"What the fuck are you talking about?" The man said again. "I just want a damn drink." The man flung his arm out in an irritable motion. "What's wrong with me, trying to get a damn drink?"

"I'm sorry sir." Hayden said again, embarrassed. He put the money back into the guy's hand, and tried to be diplomatic. "It's against the law to serve an intoxicated person."

"Everyone's intoxicated." The man yelled. "Can't you see that?"

"You're worse than they are." Hayden told him bluntly.

"What the hell?" The man screamed. "What the hell." He said again, "I'm no more drunk, than any other night." He kept blabbering.

"But I can't serve you tonight."

"What the fuck." The guy said again. "Fine." He said finally. "Fine. I don't even want your watered down, lousy swill." He continued to argue.

He swayed back and forth as he spoke. "Someone else will serve me. In some other establishment. Better than this." He said. The pitch of his voice going up and down. "I'll go somewhere else." He meandered.

"I'm sorry." Hayden called out for a fourth time, but the guy was wondering off.

"Fuck you." The guy yelled back at him. "I'm going somewhere better than this." He said again.

Hayden had to laugh. "Good luck getting in." He mumbled under his breath.

Kara glanced over at him and giggled. She pressed a button on the bar that alerted the manager.

Hayden slowly grabbed the long handled dust pan, and brush.

"What just happened?" Kara asked bluntly.

"That guy had a few too many. I had to cut him off." Hayden said confused.

"It's not easy is it?" Kara remarked.

"No, it's not."

"The first one is the hardest."

"It's not the first." Hayden clarified. "I've cut off girls before." He tried to explain. "But that was the first guy. I was worried he'd jump over the bar, and try and deck me."

Kara giggled. "Drunk guys usually can't hit." She shrugged to herself. "Usually."

Hayden sighed to himself. "I'm sorry about that. I'll pay for the drink, and the cup myself. I didn't want him to run off with it. I was worried he'd cause a scene."

"Don't worry about that." Kara said sincerely.

She wanted to know more, but she looked around irritated. It was still too busy. She turned around and served the customer on her right.

Hayden started sweeping up the glass. As he was empting it into the bin, he saw a big piece of glass, left over in the corner. It was just one big piece, by itself, so he walked over to grab it.

The girls kept serving, but they watched what he was doing.

Hayden picked it up with his hand, but he cut himself in the process. His finger started bleeding. He dumped the glass in the bin.

Corey came in behind him.

"What's going on?" He asked, concerned.

Kara motioned to Corey. "Can you serve for me? I need to talk to Hayden."

"Ok." He said cautiously.

Corey started serving the customers. He was fast and efficient. He would clear the crowds away in no time.

Hayden ran out the back to the small office, behind the bar, so no one would see the blood. He was embarrassed.

There was a first aid kit in there. Hayden washed his hands. Suddenly Kara was behind him.

She grabbed the kit off the shelf, and got out a band aid. She applied it with antiseptic cream and walked over towards him.

As she stood in front of him. She froze. She grabbed his hand.

"I thought you were cut worse than this. I thought I saw blood."

"I washed it off."

"But these little cuts, don't bleed like that."

"It's dark out there. You probably didn't see it properly."

Kara looked at him suspiciously and applied the band aid. "So…. you did start to serve that guy, and then you changed your mind?" She asked curiously.

Hayden nodded. "Yeah. I didn't see it at first." He said, slightly disorientated. "But once I saw how erratically the guy was moving, and talking. I knew I couldn't let him keep the drink" Hayden shook his head. "I knew it was a bad situation. I tried to swish the drink, back out of his reach, but then it dropped on the floor. I've seen cups drop before, and they haven't broken."

"Depends on the angle." Kara shrugged.

"Yeah. Well, I'm sorry."

"It's Fine." Kara raised her eyebrows. "You know…" She started to say. "A lot of the time we don't know exactly how drunk a person is. Or we don't know what we're seeing, until it's too late." She informed him. "You have done pretty well." She complemented him. "It usually takes a trained eye, to know when to cut someone off."

"Yeah." Hayden shrugged. "But I don't want to cause the bar profits." He said, worried.

Kara stepped back, and nodded. "Yeah, but you also don't want someone to choke on their own vomit, in the bathroom." She shrugged. "If they are too over the limit, and we don't stop serving them."

Hayden raised his eyebrows. "That's a great image."

"You're a doctor: You know what I'm talking about" She said flatly. "If anything happens to our customers, on the night we serve them. The police would question *us*. We would feel guilty for not picking it up. Or for letting it happen in *our* bar." She paused. "Usually I'm never sure what I see. I mean, it's distracting here. I think I see something, but I can't guarantee it, so I don't say anything." She said breathlessly. "How you have the confidence to do it, on your sixth day, is amazing." She looked at him curiously again.

"The guy looked kind of seedy." Hayden admitted.

"A lot of them do." She exclaimed. "You're doing a good job Hayden." She grabbed a book from the shelf, and put it down on the table. It was the incident report book

"You can take your break now." She told him. "Take extra time, because you have to talk to Corey, and the security guards. Corey will help you fill out the incident report, but I have to ask you something first."

"What." Hayden asked cautiously. The tone in her voice was very serious.

She chewed on her lip for a moment. "How did you know that I had coeliac disease?" she asked out of nowhere.

Hayden picked up the pen and starting fiddling with it. "How did I know what?"

"You diagnosed my condition just by looking at me." She said, staring him straight in the eye. "You touched Lucy, that night, in her apartment, and the colour returned to her face. You brought that kid back to life, at the rave. When you touch me, I feel like I'm floating. And also… your wound just healed itself"

Hayden shook his head. "What are you talking about Kara?"

"You really don't know?" She asked.

"You're acting crazy. I'm just a regular person." He said, as if he had no idea what she was saying.

"Hayden." She said exasperated.

"You're crazy Kara."

Kara started at him for a long time. Then she shook her head. "Fine. I'll send Corey out." She walked out the front again.

Chapter 25

Hayden was out with Lucy.

They were back, in the night club district, of Sydney City.

In this particular street alone, there were three clubs. One of them was the Joker Club, where Hayden actually worked now, with Kara. A second was The Houston Bar, where they had gone on their 'double' date. Then, the third one, which they were at now, was called The City Tavern.

Hayden felt more relaxed in this environment. Now that he worked in this industry, he was certainly more accustomed to it.

He also loved this new life. A life where he could go out all the time, and have fun.

Lucy was so full of beans, she was usually up for anything.

Right now, he was walking around the club, holding Lucy's hand. They just got off the dance floor, and they were heading off to the social side of the club. To sit with Lucy's friends.

Hayden was always nervous about meeting her friends. He knew, when it came down to it, he was still kind of shy. Still kind of awkward.

Lucy was introducing him around, as boyfriend the med student.

Hayden felt that he had to act the part. He felt like he had to be the formidable medical student, with dreams and aspirations, and brilliant future. Not the tentative guy, with social anxiety, and not a lot to talk about.

Sometimes it felt hollow though.

He didn't feel like he was being himself.

He wasn't Hayden the individual. He was, Lucy's boyfriend, Hayden.

He didn't know how to act. He didn't know how to relate to new friends, and new situations. He hung off Lucy, because she seemed to know everyone.

He couldn't make his social life work on his own terms. He had to do it on Lucy's terms.

They were moving about the crowds, and he liked the crowds. He liked the atmosphere. He loved, letting the music in. While feeling the excitement of the night.

He could tap into it all, just being in the moment. But also, with his heightened sense of empathy. He could do it professionally and socially.

Suddenly Hayden stopped in his tracks. There was a girl at the bar, and she looked exactly like... In fact it was... The red hair was unmistakable.

Hayden let go of Lucy's hand, and walked over to the bar. He walked around the people in line, and stood at the far corner of the counter.

Kara finished her order. She looked up, and saw him. She caught his eye. Then she came down the end of the bar, to talk to him.

"What are you doing here?" he asked, over the loud activity.

"This club is owned by the same company as the Joker Club." She explained. "The manager here, isn't as good as ours." She said ominously. "When they get short staffed. We sometimes moonlight here."

"Really." Hayden said, both impressed and unimpressed.

He was actually trying to avoid Kara, since last week, when she accused him of having 'magical powers'.

"Yeah, fate huh?" She commented. She smiled at him warmly, but she seemed to sense his resistance. "It's good to see you." She tried to tell him, but he looked away. "I have to get back to the customers." She left, and went straight back to work.

She was as good a worker here, as she was at 'The Joker Club.' Hayden could see how professional she looked.

"Good to see you too." He said softly. Although, Kara was already busy and preoccupied, down the other end of the bar.

He turned around, slightly disorientated, and walked back to Lucy. "Kara is here." He told her, as he returned.

Lucy seemed strangely, put out, by the news. "Yeah, she gets around." She commented.

Hayden, awkwardly took Lucy's hand again. They started heading towards Lucy's friends, but Hayden stopped suddenly.

Randy was here, with Penny Lane.

Hayden took a deep breath in. He felt a wave of adrenalin. There was something he had to do, and he finally had the courage to do it.

He put his arm around Lucy's shoulder, and whispered in her ear. "I have to go talk to Randy for a moment." He told her. "Can you talk with Penny, while we're gone?"

Lucy was caught off guard. As if she didn't quite understand. "I don't know Penny that well." She said exasperated. "But if you want me to." She added, reluctantly.

Hayden commandeered her trajectory, and pulled her over to the pool table area. Randy was talking to Penny, and penny was sipping a cocktail through a straw.

When Penny saw him, she caught his eye.

"Hey Randy. Hey Penny" He said, casually, creeping up on them.

"Hey Hayden." Penny called out. She winked at him. Then she nodded.

Lucy was too distracted to notice.

"What's going on doc." Randy asked

Hayden blinked suddenly. No one had ever used that nickname before. He had to remind himself, that being in med school, would eventually lead, to being a doctor someday.

"I'm good." Hayden said. "I'm just out with Lucy." He explained. He still had his arms around Lucy's shoulders. "You know Lucy right?"

"Ah, we live in the same building." Randy said, sarcastically.

Hayden nodded. "OK." He sighed. "Pretty busy tonight." He noted.

"It was busier last week, with the public holiday." Randy noted. "So…" He sniggered. "What's going on, with you two?" He asked, as he looking between the two of them.

Lucy looked somewhat irritated at the comment. Penny was watching on, fascinated.

Hayden shrugged. "We just having fun."

"Good for you two."

"Ok." He mumbled. He didn't have time for small talk anyway. "Actually, there is something going on." He continued suddenly. "Can I talk to you, outside? I need to ask you something?" He said to Randy.

Randy looked around. "What is it?"

Hayden tried to stand his ground, but the music was distracting. So were all voices and conversation, going on around him.

"I need to talk to you." He said again. "Would you mind?"

Randy looked irritated and confused. He didn't really want to *go* anywhere, but at the same time, he was also curious about what Hayden had to say.

Finally he submitted. He gave his cup to Penny.

Hayden kissed Lucy on the cheek, and then led Randy out, to the terrace area.

People were congregating at the outdoor tables. Hayden walked up to the furthest corner. Up the back, where there were few people around.

"What's up Hayden?" Randy asked, as they became clear of the crowds.

Hayden sighed. He didn't know how to say it. So he just came out with it. "Penny sais you're using cocaine."

Randy looked completely caught off guard. "Yeah, ok." He confessed. "So what?" He shrugged his shoulders. "So are most of the people in this bar." He deflected. "Is that what you want to talk to me about?"

"Well, yeah, ok." Hayden nodded. Also caught off guard. "I *did* already know that, and I hope you're kidding about half the people in the bar. But the point is…" He tried to get back on track. "You've been doing gateway drugs for years, but now you're past the gate. Penny's really worried. She's worried you're losing control."

"And Penny came to you, about this?" He asked confused, "That strange." He smirked. "Don't you think this is a little out of your league?"

"Why is it out of my league?" Hayden yelled back at him. "My job requires me to *literally* learn the alphabet, of every prescription, illegal, legal, and illicit drug there is." He said indignantly. "*And*" He continued exasperated. "I'm the one who has to perform resuscitation on you, if you overdose."

"As if." Randy snorted. "I don't *just* buy my coke off *anyone*. I use the most reputable dealers."

"A reputable drug dealer? That's an oxymoron if I ever heard one."

"Well, I don't know what you're talking about." Randy said irritably. "But why don't you just mind your own business."

Hayden shook his head. "The more defensive you get about it. The more I know that Penny is right."

"So what." He argued. "I do the occasional drug. I'm not hurting anybody."

"Well, yes, you are actually." Hayden clarified. "You're hurting Penny, and eventually the hospital system. Do you even know how many people overdose on that stuff, a year? Do you know how many *bad* batches go around? Do you know what they cut that stuff with?"

"No" Randy said sarcastically. "But I bet you're going to tell me."

"Well I'm not." Hayden assured him. "But the hospital system spends fortunes of money on people with drug problems, and that's fortunes of time, and money, wasted." He said bluntly. "Those resources could be better spent." He bellowed. "And don't even get me started on Ice." He cursed him.

Hayden realised he was taking his personal frustrations out on poor Randy.

Randy looked at him, awestruck.

"What's your problem?" He said annoyed, but also a little hurt.

Hayden shook his head. He was being a bit intense.

He looked around the street outside the club. There were plenty of cars going past. There were plenty of people in line, trying to get into the club. There were plenty of people staggering, half drunk. Making their way, in between night clubs. Some guy, to his right, was puking under a tree.

It was quite a different nightlife, going on out here.

"What do you want from me Hayden?" Randy asked, as if he was exhausted by the whole thing.

"I want you to stop, before you get in over your head." Hayden yelled at him. "I want you to think before you act. I don't want you to end up with fucking brain damage, because your body can't handle the reaction to the chemical you just ingested."

Hayden pointed his finger at him. "Most of all… If you decide to ruin your life. I want you to leave Penny out of it. She's scared Randy. I have a vial of adrenalin in my medicine bag at home, because she thinks you're going to overdose." Hayden took a deep breath in. "I want you to stop doing coke."

"Alright, alright." Randy shouted at him irritably. "Point taken. Can I go back inside now?" He said annoyed.

"Look." Hayden said, trying to be sympathetic. "If you need any help. I can get one of the doctors to prescribe something. I can help you through it."

"I'm not an addict, Hayden." Randy swore. "I can stop whenever I want. There is nothing to get *through*."

"Well, stop tonight then."

"Fuck off." He said annoyed. "Don't tell me what to fucking do." Randy was getting agitated.

Hayden stepped back and looked around. The doormen at the club, were looking in his direction. Hayden lowered his voice. "Do it for Penny." He whispered softly. "You treat her bad enough as it is."

"And you're the expert?" He asked snidely. "You have one girlfriend in your life, and now you think you can tell *me*, how to treat *my* girlfriend."

Hayden stared at him. "You don't need that stuff." He tried to explain. "You're lucky to have penny. You can still live happily ever after."

Randy looked up, and down the street. He shook his head. "Ok, fine, I'll stick to alcohol. It's cheaper anyway. Are you satisfied?"

"You have to mean it, Randy." Hayden pleaded.

"I do." He said irritated.

Hayden nodded. "Ok…Good." He made a sigh of relief.

"So nice of you." Randy mumbled. "To be so damn condescending." he growled.

He forcefully brushed past Hayden, and staggered back inside.

Hayden sighed. *That was pretty unpleasant.* He thought, as he walked after Randy. He hated every second of it, and realistically, he didn't know if it was effective.

It certainly killed his buzz.

Lucy was watching as he came back in. Randy had already taken Penny's hand, and had walked off with her.

Lucy gave him a look, as he walked up, but Hayden shrugged it off.

He couldn't tell Lucy what went on, because Penny had never authorised him, to make it public.

"What was that about?" Lucy asked mystified.

Hayden suddenly felt vulnerable, and uncomfortable. He didn't appreciate that fight, and as a rule, he generally avoided conflict.

Hayden looked around distracted.

As he looked up, he saw Kara staring at him, from across the room, at the bar. Her turquoise eyes were peering across at him, with such intensity. He locked eyes with her, and then he nodded.

Kara saw something was going down, but she didn't know what.

After he nodded at her, she seemed reassured, and then went back to work.

Hayden looked at Lucy. She looked at him accusingly, so he suddenly had to scramble for an excuse.

"Randy keeps waking me up, at night, with loud music." He said, lying. Although it had been true a couple of times.

Lucy smiled with glee. "Way to stand up to him Hayden." She said delighted, and patted him on the back.

Hayden nodded. He was still a little rattled.

"We should go find your friends." He said, trying to make the most, out of the rest of the night.

Chapter 26

Hayden was still avoiding Kara, and had been doing so, for the last four shifts.

He didn't know how to act around her anymore. Not since she accused him of having some form of 'magical powers', and she wished she had never said that.

He was always pleasant, friendly, and cordial to her, but that was the extent of their interaction.

He was even cosying up to the other bar maids, so he didn't have to talk to her, and that made Kara insanely jealous. Not to mention, he was dating her best friend.

Kara had some sort of anxiety about it, but Hayden would occasionally talk to her. It was always short bursts of conversation. When she asked him a question, she would get little response.

She hoped that by now, he was at least, slightly over it.

She literally had to try again, right now. So she could talk to him, about work.

"Hello." She said anxiously, as she sidled up to him. He was busy making a drink.

"Hey." He said back, apprehensively. He put the cocktail on the counter, and turned to the customer. He took their money, and finished the sale.

"I was thinking you could take your break at around eleven tonight. I know it's a little late, but Heather said she might be a late for the swing shift. As usual, I don't want's everyone dinner to pile up." Kara said wearily. "I know she's always late."

"Yeah, no problem." Hayden nodded.

That was his default answer. Nothing was ever a problem. No matter what you asked him to do.

"Ok." Kara said. She chewed on her lip for a moment.

"So how is everything going?" She asked, trying to break the ice again.

She honestly wanted to know. It didn't take much for Hayden to slip through her fingers. He would disappear into his other world of medical school, and guitar playing, and dating her best friend.

She wanted to know everything she was missing out on. She missed him.

"It's great." Hayden said, and smiled at her meekly. He actually continued speaking this time, which was a good sign.

"I finished my rotation in the orthopaedic ward, and now I'm back in the emergency department." He shrugged awkwardly. "That's where I feel most comfortable." He tried to explain.

Kara stepped back, so she could ignore all the other customers, while they spoke.

"That's great" She told him. "And you're getting good evaluations?"

"Yeah." Hayden said modestly, shrugging again. "I'm studying for my board exams, and it's so much work. There is so many systems in the human body, all connected by blood. So many different pathways in the anatomy, and I have to learn all of them."

Kara smiled. "That sounds interesting."

Hayden grinned. "Sorry. I just grossed you out didn't I?"

"Well, I didn't faint." She giggled.

Hayden nodded. "I begin my surgical elective soon." He said apprehensively. "It's going to be intense."

"I'm sure you will be good at it." She told him.

"I don't know about that." He contemplated. "We'll see." He touched her wrist.

Kara glanced around. The customers were giving her filthy looks.

"I should get back to work." She said sheepishly. She swung around, to serve one of the annoying customers. They were all stopping her, from advancing this conversation.

She tried to stop thinking about Hayden, and get back to work, but it was difficult.

Hayden had just touched her, and she was melting again, with desire. He started to serve the customer next to hers, and she could literally feel, his body heat, and his powerful presence. She could smell his aftershave too.

None the less, Kara had to put her mind on her job.

As she started serving, she didn't stop. The bar were swamped again, tonight. All the staff had to struggle, to keep up.

Quite a few times, Kara was out collecting empty cups around the club. She had volunteered for the job, and she had done quite a few runs in a row.

When she started serving again, she tried conspicuously, to flirt with the male customers. She was trying to make Hayden jealous, or even notice, and it seemed to be half-working. He glanced over at her a few times. Especially when she was putting on her most veracious act.

However, when she got back behind the bar. From one of her cup runs. Something was different. She looked up, and Hayden was staring at her.

He was looking at her, not like he normally looked at her. He was looking at her strangely. "What is it?" She asked, curious.

"I don't know." He shrugged. "Something feels off." He told her, with a strange tone in his voice.

"What do you mean?" She asked, concerned, as she started to serve another customer.

"I just have a feeling. It's probably nothing." He said softly

Kara shook her head. Nothing, was just nothing, with Hayden. It had to be something.

"Hayden, what are you talking about?" She asked incredulously. She waited desperately for a reply.

"Just keep your eyes open." He said cryptically.

That was a strange thing to say. Kara wondered, what the gravity of that statement was.

"And you've had these feeling before?" she asked, concerned.

Hayden nodded awkwardly. "Yeah."

"Have you ever been wrong?"

Hayden ran his fingers though his hair. "Not really, but I don't know what the feeling is. It could be anything."

Kara looked at him. "OK." She said cautiously.

He looked contemplative, and more concerned than he was letting on.

She decided she would keep his warning in mind, but it was so busy.

She kept serving beside Hayden, and Heather, during Bethany's break. Then once again, she went out in to the club, to do one more cup run.

It took her a while to get all around all the tables. Then it happened.

What Hayden's warning, foretold.

She was passing by, with her tray of glasses and bottles. Then she heard arguing nearby. Suddenly, a fight was braking out.

Kara summed up the situation straight away. One guy was hitting on another guy's girl. Which was such a cliché, around here.

One guy was screaming at the other to 'get his fucking hands off her'.

It was not a hard situation, to figure out.

Kara walked up to them.

The two assailants were both extremely angry.

As always, they got *so* worked up about these things.

The two guys, were right in each other's faces. There was so much energy, being tossed around.

The two guys, also looked like they were from different ethnic backgrounds. That meant, the fight was going to get bad.

The guys, both had their friends standing around. Which didn't help, and by then, there was also a growing crowd.

Kara put the tray down, on the nearest table.

She moved towards them, and inserted herself into the conversation. The truth was she loved to get involved in these thing. She loved to be part of the trouble. Her instinct was to persuade them, to break it up.

She started trying to talk to them, and this time, it took a while for her to be heard.

As she finally got their attention. She stood yelling at them, and trying to gain ground. She tried to reason with the two guys. Especially the one guy, who was clearly the boyfriend.

"It's just an honest mistake." She told him.

The guy was six foot, and stout. He had black hair, dark skin, and a distinct Lebanese look about him. The other guy, also had dark skin, with a broad nose. He looked more Arab.

"The guy is drunk." She tried to tell him. "He doesn't know what he is doing." She looked around to try to ascertain the situation. "He hitting on your girl because she's pretty. It happens all the time. You're lucky to have such a girlfriend. You should just let it go." She explained. "Or at least take it outside." She tried to persuade him.

The guy looked like he was considering his options.

She reached in the pocket of her apron and pulled out two coupons. "Here." She said offering one, to each of the two guys involved. "This will get you a free drink at the bar. Just forget about this, it's stupid."

Kara felt fearless for some reason. Guys like this didn't usually bother her. Fights made her feel adrenalin, not fear.

As she was talking, she literally stepped in between them. To separate one group from another. Amazingly it was working… but not well enough.

A friend of the boyfriend got involved. He threw the first punch. The rival group retaliated by throwing the second, third and fourth punches. Kara got pushed somewhere in the mix.

Suddenly it was out of control. Kara was getting pushed back and forth. Then one of the girls actually kicked her. She hit the wall, and then she hit the ground.

It was all a blur, but then security was on them.

Both groups got pulled back. The security guards kicked them out onto the street.

Kara was still on the ground. She felt ok, but her wrist felt funny, because she had directly fallen on it.

Then Corey was somehow next to her. It *wasn't* Hayden, it was Corey.

He picked her up and whisked her out to the office. He looked at her wrist, felt around it, appraised it, and just as quickly, he whisked her out to his car.

He took her to the hospital, to get an X-ray.

Kara kept adamantly protesting, but he wouldn't take no for an answer. It had all happened so fast.

Kara didn't know, what exactly had happened.

Chapter 27

Hayden knew that something bad was going to happen, last night.

During the night, he got this feeling in every fiber of his being. Then something did happen. Kara got caught in a fight.

It wasn't a bad fight. Nor was it a terrible result, but Hayden still felt tormented, by what happened.

The event went down, reasonably close to the bar area, so Hayden could see what was happening. He could *see* her, but he couldn't *stop* her.

Of course Kara got involved in the fight. Instead of just calling security, like she was supposed to.

Hayden just stood there watching it all go down. Then Corey got to her first. He carried her out the back. Then Hayden didn't know what happened. She went to the hospital, and he didn't even have a chance to save the day.

Heather, his co-worker, had to nudge him, to keep doing his job. Then the fuss was dying down. The customers were more amped, than ever, to get a drink.

Luckily, security had done their job well. They got in quickly, and got everyone out quickly. Luckily no bystanders had been hurt. Just one staff member – Kara.

Hayden had used his medical training a few times, in these situations, but no one asked for his help today.

The whole scene was over, almost as soon as it began. It was really just a minute or two.

Hayden, however, felt like he was immobilized for eternity, as he watched on. Then suddenly, he had to get back to work.

He just kept serving the drinks.

After that, it took over two excruciating hours for word to get back. Kara had simply sprained her wrist. She would be off work, for a couple of weeks, while it healed.

Hayden stepped up, and volunteered to stay back. He did clean-up duty for Kara, so it ended up being a long shift. It was about 5AM when he got home, on Sunday morning. He was so tired.

He went to sleep, but he tossed and turned. The sleep was restless, and uncomfortable. It didn't help that it was broad daylight.

Hayden tossed and turned some more. Then he knew he had to go see her.

He found himself back at Kara's house, one more time, on her door step.

Again, it was Kara's mother that let him in the front door.

He walked in. Followed the kind woman down the hall, and stood at Kara's bedroom door. He knocked softly.

"Come in." Kara called out.

He opened the door and walked in to Kara's room. Kara looked at him discerningly, then she smiled.

She was sitting on her bed. Reading a book. Her arm was resting by her side, with her wrist bandaged up.

"Hi." She said, awkwardly.

"Hi." Hayden looked at her for a long time. "I brought you soup"

Kara shook her head. "Why?"

"I don't know." He said nervously. "I think that's what you're supposed to do, for a sick friend."

"I'm not really sick. I just hurt my wrist." She countered him. "You really didn't need to come."

"But I wanted to." He shrugged.

Kara shook her head, again. "We've talked about this. You shouldn't have come. You probably have lots of study to do?"

Hayden sighed. "I don't want to study right now Kara. I can't physically study, all the time." He said frustrated. "I need to clear my head occasionally." He told her. "Just let me be here, with you... Please."

Kara started at him for a long time. "Ok."

"Besides, I am a doctor you know." He reminded her. He put the soup container down on her desk. "I'll give you a second opinion, about you wrist. Free of charge."

Kara smirked. "I hardly need a second opinion, to tell me my wrist is sprained." She answered him. "And you're not a doctor yet. As you keep reminding me."

Hayden nodded. Then he looked at her wrist again. "I actually was pretty worried about you last night." He admitted.

Kara looked away embarrassed. "You didn't have to be." She argued. "It was just a stupid fight. They happen all the time.

You should know." She gestured to him. "You work there now. You know what goes on."

Hayden changed tack. He decided to play his trump card. "So" He began cautiously. "Corey whisked you away pretty fast, last night." He began. "I had no idea, what happened to you."

"Yeah." Kara acknowledged. "He took me to the hospital, to get an X-ray. He's been really great actually."

"Yeah, I'm sure he took *great* care of you." Hayden commented.

Kara picked up the tone in his voice, straight away. "What is that supposed to mean?"

"I'm not judging you, for sleeping with your boss, Kara." He said, playing a hunch.

"How did you know I slept with my boss?" She asked, exasperated. "I only slept with him once. How did you know? Can you read minds?"

Hayden sniggered. "No, I can't read minds. Like I'd have to. Like it's not obvious enough anyway."

Kara bit her lip. "Ok." She looked away, slightly defeated. "I'm sorry. I'm not always a good person Hayden." She tried to explain. "Just ask my friends. I used to be a spoilt bitch actually. I know I've told you this before, but it's hard to get past my roots. I'm so used to getting, what I want."

"I never lived in that world."

Kara shrugged her shoulders. "We come from two different worlds." She looked at him vulnerably. "Seriously Hayden? Can you read minds?" She asked again, out of nowhere.

Hayden thought about it for a long time. "No." He told her. "It doesn't work like that."

Kara nodded compassionately. "How does it work?"

Hayden sighed. He finally submitted, and laid his cards on the table.

"Intuition. Empathy. The exchange of energy." He admitted. "It's all very subtle." He paused. "I certainly can't read your thoughts."

"Alright." Kara accepted that. "All the more reason that you shouldn't be here." She explained. "I'm sure you have better things to do, than visit my house, in the sticks." She said softly.

Hayden sat down next to Kara, on her bed.

"There is nothing wrong with this house. It's not in the sticks."

Kara swung her legs over the side of the bed. She sat up straight next to him. She looked in his eyes for a moment. "Yes it is."

"I like it here." He smiled at her. "This is like my mom's neighbourhood."

Kara nodded again, and her face softened. She looked at him longingly "I lied before." She acknowledged. "I'm glad you came." She looked at her bandaged wrist. "But let's not talk about this." She held up her damaged arm.

Hayden nodded. "We don't have to talk about that." He sighed. "And I lied before too. It's not that obvious between you and Corey." He paused. "I mean, I sensed it, but I don't think anyone else can tell."

"It just happened." Kara mumbled. "We both wanted it. Since it's happened, he's been more attentive to his wife…"

"Don't explain." He told her.

"Alright." Kara eagerly stopped talking, and then looked him musingly. "So, how's Lucy going?" She asked. There was a definite tone in her voice. It could have been considered resentful.

"She's good." Hayden said slowly, awkwardly.

Kara nodded.

"But that's not the conversation we want to have either." He ventured.

Kara turned away, and looked out the window. "Tell me something, while you're here" She said, changing the subject completely. "Tell me about the world again, and about history. Tell me why the world is so violent. Last night, that girl at the club, kicked me, for no reason."

"I don't know." Hayden started to say. "I don't know, why the girl would do that."

"But you have an idea."

"History was always violent." Hayden told her flatly.

"But when was it not violent? Surely it couldn't have always been like this"

"Are you serious? Have you read the bible?"

"But life is supposed to be fun, and exciting." She tried to explain.

"It is." Hayden whispered. He thought about it for a moment.

Kara was vulnerable at the moment, so he had to say something. He wanted to try and make her feel better.

"The Renaissance." He said finally. "That's the answer. The Renaissance." He slowly laid back against the pillows.

Kara fell back too, and she laid up against him.

"What's the renaissance?" Kara asked softly.

Hayden thought about it for a moment. "It was a time of emotional awakening. It *wasn't* specifically about war or conquest. It was a time in history, when beauty became beautiful."

"I like the sound of that" She said softly. She closed her eyes. She lay with her head against his chest.

"Suddenly people started to celebrate, and appreciate, beautiful things. Things like artwork and paintings. Music and philosophy. People were not so steeped in a historical way of thinking. It was no longer masters and slaves, the aristocracy and their serfs, the ruling class, and the peasants. People suddenly became free to make up their own minds about science, and religion, and politics."

Hayden spoke emphatically, so she understood. "People were somewhat liberated during the renaissance. The human mind was free to roam, and create, and be artistic. People stood to explore their own essence, against the essence of others. They could celebrate their individuality."

"Sounds nice." Kara whispered.

Hayden held onto Kara with a soft grip. She had a strange effect on him. He found himself becoming tired, and slightly lethargic. None the less, he continued with his story.

"The Renaissance opened the doors for the Enlightenment. People had ideas, and could debate ideas. The main idea was that all men had rights. People did not have to be born peasants or slaves. People *could*, and *should,* have all the same opportunities. Philosophy spawned ideas about self-worth, and individualism. Then, the invention of the printing press, carried those ideas, all throughout the countryside, as well as different nation states."

Hayden took a deep breath in. Suddenly he felt like a glass of water. Like he was dehydrated, or something.

"Then after that, women started to get rights, and assert their independence. Then the flavour of the day was economics, and the value of labour. Capitalism flourished. The world was being explored, and conquered by ships. Commodities increased. Commerce grew sharply"

Hayden was suddenly really tired. He was trying to explain world history to Kara, but he had a headache. It was getting worse, and it was hard to concentrate. He didn't know what was happening. He kept forcing himself to speak.

"Britain turned to industrial revolution, and the division of labour. France overturned the monarchy and aristocracy, to become a republic, with democratic values. Russia turned to Marxism and communism - but that's a whole nother can of worms."

"So you're saying: Our modern world really started, when beauty became beautiful." Kara said blissfully, snuggling up against him.

Hayden found the strength to nod his head. "Yeah." He said softly, but his voice was raspy. He was so tired. "The problem is: *We* are living in the enlightened age, but there are still people out there that live in the dark ages. Muslims under Sharia law. The world is divided, and it's scary."

"Yeah. I know. I can see it at the club." Kara agreed.

"But for us." Hayden changed the subject quickly, to something more uplifting. "Art and music and literature, are so immersed in our culture now. It's a part of us. What we turn to now, is something else to awaken us."

"What is that?"

"The environment" He finally answered.

Hayden could barely move a muscle any more. He rested his head back on pillow and stared at the ceiling. He answered her question, stagnantly.

"We are starting to appreciate the environment, and the scenery, and all the animals that we took for granted before."

He found himself drooling, as he talked. It was getting out of control, but he tried not to let his weakness show.

"The World Wildlife Fund, and Greenpeace, and Animals Asia, and so many environmental groups are trying to save our natural world. It's so beautiful and you can see it on the BBC Earth, and David Attenborough documentaries. They are trying to show us, what this world is really made of."

"The environment." Kara repeated.

She laid there silently on the brink of sleep. Hayden laid there, feeling slightly disorientated, and almost like he was sea sick. He was hardly able to move, or talk, anymore.

Then Kara realized.

She looked at him, and screamed to herself. "What the hell? Hayden! You're pail as a ghost." She jumped up, and stared at him, exasperated.

"Hayden are you Ok? You're practically green. You look so sick"

"I'm fine." He said lying.

"No you're not!" she screamed back. "You're sick! If you could only see yourself." She told him.

Hayden tried to move, but he was hardly able to. "I feel like I haven't got any energy." He finally admitted. "I think my electrolytes are low. Do you have a sports drink around, or any hydrolyte? Maybe something to eat, like some carbs or something?"

Kara ran out of the room.

Hayden lay there incapacitated. He curled up in the fetal position. He was incredibly tired and exhausted.

Kara ran back, in a few minutes. She had a sports drink, and a chicken sandwich. She put it down on the bedside table, and sat down, next to him.

He pooled his effort to sit up, grab the drink, and take the top off. He glugged it down quickly.

"You were healing my wrist, weren't you?!" Kara asked him point blank. "That's why I forgot it was hurt." She exclaimed. "It didn't bother me, when I made that sandwich."

"I didn't know that would happen." Hayden whispered. "I didn't know that I was doing that."

"Didn't you?" she accused him. "You didn't made yourself sick, to heal me?"

Hayden didn't have the strength to argue. The fact was, maybe she was right. He had channeled his own life force into Kara, because he couldn't bear, seeing her like this.

This situation didn't always happen. Not to every person he touched. He had to want it. He had to want to save her. It was his subconscious. His subconscious did this.

"No." Hayden told her. "I didn't." He insisted. He didn't want Kara to think this was her fault.

Kara shook her head "I'll borrow my mom's car, and drive you home. You can't be around me like this." She cried. "You'll kill yourself." She shook her head, and walked out of the room again.

She came back in a moment, with her mom's car keys.

Hayden finally nodded. "I just need to sleep." He said, blearily. "If you can help me home. I'd appreciate it."

Kara helped him up. She walked him out of her house, and got him into the car.

She drove him home, slowly. She was quiet, and very pensive. The trip in the car just made him car sick.

Kara managed to help him up, into his apartment. Then straight into bed.

This time *she* slept on the lounge chair, while *he* was sick, and slept in his bed.

Chapter 28

Hayden woke up slightly disorientated, in his bed.

He didn't feel entirely well, and he distinctly had a hangover feeling.

He felt like he was famished, from yesterday. He needed some kind of sustenance.

His first instinct, was to actually go to McDonalds. He wanted to eat six hamburgers, which would give him an iron boost, and 2 large thick shakes for the calcium.

He looked around, and he realized Kara was there. She was running her fingers through her hair.

She was lying in the lounge chair, beside the bed, staring out the window.

As he woke up. He moved, and she noticed it.

"You shouldn't have done that yesterday." She yelled at him straight away. "It was just a sprain. It didn't need your assistance to heal."

"Good morning." He said, trying to change the subject.

Kara looked at him, confused.

"I swear Kara." He told her, adamantly. "I didn't know that was going to happen. It just happened."

Kara took a deep breath in. "You scared me last night."

"I'm still learning how to control it." He mumbled.

"Don't practice on me." She said flatly.

"I usually practice on Lucy." He said, not holding back.

Kara sighed. "I stayed here last night, to make sure you were ok." She chewed on her lip. "You still look a bit pale."

"I just need some food… and vitamins. I'm hungry." He told her. "I'm going to go to McDonalds, in a minute."

"McDonalds?" She said surprised

"Yeah, I feel like McDonalds." He explained. "They make the food for me, and I don't have clean the Kitchen afterwards." He told her. "I'm starving."

Kara looked at him for a long time. "Ok." She shrugged her shoulders. "I'll come with you?"

"Sure."

"Shouldn't you eat some fruit, or something?" She asked him, curiously.

"Yeah, I'll have a banana in a minute, and eat it on the way."

Kara thought about it. "When I go to McDonalds now. I have to take Gluten free bread, and substitute it for the bun, or the McMuffin."

"Yeah." Hayden nodded back. "The café down the street, serves gluten free." He suggested. "Maybe we could go there, instead."

Kara shrugged. "No." She shook her head. "You've put McDonalds into my head. I want McDonalds." She mused. "I can take the bread with me."

Hayden sighed. "Maybe they will toast it for you." He smiled at her.

Kara shrugged. "I hope so." She looked at him timidly. "I'll be glad to go with you. I wanted to talk to you anyway. I wanted to tell you about something."

"What."

"About a car."

"What?" Hayden asked, surprised.

Kara shrugged. "I think, if I keep saving. I can afford to buy my first car!" She exclaimed.

"Wow." He nodded at her again, encouragingly. "That's so cool."

"Yeah it is." She smiled at him.

"In fact, I'm jealous." Hayden continued. "I don't even have a car. I usually walk everywhere. Or ride my bike."

"Yeah, I know." Kara grinned. "But you do live in the city. It's a good transit area." She acknowledged.

"Yeah." Hayden nodded again.

"I really want one." She told him.

Hayden stared at her, bemused. It was as if she was trying to persuade him, that she deserved a new car, and really, she deserved anything she wanted.

"I'm sick of trying to borrow my mum's car, or taking a taxi to work." She continued, explaining.

"Yeah I don't blame you." He grinned. "*The fast and the furious*, was on TV the other night, and I felt so inadequate." He told her. "Just looking at my push bike, in the corner."

Kara giggled to herself softly. "Sometimes I get jealous of people *our* age." She began to explain to him, precariously.

Hayden wasn't sure how to reply, so he stayed quiet.

"I mean, all my friends got their own car." She told him, frustrated. "They got handed the keys to a car, when they were, like, sixteen. Some even got their car, before they even got their license"

Hayden nodded. "Yeah. I know what you mean." He told her. "I had a few friends like that, in high school."

"They got love, and support, and encouragement, and everything got handed to them, on a silver platter." Kara murmured. "It looked like everything came so easy to them, and sometimes I feel myself being so resentful."

"I do know what you mean Kara." Hayden agreed.

"And you can always see who they too." She continued. "The ones at the club. The entitled ones, who walk around, and splash their cash around."

"There are lots of unentitled ones too." Hayden said softly, very truthfully.

"Yeah, I know." She looked into space. "Not to mention, I used to be one of those spoilt girls"

"Well. You're different now." Hayden told her. "And don't forget…. You're the one who talks about the third world. You still have it a lot easier, and better, than most people in this world."

"Working five nights a week, at a club, when I was eighteen, is a lot easier?" She asked, still slightly resentful. "Helping my parents pay off their mortgage." She mumbled. "Although I do know what you mean." She turned to look at him. "I feel like we're in this together, because we both struggle, for what we want."

Hayden looked at her for a long time. "Yeah." He agreed finally. "And who cares what other people have, or do, or think." He nudged her, with his elbow. "We can make it on our own."

Kara smiled, and nudged him back. "*To thy own self be true*, Right?"

"Yeah." Hayden grinned. "You're right!" he told her. "And when you earn it all yourself, it's so much sweeter." he added hastily. "Just like you are." He told her. It was corny, but he said it anyway.

Kara rolled her eyes. "You're so funny."

Hayden looked away.

"I could use some help." She hinted. "Going, car shopping." She paused. "I would get the worst deal, if I went by myself." She said, unsure.

"I could go with you." Hayden answered. "If you don't mind, that I don't know anything about cars."

Kara smiled. "I don't mind." She said quickly. "That would be great… Just when you're not busy. I mean… when you're not busy with Lucy, and stuff." She said nervously. "But, I mean, I still have to save up a little."

"That's Ok." Hayden told her. "Anytime."

Kara suddenly pushed forward, on her chair. She leaned over, and kissed him on the lips.

"Thank you, for healing my wrist yesterday." She told him, mesmerized.

Hayden started at her, confounded.

Kara shook her head again. She looked embarrassed.

She immediately jumped out of the chair.

"You're pail. You need to eat." She said quickly, and shrugged again. "I'll get out of your room, so you can get dressed." She smiled. "So we can go to breakfast."

She looked at him for a moment, as she walked out of the room.

"McDonalds." She said abruptly. "And then you could study. Or go see Lucy or something." She mumbled.

Hayden watched her. She looked completely frazzled, and Hayden felt suddenly confused.

"Yeah." He said softly. "Actually, I was going to go to the movies, with Lucy, this afternoon." He said, as he just remembered.

Kara nodded her head, uncertainly. "Good." She said flatly. "That's really good."

Hayden nodded at her.

Kara shrugged. "You know what" she began telling him. "I'll just toast my bread here, before we leave." She said simply. "It's just easier that way." She tried to explain to him. "I'll go find your toaster."

"Ok." Hayden said, casually.

She smiled humbly, as she left the room

Chapter 29

Kara's world, had changed somewhat, in the last couple of weeks.

She was still thinking about Hayden, but she was doing it from another part of town. She didn't tell anyone at the time, but she applied for a second job, and she got it.

She needed her space, from her night owl ways.

Working at the club, five nights a week, was simply too much for her mind and body to handle. It was causing her stress, and her REM cycle wasn't coping, with the late night fatigue.

Besides that, she felt too decadent, sleeping every day and working every night. A few weeks ago, she had applied for, and got a second job, at a café.

Now she was both a waitress, and a bar tender.

It wasn't much to speak of, but she was proud of it.

Variety was apparently the spice of life, and she finally felt she was getting in control of her life. She worked three days at the club, and two days at the café. At the café, she was lucky enough to get morning, and day shifts.

She was also, especially happy with her jobs, because the café shifts were Wednesday and Thursday. That meant, she still got to work, Friday and Saturday, at the club with Hayden.

She was completely falling in love with him, although she constantly tried to deny that, for obvious reasons.

She liked being near him. She like the sound of his voice, and the smell of his aftershave. She liked his humble and kind manner. She liked his thoughtful words, and his sense of optimism.

Kara sighed as she fulfilled her work at the café. She cleared a small, quaint, table by the window. It was just a nice, two seater table. With a red and white table cloth. Salt and pepper shakers, and a pleasant small vase, with a sunflower in it.

Kara felt like this was a very pleasant place to work, and so much less stressful than a roaring night club could be.

She loved both worlds, but she especially loved the balance of having both in her life.

She cleared the cups, and plates, and looked around at all the people in the café. It was a slow morning but the sun was shining through the window, and the customers were friendly regulars. It looked like it was going to be a beautiful day.

This was the Buttercup café. She worked here, very happily, in her off white waitress uniform, with sand shoes, on her feet.

Everything was new and fresh. Even the quiet undertone of the café, blended in with the heavy aroma of coffee beans. It made her job, all the more peaceful, and welcoming.

As she worked, Hayden crossed her mind again, and that was a problem, for many reasons. Mostly because he was dating her best friend.

It was a major problem *right now*, because Lucy was *here*, at the cafe.

Lucy had come this morning, to give her moral support, at her new job. Even worse than that, was that Lucy was smitten. She ordered pancakes with cream, and a bottle of water, and had been eating it for the last fifteen minutes. She was waiting patiently, for Kara to take her tea break.

Kara gulped down her jealousy, then went and sat at Lucy's table.

"I've only got fifteen minutes, so you better make this quick." Kara said, as she slipped into a chair. She put her notepad down, and looked at her waiting friend.

Lucy grinned at her. She gave a cheeky smile, and then nodded. "I think tonight's the night."

Kara's face fell, almost to the floor. "What."

"We've been getting pretty hot and heavy lately. I think it's actually going to happen tonight. I think *I'm* going to make love to Hayden."

"Oh." Kara said. She forced a smile like shape onto her mouth. It was so strained, it was hurting her entire face.

"You know Kara." Lucy said excitedly. "He hasn't pressured me at all, and his love is so addictive. We he touches me, I feel like I'm floating." She insisted. "I know that sounds like a metaphor, but I swear it's real. I'm addicted to his touch. I never feel better than when he is with me."

Kara looked away for a moment. "No, it doesn't sound like a metaphor at all." She gritted her teeth, one more time.

Lucy grinned. "What do you think?" She asked Kara, directly. "I mean, you're probably amazed we haven't done it already, but since you stole him away, at the club. I hardly have time to see him." She paused. "I really feel like I'm ready."

"Is he ready?"

"He's a guy, Kara. He was born ready."

"So, has anything happened?" She asked, exasperated. "Have you guys talked about this?"

"No, we haven't talked about it, but he finally unhooked my bra strap last night, so I'm guessing it's time."

"Oh." Kara said again, for lack of better words. She wearily ran her fingers through her hair. "Well I hope you have protection. I mean he's in med school. You can't tie him down. You really shouldn't monopolize his time too much"

"Kara, for crying out loud. He's my boyfriend. I think I should at least spend time with him, and you know I'm on the pill anyway." Lucy looked at Kara incredulously. "Are you even still friends with Hayden?"

"Yeah." Kara asked concerned. "Why?"

"He hasn't mentioned you at all lately." Lucy proclaimed. "I asked him if he wanted to go on another double date, and he said no pretty fast."

Kara bit her lip. The truth was hard to hear.

Hayden was still uncertain around Kara. Not just because of what she said about his 'powers', but this time, he was standoffish, since he healed her wrist. When they had shared another moment, in his room... again.

Kara was never sure what was going on with Hayden. However, she was the one that was often confusing the situation.

"Yeah we're friends." She said simply.

"And everything is good at the club?" Lucy asked.

"Yeah." Kara replied, unsteadily.

"I mean, he really seems to like the job." Lucy elaborated.

Kara felt a wave of happiness. She was glad to hear that.

"Yeah, everything's good." She smiled. "He's doing a really good job. He's quick on his feet, and he tougher than I thought." Kara admitted. "He doesn't back down from a fight, and it surprises me sometimes." She answered humbly.

"Yeah." Lucy grinned. "I concur with *all* those statements."

Kara swallowed thickly. "Yeah." She said, with a fake smile.

"And you guys, work well together?" Lucy queried.

"Yeah, of course we work well together." Kara snapped, a little too boldly. "I guess he doesn't talk about it much, because he's busy focussing on you." She said, swallowing her jealousy again.

"Yeah. He has been so sweet lately." Lucy swooned.

Kara nodded her head, apprehensively.

"She slowly got up, out of her seat. "Well good luck." She said, trying to grind the words out of her mouth. She tried to seem positive, at the same time.

"Good Luck? That's all you can say."

"What do you want me to say? I told you I only had a few minutes, and this is a new job. I want to make a good impression."

"Well, I just wanted to tell you."

Kara forced the same hollow smile. "Good. I'm glad you did. I'm sure he'll be magic between the sheets."

Kara gulped down another lump in her throat. "Call me later." She said patting Lucy on the back. "I have to go my locker." She murmured, as she quickly walked off the café floor.

Kara turned around, and disappeared out the back, as quickly as she could.

She went out employee bathroom. She was devastated. She slowly washed her hands in the warm water from the sink.

When she looked back up in the mirror, there was something in her eye. It was a stupid tear. How could she let this happen? How could she let herself get this wrapped up in someone, other than herself? It was so unlike her.

As she went out again, on to the café floor, Lucy was gone, thank goodness. Kara might not have been able to control her emotions, if she was still there.

It occurred to Kara suddenly that she was only working five hours today. She could work anything between five, and nine hours shifts, but today was only five. It was the perfect shift: 6AM to 11AM.

Kara felt sick, and disorientated. She watched the clock for another two hours, and ten minutes. She tried desperately to focus on her work. She chatted with the customers, and brought them their food, and cleaned the tables.

When she finished work, she knew what she had to do.

She slowly walked, to Hayden's apartment. She didn't even stop to think, before she found herself knocking on his door.

Hayden was surprised to see her. "Hi Kara."

"Hi." Kara said back. She was surprised he was home, but he must have had a late class. She walked in, and stood before him, in the living room.

"How are you doing?" He asked, slightly confused.

"Good." Kara said, distracted.

"Ok." He said distractedly, watching her.

Kara wondered around the apartment for a moment. She was trying to focus. "I'm here because of what Lucy said."

"What did Lucy say?"

"Tonight's the night."

"The night for what."

"Are you serious?" Kara started pacing. "For you two to have sex."

"Oh." Hayden looked around shocked slightly. Then he nodded.

Kara continued pacing, and then stopped. "You know, Hayden. I don't care what you do with Lucy tonight... but she's not taking something that was meant for me."

"What was meant for you?" He asked confused.

Kara closed her eyes. She had to say it. "Your virginity."

Hayden laughed awkwardly, and tried to sound tough. "What makes you think I'm a virgin?"

Kara looked in his eyes. "The way you touch me."

Hayden froze, and looked at the floor.

"The way you look at me. The way you never made a move, when we slept together so many times. The way you get nervous look on your face, whenever you think something might happen. How tender you are. How patient you are."

Hayden raised his eyebrows. "Am I really that pathetic?"

"No." Kara shook her head. "You're really that wonderful actually."

"And what you saying? You want to be with me."

"I want to be your first" Kara said bluntly. "It should be me. I want it to be me." She looked at him desperately. "I could show you Hayden."

"Show me what?" He asked exasperated. "How to be good in bed?"

"No." She cried. "How good it *could* be. Don't you see?" She told him desperately. "Being experienced doesn't make you good in bed. Having passion makes you good. Wanting it, makes you good. Desire makes it good. There has to be love. There has to be passion. There has to be lust. When you have all of those things, at the same time, it would be amazing, and we have that."

"We do?"

Kara looked out the window. "I hope we do. I know I do."

"And there is love involved?"

"Was I not clear enough at the rave?"

Hayden shook his head. "You said you were high at the rave. You didn't know what you were saying."

Kara shook her head, back. "Of course I knew what I was saying. I was hoping you would get that. You're smart enough in every other way."

"But you said you didn't want to date me, until I graduate. You said you didn't want to distract me."

"I still believe that Hayden, but I can't bear it. Not Lucy. Not now." She stepped towards him. She cupped his right cheek, with her hand. Then she looked deep into his eyes. "It has to be me. I want you, to want it, to be me."

Hayden was stunned. He didn't say anything for a full minute. Kara held her breath.

"I want it to be you too." He said softly.

Kara nodded, and continued to look in his eyes, for a long time.

She reached back, and undid the zip on her dress. She let the dress fall to the ground.

Hayden stared at her.

She reached back, and undid her bra strap. Then she let the bra, drop to the ground, as well.

Hayden reached out, to take her in his arms. He kissed her long and hard.

He slid his hands down her body, till they reached her lower back. Then he quickly picked her up, so he legs went around his waist.

He carried her to the bedroom, and he laid her down on the bed.

He quickly flung off his own clothes, and then they were together.

He was hungrily, making love to her. It was like nothing she had ever experienced before.

He really was magic.

Chapter 30

Two days had passed, since Kara had turned up here, at Hayden's apartment. Then they had been together.

Now Hayden had invited her back, and she was here with him, again.

Hayden sat across from her, as they both sat cross legged, on top of his queen sized bed.

"So what's going on?" he asked her.

She shrugged. "You tell me. You invited me over." She paused "Even though we worked together last night."

"We saw each other last night at work, but we didn't get to talk."

"We didn't get to talk, because it was a crazy weekend. We were way too busy." She began. "But, even though you didn't say anything. You kept grinning at me the last two days." Kara giggled. "I'm sure everyone knows what happened by now. Just by the look on your face." She sighed. "That goofy grin. I know Corey does."

"Did he say something?"

"Sort of. Let's just say he guessed." Kara said, and gave him a knowing smile. "I just confirmed it."

"And you told him, that you were my first?"

"No." Kara shook her. "I never would have said that. That is no one's business, but yours." She looked out the window for a moment.

Hayden shrugged his shoulders. "I just called you over today, because I wanted to see you." He said simply.

Kara nodded. She looked at him curiously for a second. "So how did it go, with Lucy?"

Hayden looked at Kara closely. He noticed that she was holding her breath. The question had clearly been on her mind.

Hayden thought about it for a moment. "I couldn't do it." He shook his head. "I could have done it, but there was no going back from it." He said, nervously. "I didn't sleep with her. I broke up with her."

"Wow." Kara raised her eyebrows. "I thought you would do it." She said frankly. "I thought you would be with two girls, in one day."

"I'm not that kind of guy."

"You know it would have been ok, right?"

"Not for me it wouldn't have been. Not for Lucy it wouldn't have been."

Kara took a deep breath in. "How did she take it?"

"Not well." Hayden lowered his head. "She cried. It was kind of awful, actually."

"She's pretty emotional. I'm surprised she hasn't called me yet. I'm sure she's just off licking her wounds. Ballerinas are like cats. They bounce back."

"You mean they land on their feet." He articulated the metaphor. "And you don't sound too concerned, about your friend."

Kara nodded. "That's because you didn't sleep with her. If you slept with her, it would have been a different story."

"Were you testing me?" Hayden asked, suddenly.

"No. No Hayden." She said adamantly. "I was the one who came to you. You should have done what you wanted."

"What if what I want… is you?"

Kara shook her head. She looked slightly annoyed for a second, then changed the subject.

"It would have been worth it to Lucy." She proclaimed suddenly. "You don't know what you're capable of. Or how you make people feel."

Hayden stared at her for a moment. He knew what she was getting at, but he ignored the comment. "You were pretty good yourself."

Kara laughed. She shook her head, then stared up at the ceiling, for a moment. "You know Hayden… I can't go out with you."

Hayden took a deep breath, and looked at the ground. "I hadn't thought that far yet." He said, wounded.

It was hurtful, to hear her say that. Especially after everything that had happened, but he continued with his story. "Lucy didn't call you, because I told her I was in love with someone else. I told her it was you."

Kara gasped. "Why did you do that for?"

Hayden shrugged. "Because it's the truth." He whispered.

"Yeah." She gestured. "But since when do people tell the truth, in that situation?" She argued. "I mean, you had to know, I can't go out with you." She paused. "Not while you're still in med school."

"But you will, sleep with me?"

"I was being selfish." Kara broke eye contact, and shook her head. "You're love is like a drug, Hayden." She informed him. "Lucy knew it too. I wanted it for myself."

"But you don't want it enough, that you would date me?"

"No." She said flatly. "You need to focus on your studies. I couldn't help you with that. I'm not that smart."

"You're very smart." Hayden cried desperately. "You could run the club, with your arms tied behind your back."

"Yeah, but that doesn't mean that I could help you with your med school homework."

"You wouldn't need to." He pleaded with her. "I don't get it Kara? I just want to be with you."

Kara shook her head. "I don't get it either Hayden. I just know that I can't. It's like the universe is telling me not to. You need to focus on something bigger. Bigger than this. Bigger than us."

"The universe is telling you that?" Hayden said sarcastically.

"Well, *you're* obviously hooked into the universe." She cried. "Why can't I be?"

Hayden paused. He uncomfortably turned away. "So we're back where we started from."

"Yeah." she said softly.

Hayden looked at her for a long time.

He didn't know what to say, but there was nothing else he could say. Her expression was adamant.

Suddenly Kara turned to him, and conspicuously changed the subject. "What were you talking to Randy about, at the starlight tavern?"

"The city tavern?"

"That's not what I call it." She meandered. "What was going on?"

Hayden shook his head. "That was about two months ago." He said incredulously.

"Yeah, well, I'm finally catching up." Kara explained.

Hayden sighed. He practically got whiplash, from the topic being redirected so quickly.

"Penny asked me to talk to Randy." he conferred.

"Why?"

"Because she's worried about him." He said tactfully.

"Yeah, about what?" Kara asked, not being able to contain her curiosity.

"He's doing cocaine." Hayden finally admitted.

"Yeah I've seen it." Kara said cryptically. "Didn't Penny already get that message? When she started going out with him?"

Hayden scratched his head. "I don't know Penny well enough."

"Nobody does." Kara commented.

Hayden wasn't interested in that. He leaned in quickly, and changed the subject, back to where it had been.

"So you're just telling me…You don't want to go out with me, and I can't touch you again." He asked her, point blank.

Kara looked at him. Trying not to smile.

He put both his hands, on the outer thighs, of her crossed legs.

"Yes." She muttered, confused.

"And I can't kiss you again." He asked.

He leaned in close, poised to kiss her, but stayed just enough away, so their lips were an inch, or two, apart.

Kara was clearly trying to stay resolved. "Yes." She tried to say, but her voice had an unresolved, whiny tone in it. She continued. "I mean, this time, I might have to start ignoring you, because this isn't working."

Hayden watched her for a long time.

She looked confused. More confused than he was. He leaned forward, and kissed her on the lips.

Kara grinned, and shook her head. "That's no fair." She said playfully. "You're playing dirty." She told him, although she couldn't wipe the smile off her face.

He moved his right hand to her face. He streaked it down her cheek, down her neck, over her breast, then settled it back on her leg.

"One more time." Hayden whispered to her.

Kara grinned at him again.

He kissed her on the lips again. Then he kissed her down the length of her neck, over her collar bone, and his hands caressed her, up and down, her back.

Kara finally smiled, and fell back on the bed.

He watched her breathlessly. She was powerless against him. He had that power. It scared him, and exhilarated him, at the same time.

Kara was mad with desire, and he was instigating it. That power overcame both of them.

Chapter 31

Hayden had a strange feeling.

He was coming home from breakfast, at a coffee shop down the street, when he entered the elevator up to his apartment.

There was someone else in there, but that's wasn't what was distracting him.

He cautiously got in, but as he looked up. He was just *out* of time, to see *who* he was standing next to.

It was Lucy's roommate, Bianca.

Hayden huffed.

Bianca looked at him cautiously, but also judgmentally.

The truth was, they had never really spoken much. Nor had they ever been much acquainted. They did exchange pleasantries sometimes. Specifically when they were caught in this type of situation, but that was before he broke up with Lucy.

Bianca was not the forgiving type, nor was she especially friendly. Hayden dreaded what she had to say to him, but whatever it was, he probably deserved it.

The girl was shrewd, but at the same time, she constantly surprised him. Her mind was always burning with questions, every time she came into contact with him.

Those moments were rare when they were together.

Moments like this elevator ride, or passing on the street, but her scrutiny was never long enough, to get to the bottom of anything.

Bianca was just as rich as Lucy (and just as rich as Kara's used to be.) They had all gone to the same school, originally, when Kara had gone to a fancy private school.

As the elevator doors closed, Hayden instantly knew that something was about to happen. He felt the sensation more keenly now.

If he had felt it, any earlier, he never would have got on this damn elevator.

"Did you go out for a jog?" Bianca asked quickly, looking at his track clothes.

"Yeah, but I stopped for breakfast." Hayden acknowledged. Then he nodded awkwardly.

Bianca nodded back. Still looking at him accusingly.

The elevator started its ascent. Hayden held his breath, sub-consciously.

Then it happened, somewhere around the seventh floor. The elevator slammed to a halt. The lights went out.

"What?"

Hayden waited anxiously for a moment. Then the auxiliary power kicked in. The lights came back on.

"What the hell." Bianca yelled.

"Must be a blackout." Hayden told her, trying to keep his voice smooth.

He was silently grateful that he wasn't alone. He always had a fear that he would be trapped in an elevator, alone.

He was *less* grateful, however, that the girl he was stuck with, wanted to throw javelin like, questions at him.

"Why is there a blackout at 8 in the morning?" Bianca asked annoyed.

"Maybe a tree fell over a powerline, or something?" Hayden suggested, completely guessing. He immediately started feeling claustrophobic.

Bianca nodded her head, as if that scenario was in some way possible.

She got her phone out of her bag, and looked at the time. "I have to be at Uni soon."

Hayden shrugged, and glanced at his wrist watch. It was 8:16. "Yeah, so do I." He told her. "My work experience, at the hospital, I mean."

Bianca looked at him shrewdly again.

She was wearing a designer outfit; a purple blouse, black skirt, and high, black boots.

Her brown hair was still hanging at her shoulders, but her fringe was immaculately combed over to one side.

She had a tall coffee cup, in one hand. Which she sipped, slowly, and a designer bag, hanging off the other shoulder. She look pretty, and very rich.

"Why did you hurt my roommate, Lucy?" She asked him, suddenly, out of nowhere.

Hayden gulped down a lump in his throat. "I didn't mean to." He said exasperated.

She waited for a better explanation. That one didn't particularly impress her.

"I wanted to see what it would be like, to go out with Lucy." Hayden finally opened up. "And I did… She was a really great girl." Hayden paused. "But in the end. I had to force myself to admit that I was in love with someone else. I couldn't go out with her anymore." Hayden explained slowly. Trying to be diplomatic.

"Kara." Bianca said flatly.

"Yeah." Hayden nodded. "I like Kara. I love her."

"But why go out with Lucy at all?" she queried him. "If you knew, you liked someone else?"

That was an excellent question.

"It all happened really fast." Hayden began to explain. "I met them both around the same time. I didn't know what I was feeling." He tried to be articulate. Although he was kind of lying. He knew Kara was the right one, from the start.

"It's just…" Bianca insisted. "You just really hurt her."

"Yeah. I'm sorry." Hayden bowed his head.

Bianca was right. He did hurt Lucy, and he was a terrible person. In fact, he was so terrible, he was taking his sexual frustration out on Lucy, while Kara was always so elusive.

He never realized he could be such a terrible person. Not until it was happening.

"So." Bianca sighed again. Now Kara's working two jobs, and she's got a boyfriend in med school." She shook her head. "She always did work hard… to get everything she ever wanted."

"She's got what?" Hayden asked, suddenly, confused at both parts of that statement.

"She's got two jobs." Bianca said warily, and then sipped her coffee again. "She works as a waitress. At a café, downtown, as well."

Bianca shrugged her shoulders. Did you not know that?" She asked him confused. "Don't tell me, you two broke up, already?" She asked baffled. "Don't you both work at the same night club?"

Hayden sighed. "We never actually dated." He clarified.

"But you slept with her though." Bianca interrupted. "She's been walking around on cloud nine, for a month now."

Hayden blushed, and couldn't wipe the smile off his face.

"She thinks I should focus on my studies." He explained. "She won't talk to me about anything personal anymore. She's been keeping her distance" He continued. "We only talk about music, and movies, and stuff on the surface. I didn't know she had another job."

"Yeah, well…" Bianca smirked. "Don't take it personally. Kara can be pretty guarded when she wants to be." she mused.

"Well." Hayden shrugged. "I have been doing what she asked me to do." He confessed. "I have had my nose in the books. I don't know what's going on around me."

Hayden felt slightly off balance. He didn't know that Kara had another job. Evidently, he didn't *care* enough to know what was going on with her.

"Do you like it at the club?" Bianca asked curiously.

"Yeah I do. It's a lot of fun." Hayden answered her, and smiled to himself, because it was the truth. "I get to go out, to a club, every Friday and Saturday night, and I get paid to do it." He exclaimed. "It's more than I ever used to do." He admitted.

He reflected back to the time, when he used to sit at home, on his couch, every Friday and Saturday night.

"Yeah." Bianca nodded. "My dad's threatening to cut me off if I don't find a job soon." She mumbled. "He thinks I've had it too good, for too long."

Hayden laughed at her. "What do you mean?"

"He's a philanthropist." She explained. "He thinks I should be more proactive about being employed."

Hayden grinned and nodded. "What do you want to do?"

"How should I know?" She cried. "I'm studying media and communications. Where the hell, is that supposed to get me?"

"You'd probably be a good publicist?" Hayden suggested. "Or work at a fashion magazine." He looked down at her outfit, one more time.

Bianca smiled at him. "Thanks Hayden." She said grinning. "I suddenly know why Lucy and Kara like you."

"How is Lucy?" he asked cautiously.

"Dating one of ballet boys." Bianca shrugged. "She's going to be fine."

"I knew she'd land on her feet." Hayden commented. "So did Kara."

"Yeah, well, Lucy just coasts along. I, on the other hand, haven't found a boyfriend since I got back from Europe." She said, as a matter of fact. "I hooked up with two gorgeous specimens on the Swiss Alps. Then, I get back, and every guy is either covered in tattoos, or doing drugs. I don't know what is wrong with this country." She mumbled, frustrated.

Hayden laughed softly, then he shrugged. "That's not true." He tried to tell her. "I'm sure there are lots of guys out there, who are just right for you. I know they'd be lucky to have you." He said optimistically. "There are heaps of guys at the club, who have their eye out. Why don't you come by some time?" He asked her. "I'll buy you your first drink. Get the ball rolling?

"That's sweet Hayden." She smiled at him. "But I don't want just *anyone*. My ex-boyfriend was awesome, and he was the perfect blend of sugar and spice." She giggled to herself. "And, he didn't have any tattoos." She emphasized. "I'm not sure guys like that *exist* anymore."

Hayden thought about it.

He looked around contemplatively. He was looking at the four incredibly enclosed walls around him. He wondered how long they would be stuck in something that resembled a tin can.

"There is a stigma about today's youth." He acknowledged slowly, "But I think young people are disillusioned, these days." He said finally, offering his thoughts. "Before, when kids finished high school. They used to have an option of going to university or TAFE, to learn a skill. But now, however, half the TAFE institutions are closed down. The ones that are left are mismanaged, and too expensive. People can't afford to go to them anymore. I think some kids have nowhere to go. So they turn to drugs… That's sort of the impression I get."

Bianca sort of nodded. "How did you gain that wisdom?"

"One of the girls I work with at the club, goes to TAFE." He answered her, "She is always complaining about it." He sighed. "I've always thought it was a shame." He continued. "TAFE should have been opened up, not shut down. It should have incorporated sustainable technology. They should have included new courses on environmentally friendly infrastructure, and innovation. As well as, so many other trade courses, they have cut." He said discouraged. "As for the tattoos." He returned to the subject. "I guess you either get it, or you don't."

"Do you get it?" She asked inquisitively. "Do you have any tattoos?"

"No." Hayden said quickly. "I wouldn't. I don't like them either."

"Yeah." Bianca nodded. "Hopefully there is another one of you around."

Hayden blushed for the third time.

Bianca finally sighed, and looked around the small elevator. "It feels like everything's going to hell in a handbasket. As my dad would say." She shrugged. "I mean, if we're not worried about jobs, we're worried about global warming, severe weather, and our future." She nodded at him. "And there is nothing at all, we can do about it."

"You really feel that way?"

"Yeah." Bianca nodded, as if it was obvious.

Hayden sighed. "I guess the government are stepping back. Letting the corporations take over. Letting the media set the agenda. Not enough participation in cultivating people, or the environment." Hayden shrugged.

Bianca looked at him, curiously again.

Then suddenly the elevator jolted. It started moving upwards again.

Hayden sighed, and smiled at Bianca. She joyfully smiled back at him.

Obviously the elevator reached the eleventh floor first. That was his floor.

"We'll, I'll see you around." He said idly.

"Yeah. I'll see you around." She replied quickly.

Bianca's face looked blank. Then she did something that surprised him. She stepped over, and gave him a hug. "Thanks for talking to me."

Hayden hugged her back warmly. He felt surprised. "Any time." He told her. "You know where I live. Any time." He repeated.

Bianca smiled again. Hayden stepped back, and the elevator doors closed.

Hayden thought that was strange. He didn't know Bianca had a softer side. She turned out to be a really nice girl, and she was funny too.

Hayden suddenly felt really happy.

It seemed like lots of girls liked to show him affection these days.

Penny did, Kara did, and all of his female co-workers at the club, loved to talk to him as well.

He was making so many more friends than he used to.

However, scholastically, he still had a long way to go. He knew he had to step back from his social activities, if he was going to make it through med school.

Things were getting very intense, with his education. His board exams were coming up soon. The hours at the hospital were long. The work was ever challenging.

Hayden had a feeling it was going to get even more intense, in the next few months.

Chapter 32

Kara took a deep breath in, and finally knocked on Hayden's front door. It was strange to be here again. She promised herself she wouldn't come. But here she was

It had been sixty two, agonizing days, since she had slept with Hayden.

Since then, she woke up, every morning, yearning for him.

Then every morning, she would compose herself. Then remind herself, that she had to stand her ground.

She also had to remind herself of that, at the club. Every time she saw him. Every time he was there, and he would look so handsome, and he was so kind… and sweet… and thoughtful, and the staff loved him, and the girl customers swooned over him.

Kara knocked on Hayden's door again.

She was here, at his apartment, at five o clock in the afternoon.

As Hayden answered the door, he looked slightly confused. He had a blanket around him.

"Kara." He said surprised. "You're here"

"Yeah, of course I'm here." She told him, emotionally.

He looked at her for a minute. Then he turned his back on her, and started walking away.

Kara couldn't help but see, that he was acting erratically. It was eerie. She never thought she'd see him like this. He was usually so grounded.

She honestly didn't know what was going on.

She invited herself in, and followed him to the kitchen. She followed him, reluctantly, not knowing what else to do.

"I was making a cup of coffee. Would you like one?" He asked distractedly. He was still barely looking at her, or acknowledging her.

"No, I don't drink coffee." Kara replied steadily.

Hayden poured himself a black coffee. "How are you?"

"I'm Ok." Kara said softly. Although, truthfully, she felt completely thrown off guard.

"What are you doing here?" He said restlessly.

Kara wasn't sure how to take that. She took the phone out of her bag, and read the text message, that he had sent her last night, at 3 o clock in the morning:

"It's after 3, and I can't sleep, and I need you" she looked at him worried. "What did you mean by that."

"I don't know." He said, confused. "I was *not* myself last night."

"You're not yourself, right now." She countered.

He looked at her, even more confused.

Kara decided she should use caution, and not get defensive. There was something wrong with him.

"What's the matter?" she enquired further.

"I just wanted to see you, but I was wrong. You should go." He mumbled helplessly.

"What's the matter Hayden?" Kara insisted. She put her hand on his arm, to get his attention.

Hayden shook his head, took a sip of his coffee. And then walked off again, to the lounge room.

"Hayden what's the matter." She yelled at him. She was sternly standing at the entrance to the lounge room.

Hayden put the coffee down on the coffee table. He stood in the middle of the room. He seemed unsure of what to do next.

Ordinarily he would have looked good in his blue jeans, and a purple striped shirt. His thick brown hair was a little messed up. The blanket around him, however, made him look a bit like he was crazy, or high, or something.

She moved over to him. Standing face to face. "Tell me Hayden." She whispered.

"I can't."

"You have to tell me, or I can't help you." She grabbed on to his arm. "Tell me what's wrong. Are you high???"

Hayden shook his head. "No." He sighed. "I don't want you to think I'm crazy." He looked away, distracted again.

Kara looked him deep in the eyes. "I would never think that."

He shook his head. "Not yet."

Kara continued to stare in his eyes. Refusing to back down.

"Ok." He finally agreed. "You know that I'm doing my rotations, in the hospital, right?" He asked carefully.

"Yeah." She answered. "You're in the Pediatric ward?"

"No, pediatrics was ok... I mean, I'm not sure I'm good with kids, and I have no interest in being their doctor, but I moved on from there." He told her adamantly. "I'm doing my rotation in the psychiatric ward."

"Yeah. Ok."

"So, that's the problem." He turned to her, and looked at her desperately. "Don't you see?" He asked her. "You know what I am. You know there is something wrong with me. I have a heightened sense of empathy. I feel what they are feeling."

"What do you mean?" She asked carefully.

"I feel what they're feeling." He said again. "If the patients are crazy, I feel crazy. If they are severely depressed, I feel severely depressed. If they are anxious, I am anxious. I can feel all of it. All around me. Every day." He looked into her face, and cupped her cheeks with his hands. "It creeps in. I can't keep it out." He looked at the ground. "And if they are disturbed…"

Kara nodded. She was surprised by the frankness of what he was saying. He never usually showed his feeling.

Hayden collapsed down on the very edge of the couch. He nestled in, against the arm rest. He curled up his legs, and sat in a ball, as he leaned against the back of the couch.

"I have to get out of there Kara. I have to get out of the psyche ward. I can't handle it. I feel sorry for those people, I really do, but I can't handle it." He emphasized. "I feel cold and empty and so… sick to my stomach. I have a ten day rotation in there, and I have three, whole days left. I can't handle it. I can't go back. The longer I stay there, the more emotional I feel."

Kara watched him closely. He was so caught up in this. It was so real to him.

To her, she was completely thrown by it all. She had to down-shift her emotions, to sync with his brittle mentality.

"You can handle three days. You're stronger than you think." She tried to persuade him.

"Look at me Kara." He said desperately. "I've got the air condition up to twenty five degrees in here, and I've got a blanket around me. I'm treating myself for shock. I haven't slept for days." He shook his head. "I'm scared. I can't stand it in there another second." He told her, desperately.

He ran his hands through his hair again. "I have to go to work, on Friday night, when I finish in the ward, and I'll be so unstable." He shook his head. "I can't do this. I can't do this Kara. Something's got to give."

Kara bit her lip. "So... Call in sick on Friday night." She told him, compassionately. "In fact... don't even do it." She shook her head. "I'll do it for you. I just tell Corey that you can't work."

She shrugged, as if it was obvious. "You can't go in there acting like this. Besides, you *haven't* called in sick once, since you've been there." She looked at him, longingly, for a long time. "In fact." She suggested. "Take Saturday night off too."

Hayden looked at her doubtfully.

"It's ok Hayden." She assured him. "Corey won't mind."

"Are you sure." Hayden said, scratching at his head. "I don't want to let anyone down."

"Yeah." Kara nodded. "Bethany has been nagging Corey for more shifts anyway. She wants to go on holidays."

"Holidays?" Hayden acknowledged suddenly. "That's right. I heard you wanted to go with her." He asked. His voice was completely raspy.

Kara sighed. "Yeah." She whispered. "I need a holiday."

"To the Whitsunday's – The Great Barrier Reef?"

"Yeah." Kara acknowledged. "I haven't had a holiday since I was sixteen." She tried to explain.

"Good I'm glad." Hayden looked at her for a long time, then nodded. "Yes." He said suddenly. "Yes." He said again. "If you could, get me off work this weekend. I would really appreciate it" He shook his head. "I really mean that." He looked at her desperately. "I'm so sorry Kara. I'm sorry if I was rude to you, when you came in."

"No, it's ok." She tried to tell him.

She wanted to hug him, but he was a little bit jumpy

"I know you. I know how powerful your emotions are. I just want you to concentrate on feeling better."

"I'm not powerful Kara. It's just susceptible. I avoided people for so long. I hated feeling what they are feeling. Eventually I learned to handle it, but now I can't handle it at all." He looked at her. "Except when I'm around you." He sighed. "I like being around you. I knew you would make me feel better."

Kara smiled "Thank you for saying that."

"No, it's true." He explained desperately. "You feel calm, and quiet, but for the people in there… I'm supposed to help them, but I can't do it Kara. I can't help them. I don't know how."

"That's Ok Hayden. Really, you *don't* have to be a psychiatrist. It's going to be ok." Kara tried to assure him.

She sat down on the couch next to him. She very slowly put her hand on his back.

"I feel like I'm going crazy." He said squeezing tighter in his ball. "I act like its ok, when I'm at the hospital, in the ward. But I'm breaking down in there." He cried desperately. "If I don't stop…" He paused. "If I don't stop, I'm going to end up in there, with them."

"It's ok." She said one more time. "That would never happen. You're too strong."

"No I'm not." Hayden cried. "I thought I was, but I'm not."

Kara nodded. She turned inward, towards him. "But you said *I* can make you feel better, right?" She asked him carefully.

Hayden very slowly unwound himself. He sat up a little bit straighter. He looked at her uncertainly. "Yes, but my condition is like hypothermia. I have to come out of it slowly."

He suddenly dropped his hands. Then quickly he jumped out of his seat, and stood up. He was running his fingers furiously though his hair, one more time.

"How can you like someone so crazy?" he begged her. "I can't sit still, or think clearly. I can't handle this. You shouldn't have to deal with this."

Kara nodded. She got up and stepped closer to him. She looked into his eyes one more time. Then she put her arms around his neck, and leaned in. Giving him the most embracing hug, she had ever give anyone. She held him so tightly and close.

"Can you feel my love for you?" She asked him softly. "Can you feel *my* emotions?"

He tried to wriggle out of her arms at first. Then he stopped, and went silent. "Yes. I can feel it."

Her arms continued to hold him closely. Then he started to hug her back.

She just kept holding on. After a long time, she finally felt some of his weight collapse on her.

He put his chin on her shoulder, and she felt his head, rest against hers.

"Your body is so warm." He said softly. His fingers were moving quickly up and down her back. They were twitching, because he still couldn't stand still yet.

"I'll bring you back." She whispered.

She stood there for an indeterminate amount of time.

Their bodies started to sway, a little bit. Like they were dancing without music. Finally he stopped scratching up her back.

Kara kissed him on the cheek. He seemed like he was starting to calm down.

"I'll stay here, while you need me to." She offered "You can hold me." She told him. "You can hold me close. Like you used to do. You can feel my emotions. No one else's."

Hayden held her tighter, if that was possible. "You would do that for me?"

"Yes."

"Thank you." He whispered.

Kara nodded. She pushed back, out of his embrace.

"We'll go lie down." She told him, and ushered him towards the bedroom.

Kara helped him back into bed.

While she was so close to him, she could feel his heartbeat, going like a rocket. He was clearly having an anxiety attack.

Kara knew that, because her mother had had a few of them. When the family lost all their money.

Hayden lay down slowly. Kara took off his shoes, undid the buttons on his shirt, and took it off. Then she pulled up the sheets and quilt. Then she took off her own shoes, and lay down next to him.

He lay on his side, still wriggling, and twitching.

Kara slowly had him nestled, into her arms. He was holding her back, but his hands were still moving erratically. After some time they slowed, and calmed down, but it took an even longer time, for him to get to sleep.

Kara just laid there. She felt every move he made, and every nervous twitch. She just held him tighter, when he needed to be held.

She was really getting in deep. Hayden was sensitive, and apparently, so was his magic.

Maybe he needed help with this. He was so alone in this world, and this apartment building. He needed someone to lean on.

She just had to hold her ground, and support him, until he graduated.

Then he could make up his own mind. As for now, Hayden had to get through the night, and she had to help him do it.

Chapter 33

Hayden walked around his apartment, and he felt like he was dancing on air. Today was his last shift in the psych ward, ever, and now, he got to move on with his life.

Yesterday there was a thousand ton weight on his shoulders. Then this afternoon, as he walked home from the hospital. It simply disappeared.

It took him time, to get his bearings, but after that he felt pretty good. Not only that, but he felt pretty excited about his future.

Luckily, today, he didn't have to go to work at the club. He knew that would have been too overwhelming, but Kara had cleared his schedule.

It turned out, Kara was right about all of it.

Hayden was busy, and he was tired, and he was exhausted, all of the time.

Work and study, were all he could handle. Kara had been accurate, when she said that he didn't have time for a girlfriend.

Hayden jumped into bed, with his t-shirt and track pants on.

It was cold tonight. He laid flat on to his back, and thought about everything that had transpired, since he had first met Kara. It had been such an adventure, since she came into his life.

Now, he was going to graduate soon, and it would all be worth it.

After a while, he was starting to drift off, when there was a soft knock at his front door. Hayden stared at the ceiling for a moment. He rubbed at his eyes, and practically fell out of bed. His muscles were so stiff and sore.

"What's going on penny?" He asked, surprised, as he opened his door. Penny stood at his doorway. She looked somehow sad, and deflated.

She looked away. "Not much." She said without explaining.

Hayden looked at her for a long time. "Ok." He shrugged. "Is everything ok?"

Penny shook her head. "Sort of." She pondered, looking into space.

Hayden wasn't sure what to make of that. "Do you want to come in?"

Penny nodded weakly. She meandered in, and Hayden directed her to the couch. He sat next to her, and tried to smile reassuringly. "Is this about Randy?" He asked, trying to figure out, what her problem was.

Penny shook her head. "I think he's still using, but I don't even care about that." She said irritated. "That's not what's bothering me."

Hayden wasn't sure what she meant. He sat close to her, as he gave her all the time she needed, to explain herself.

"My dad's being deployed." She told him.

"What."

"My dad" She said again. "He's going to Iraq."

Hayden could have been knocked over with a feather. He didn't even know that Penny's father was in the military, in the first place.

He's already had two tours of duty." She explained. "First in East Timor, then in Afghanistan. He came back all screwed up, after the last one." She told him. She leaned closer to Hayden, as if she was telling him a secret.

"PTSD?" He asked softly.

"PTSD, stress, paranoia. You name it, he suffered it." She said, and then looked back at the floor. "You're a doctor" She shrugged. "You know what I'm talking about."

Hayden looked away embarrassed. He obviously did not cope well with the, mental health field of medicine, and suddenly he felt ashamed about that.

He also knew that military combat fatigue, was a different monster entirely. This condition hit very hard on its victims, and it was extremely chronic.

Judging from the last couple of weeks. Hayden felt like it was one of the few, mental health areas, that he could actually treat.

"He was getting better." Penny started talking again. "He was coming out of his funk, and now they're going send him back."

Hayden spoke carefully. "I can't imagine Penny. It must be so hard on you." He said delicately.

"No. It's hard on him." She said desperately.

Hayden took a deep breath in.

He was out of his depth and he knew it. He didn't know how to console her. Not in this instance.

"I don't really understand." She continued. "We just got out of Iraq. Now they want to go back in? I don't understand! If they have to go in now? What the hell did they achieve the first time?"

Hayden sighed, he was so caught off guard.

Penny buried her face in her hands. "Everything is so screwed up." She whispered. "What if he doesn't make it out this time?"

Hayden tried to console her, by rubbing her back. "It's ok Penny."

"Is it ok?" she asked, confused. "I just wish I understand better. What is really going on over there?"

"Islamic state is going on over there." He told her, softly.

"So what?" She yelled, annoyed.

Hayden changed tack. "You're right Penny. Going into Iraq, the first time, was a colossal indignation. Both for the troops, and the nation state." He informed her. "They had oil, and we wanted it, and we went in, under the guise of Al Qaeda, to get it." He sighed. "At least in my opinion."

Penny looked up at him, from behind her fingers.

"The global elite establishment had political and economic ties, into contracting out Iraq, after it had been invaded." He posited.

"What does that mean?" Penny sobbed.

Hayden took a deep breath in. "Iraq was one of the few Middle Eastern countries who controlled, and distributed, their own oil." Hayden tried to explain. "They had their own national oil company. So Iraq was able to keep their own slice of the pie."

Hayden took another deep breath, because this was a very controversial subject.

"But" He continued. "That did not sit well, with a lot of powerful people." Hayden told her. "So then, of course, we went to war with them." He huffed. "We declared them the axis of evil. Labeled them a threat to civilization, and we went to war."

"Ok." Penny said, listening closely.

"So." Hayden continued. "Iraq instituted a new regime, to rightly overthrow a dictator, but at the same time, western oil companies suddenly had the rights, to most of Iraq's oil fields." Hayden hesitated. "And Western companies had the contracts to fix up the oil infrastructure, and oil mining systems. The same infrastructure systems that had been crumbling for decades, because Iraq had been slapped with sanctions, for so long."

Hayden sighed. "Iraq was languishing for a long time. Ready for the taking." Hayden shook his head. "There is no way Iraq was making weapons of mass destruction." He proclaimed. "They couldn't even get equipment in, to fix up their own oil pipelines." Hayden took another deep breath in. "That war was fucked up."

Penny took her hands away, and started at him.

"But now it's for real Penny." He told her.

"What do you mean?"

Hayden spoke as forcefully as he could, without upsetting her.

"Islamic state are a terrible organization." He tried to explain. "The first thing they do, when they invade an area, is terrorize, kill, and rape. Close down the schools, and subjugate all the women."

Hayden put his hand under Penny's chin, and forced her to look up. "They would keep girls like you in servitude in the household, and never let you out. Or marry you off to their soldiers, who would mistreat you, and oppress you unbearably." Hayden took another deep breath in. He didn't want to scare her, but he wanted to help her understand.

"Every aspect of society is suffocated, and coerced, by some fucked up interpretation of their wayward ideals, and religious philosophy. Everything they do is about living in their backwards, uneducated, and unenlightened society. Where every thought is about hating the West, and modernity. Every action is some strict code of conduct of male domination, and a state of prohibition, anger, frustration, and condescension."

Penny looked at him, desperately with her mouth open.

"Penny." Hayden lowered his voice, and tried to sound supportive. "If your father is going over there… Then I am with him all the way! And you should be so, so, proud of him."

"Really." She mumbled.

"Yes. Penny." He said emphatically. "I am usually against war, but not this time." He told her definitively. "We can't let IS stand. We can't let them try and take over this world."

Penny lost it.

She started crying uncontrollably. "I am proud of dad." She snuffled. "I love my dad."

Hayden leaned forward. He reached for the box of tissues, on the coffee table, and offered one to her. Penny wearily took it.

She blew her nose, and continued crying, while wiping at her eyes. Then, suddenly, she threw her arms around Hayden's neck. She cried, tearfully, on his shoulder.

Hayden took her small, thin body, in his arms, and held her. He thought about if for a long time. "If only I was that brave." He told her. "To go over there, and be a doctor on the front lines." He held her tighter. "Your father is very brave. He's a true hero." He encouraged her.

Penny looked up at him with bleary eyes. "Thank you Hayden."

Hayden shook his head. "No, don't thank me. Thank your dad, for me. He's one of the brave soldiers, who defend our freedom. Since we live in the best country in the world."

Penny continued to nuzzle into his shoulder, and his arms.

She sniffled, and sobbed in his embrace. Then finally she looked up at him again. "Thanks for explaining it." She said delicately.

She buried her head, back into his shoulder. Hayden held onto her tightly, until she finally stopped sobbing.

Then she looked up at him. She looked deep into his eyes.

He looked back at her. Then suddenly, something took over him.

He never saw it coming.

He found himself kissing her. He didn't know how it started, but he was kissing her on the lips. Then, his lips were all over her, and she was all over him. Then they were laying back on the couch.

Then she was tearing at his clothes, and he found himself tearing at hers.

Then, before he knew it, he was making love to her. It happened, barely before he even knew what was going on. It just happened.

It was such an emotional outpouring for both of them.

Then they were together.

He never expected this, but then again, his whole life was being turned upside down lately. He never expected any of this.

He was making love to penny, and it was so passionate.

Chapter 34

Hayden felt strange, as he stowed his gear, in his locker, at the club.

He wasn't sure how to act around anyone anymore. Specifically after what had happened last week.

Last week, when Kara had comforted him, and Penny had slept with him.

He hadn't told anyone, about either event, since they happened.

He slowly made his way out behind the bar. Kara was pouring a beer for some young kid, who looked so juvenile, his eighteenth birthday might have been today.

Kara smiled at the kid, as if she noticed it too. He had that wide eyes and starry look. The kind of look you got, when you came to a nightclub for the first time. Hayden waited as the young guy paid for his drink, collected his beer, and wondered off back to his friends.

"Hi." Hayden said nervously.

Kara nodded at him. "Hi."

He took a deep breath in. "Thank you for helping me last week."

Kara shook her head as if it was nothing. "Your welcome." She told him. "I'm glad you're ok."

"Yeah. I'm fine." He told her.

"So you're out now?" She asked him cautiously. "You've finished your psyche rotation?"

Hayden nodded vigorously. "Yes, I have." He paused. "I had the conviction to get through it... because of you." He looked at the ground. "Thanks again for everything." He paused. "Thanks for getting Corey to replace my shifts."

"You're welcome." Kara smiled to herself.

She acted like it was no big deal. Hayden suddenly felt self-conscious.

He felt like *he* was making too big a deal about it. But it was a big deal, and he was still embarrassed about it.

"You know what?" Kara asked suddenly, out of the blue. "We should drink to this."

Kara quickly turned around. She picked up two shot glasses from the bench, and put them on the counter. She took the bourbon bottle from the rack, and poured two shots.

She picked one up, and gave it to him.

"Nostrovia." She said to him cheerfully. "To your freedom from the psyche ward." She clinked glasses, and gulped down the shot in one go.

Hayden laughed to himself, and downed his own shot.

Nostrovia - was a Russian word. It meant - cheers, and to good health. Every now and then, they would get some crazy Russian in the club, who wanted to toast them.

"So you're staying back for clean-up duty, with me tonight." Kara asked happily.

"Yeah." Hayden acknowledged. "I am."

Usually Kara would stay back with Corey on a Saturday night, but Corey was out of town at a christening. Hayden said he would fill in.

"Good." Kara smiled at him again.

After that, Kara finally turned around and got back to work.

Hayden took a deep breath in, then served his first customer. The bourbon had warmed his blood, and it made him feel good.

The usual craziness of the night, set in pretty quickly. He got to work, and didn't stop until it was closing time.

As usual, on a Saturday night, the staff practically had to drag the patrons out by the hair. To make them get out.

Closing time was always a nightmare on a Saturday night/Sunday morning.

When everyone was out, he cleaned up with Kara.

He tried to do his work quickly, but for some reason, it felt like Kara was resisting him again. She didn't say much.

Hayden mopped up his section of the club, and stowed the mop buckets away. Kara made sure the bar was moisture free. She was letting the radio do the talking. It seemed like every song that came on, was strangely on par with what Hayden was thinking about.

Hayden looked over at Kara and watched her work. She was so proficient.

Kara walked into the office and completed her office duties, then locked the safe. She walked back out with her bag over her shoulder. Her uniform was untucked, and her hair was up in a ponytail.

"Do you want to walk to the cab rank?" She asked causally.

Kara had *not* bought her car yet. Her holiday fund, was setting back her car fund, just a little bit.

Hayden shook his head. He moved forward and put his hands on her waist. "I've done something, and I need to tell you about it."

Kara looked around distracted.

She smiled awkwardly, then settled her vision on the security camera. The whole club was wired with them. The monitors were in Corey's office. Kara instinctively stepped back, out of his grasp.

She nodded her head. "What?"

Hayden grinned.

He actually had an announcement, and he knew it would blow her away. It had nothing to do with Penny though. Hayden had done *other* momentous things lately, and no one else knew about them. Except for his mom.

"I bought a Jeep."

"What?" Kara asked incredulously.

"A jeep." Hayden said again. Amazed at his own sentence. "I bought a black, Rubicon, 4by4, soft top, Jeep."

Kara fluttered her eyelids. She was completely astonished. "What?"

"A jeep." Hayden said again. He could feel himself grinning like a Cheshire cat.

"When?"

"Two weeks ago."

"You've been driving around in a jeep, for two weeks, and you didn't tell me?"

"Yeah, I'm sorry." He said, exasperated. "I just couldn't believe it myself. And my life got a bit crazy." Hayden shook his head, humbly.

Kara stared at him, amazed.

Hayden continued his story. "After driving around in Lucy's

BMW last summer. *Then* I was jealous of you, when *you* said that you were getting your own car." He explained. "There was no going back after that. I applied for a loan, and they gave it to me." He smirked. "When the bank saw *med school* on my application, they practically threw the money at me."

"And you bought a jeep?" Kara said again. Stunned.

"It's my dream car." Hayden said, smitten.

Kara got a light in her eye. "Is your car here? Right now?"

"Yeah." Hayden answered. "It's parked out front."

Kara grinned, amazed. "Take me to see it."

Hayden nodded. He led Kara out of the club. They locked up the entrance tight, and he led her down the street. He got his keys out, and gestured to his new car.

As she walked towards it, and came up to it. She couldn't believe it. "Wow." She said again, as she walked around the entire car. "It's brand new."

Hayden grinned.

The Jeep was big, black, sleek, and quite frankly awesome. The car had big wheels, and the soft top. Inside, it was beautifully furnished with leather seats, cup holders, plenty of space, and a satellite navigation system that came standard.

"It's amazing Hayden."

"You really like it." Hayden gleamed.

Kara nodded her head. "Are you kidding, I've never been more turned on in my life."

Hayden was caught off guard. Kara giggled to herself

Kara threw open the car door, and jumped up into the passenger seat. She studied the car from the inside out.

She looked at all the nooks and crannies, and breathed in the new car smell. Then she looked around, from the back to the front.

Hayden jumped in the driver's seat next to her, and looked at her. She looked like a kid in a candy store.

Kara started inhaling, and exhaling, the sweet aroma of new car, and leather. She breathed in slow and deep.

"Wow." She said again for the third time.

"Yeah, it's pretty cool." Hayden exclaimed.

"I'll say." Kara smiled again. "Turn the ignition on." She yelled at him suddenly. "So we can put the top down."

"What?" Hayden asked, surprised.

"So we can look at the stars!" Kara yelled out, gleefully.

Hayden shrugged. He turned the ignition over, and the car purred to life. He fumbled over the instruments for a moment, then found the correct button. The soft top, steadily started reclining.

Kara grinned back at him. "This is so cool."

She suddenly reached back, and adjusted the seat position. She put her seat all the way back, as far as it would go, and laid back on it.

She was staring at the night sky above her. "We can watch the stars from here." She said looking deep into abyss, from the not-so-clear, night sky, from a city street.

Hayden watched her. She looked so excited.

He put his own seat back too, and looked at the stars.

"This is so perfect." She glanced at him. "It suits you."

"I hope so." Hayden blushed.

"I'm so glad you bought it."

"Thanks for saying that."

"You deserve it." She insisted. "You work so hard." She looked around the broad night sky. "So do you know any of the constellations?" she asked, gesturing to the panoramic view.

"No, not really Hayden said, shrugging. "I can see the Southern Cross."

"So can I. That's the only one I know too." She shook her head. She looked wistfully around the car again. "Can you take me for a ride?"

Hayden nodded. "Of course I can. I was going to take you home, anyway." He proclaimed. "It's nice that we can cruise around. Especially at 4:30 in the morning." He laughed.

Kara laughed too. She was so genuinely happy for him.

He adjusted his seat into the upward position, and waited for Kara to do the same.

Kara suddenly lost her smile, and took a deep breath in. "We haven't... We haven't' talked about the *other* thing tonight." She said, slowly, uncertainly

"What other thing?"

"Penny."

Hayden froze in his seat. "What about Penny." He asked carefully, as if he didn't already know.

"Come on Hayden." Kara said, ironically. "You know the grapevine leads straight to the Joker Club."

"Yeah." Hayden sighed. He wasn't sure how to tackle this particular subject. "Yeah. I know."

"Was it lust or love?" Kara asked, very slowly and cautiously.

Hayden chewed on his lip for a long time. "Lust."

Kara nodded her head. "Ok."

"I'm sorry Kara. It was late at night, and we were both vulnerable, and ..."

"No." Kara explained. "You don't have to explain it to me." She told him definitively. "You should do what you want to do... and what makes you happy. Honestly, I'm glad that I'm not the only girl you've... Well anyway. I trust you. I believe in you. *To thy own self be true*, right?" She said again.

"Right." Hayden said exasperated.

He didn't know why she kept coming back, to that particular phrase. The sentence always just felt right, at the time she said it. Just like it felt right, when he was with Penny that night.

"So, what about you?" He asked tentatively "How is you job at the café going? The Buttercup Café? I believe." He hesitated. "You never told me you worked at a café, in the first place."

Kara looked away embarrassed. "My little secret." She told him, and then blushed. "Yes, it's going very well."

"Why didn't you tell me?" He asked confused.

"I don't know. I just wanted to see how it would work out first." She explained. "Before I told anyone."

"And how *has* it worked out."

"Good." She told him again. "Really good." She hesitated. "I get to work the morning and days, and it's just a quiet, fun, little job. I like it."

"I'm glad for you." Hayden told her earnestly.

Kara nodded sheepishly. "It's a nice balance, and I still get to work with you, at the club. I still love working at the club."

"Yeah." He grinned. "You sound like you're way ahead of the game." Hayden encouraged her.

"Yeah, and I'm explaining that to a med student, who is already miles ahead of the game!" She grimaced. "It's a little intimidating."

"Have we met?" Hayden asked her. "You know how awkward and shy I can be. I still have an awkward bedside manner at the hospital. I haven't found my way yet."

"But you will." She told him thoughtfully.

"I'm glad you think so."

"I know you will." She looked him in the eyes, for reassurance.

"And you will be just as successful, in whatever you do." He informed her.

Kara shrugged. "I hope so." She said timidly. "Because I might be able to afford, part-time university, next year."

"What?"

"Well." Kara grinned. "I haven't *just* been saving up, for a car, all this time. I've been saving for University as well. I think I can afford to go to university next year."

"That's awesome, Kara." Hayden said excited.

"Yeah. I really want to go."

"You will definitely be a good student." He told her.

"I want to learn about the world." She giggled. "Since you've given me, such a head start."

"I hardly explained anything."

"You explained everything." She said sincerely.

"I'm so glad that you want to do this." He said adamantly. "You can learn whatever you want to learn. You can cross faculties, and find what you're passionate about."

"Thanks Hayden." She looked at him, earnestly. "But it will be part time. So I will have plenty of time, to figure out what interests me."

Hayden smiled. He wanted to lean over and kiss her, but he knew she wouldn't let him. She remained vigilant about him finishing his studies, uninterrupted.

"We should go." Hayden told her. He turned over the ignition, and put the Jeep in gear. He started driving around the city streets.

Kara adjusted herself in her seat, and she smiled again. "I love you Hayden." She said softly, as he drove.

Chapter 35

Hayden's fifth hospital rotation was a surgery elective. He had just finished a shift in the operating room, and he was exhausted.

Being in the O.R. was intricate work. It was less about sensing the problem, more about fixing it.

This rotation was extremely different, to working in all the other fields. Not like the ER, and orthopedics. All of his rotations so far, were very different, and challenging.

In surgery, by the time the patient got to the operating table, the diagnosis had already been made. What the surgical team had to do, was assess the damage to the tissues, and the organs, and then repair it.

The human body was fragile. There were sometimes complications in the body that were interrupted by a man made, or an organic process, and they had to be corrected.

The only word Hayden could use to explain surgery, was *intricate*. The human body was composed of so many different elements. To fix one thing. You had to work around a thousand others. Including a lot of red blood.

When he was allowed to step in to assist, there was no room for mistakes.

It was getting better though. The longer Hayden spent in the operating room, the more he was beginning to feel it. The more he was drawn to the specific artery that had to be repaired. The specific incision that had be made. The specific aortic tear that he had to smooth over. The specific suture that he had to stitch in.

His hands, and attention, were starting to move to the problem area, without him knowing it. Whether that was from gaining experience, or from his intuition kicking in, it wasn't clear.

He was starting to see what he had to do, in order for the body to be able to heal itself. His reviews so far had been good, and he was really proud of that.

Today had been a long shift in the operating theater. After he was finished, he walked home quickly. Then he crashed on his bed, and went to sleep.

The only problem was; he woke up again.

He sat up in bed and looked around his bedroom. Something didn't feel right.

Maybe he felt out of place because Kara wasn't here, and he so desperately wanted her to be. Maybe he was scared about the future.

He was going to graduate in eight days. He was going to get his board exam results, in one.

Hayden checked his watch. It was 1:02AM. It was so dark and cloudy outside. There was no moon or stars, and it looked like there was a storm brewing. Hayden couldn't sit still. The feeling was growing stronger.

Something was coming, but it wasn't exactly that. Maybe something had already happened. Hayden wondered where Kara was. Hopefully she was ok.

Hayden jumped out of bed. He paced the floor for a moment. Then found his way to the bathroom. He threw some water on his face, and looked in the mirror.

As he was washing his hands, he stared in the mirror for a long time. He actually started to feel nauseated, and his breathing was labored.

Was he having an anxiety attack, about nothing?

Hayden shook his head. He had to snap out of this.

He couldn't seem to move. All he could do was just breathe in and out. His muscles were so tight.

He had to figure this out, but he couldn't. He went back to bed, and tried to lay still, but his heart was pounding.

He was laying there for another five more minutes, trying to calm down.

Then it happened.

An inflamed banging, started pounding on his front door. It was so intense and loud, it felt like the person was trying to knock his door down.

Hayden realized immediately, the sense of urgency, and jumped up. He went to the door and answered it.

Of course it was Randy. Of course it was. One of his worst fears had been realized.

Randy was hysterical. He opened his mouth to start screaming, but he didn't have to.

Hayden knew instantly what was wrong: It was Penny.

Randy grabbed Hayden's arm. "You have to come to my apartment! It's Penny! She's taken something! I mean I gave her something, and she keeled over right in front of me! I called the ambulance, but *you're* here. You have to do it. You have to save her!" Randy screamed, chaotically in Hayden's ear.

Hayden felt like the room was spinning. The words were just a formality. Hayden understood what was happening now. He understood what he was feeling. The picture started to make sense.

He staggered backwards. He hardly had time to react, or get his thoughts in order, but he knew what to do. Even before Randy even started screaming.

He sprinted into his room to get his medical bag, and went to the fridge where he kept the vial of epinephrine, AKA, adrenalin.

Hayden had swiped the vial from the hospital in case Randy overdosed. He did it because Penny had asked him to.

Amazingly no one at the hospital, had discovered it yet, or had accused him of taking it. He did it because Penny's speech had been so desperate. She had convinced him he might need it one day, and now he did. Except it was for the wrong person.

Hayden shook his head in disgust. He ran across the hall, into Randy's apartment.

He saw Penny, and she was passed out on the couch. Her nose was bleeding. Her long blonde hair, feel down to her lower back. She was wearing a pink top, with a black skirt. She looked so delicate and vulnerable.

"What have you done?" Hayden swore, profoundly shocked.

This was clearly an overdose, or an anaphylactic shock.

Randy put his head down, ashamed. He had clearly dealt her, whatever she had taken.

Hayden checked Penny's slow and irregular pulse. She was in V-tack. He could feel it.

Suddenly Hayden felt implored to check the rest of her body. There was something else going on here.

He moved his hand. It brushed past her breasts, and landed on her stomach.

Suddenly Hayden was knocked back.

The force was so strong, it was like getting hit by a freight train. He was knocked so far back that he must have landed six feet away. Then he hit the wall.

He lay there for a moment, in stunned silence. Staring at the ceiling, breathing in and out.

"What just happened?" Randy asked, astounded.

Hayden took in one long breath. He slowly got up, and stood there in shock.

He finally shook his head. "We have to save her."

Randy stared at him desperately. "What's wrong?"

Hayden shook his head. Stunned. "There is life inside of her."

Hayden got up. He went to Penny, and grabbed the needle. He took a deep breath in, and injected the adrenalin into her radial artery. He administered it, threw the needle away, and quickly started compressions.

He continued for two minutes. Then he checked her pulse again. Luckily it was steady, and getting stronger. Hayden gave a sigh of relief, and looked at Randy.

A moment later the paramedics came in the open door. Hayden gave a stern look to Randy, to keep his mouth shut.

"We've got an overdose here." One of paramedics shouted over to the other one. "Sir, can you tell me what this girl has ingested." He asked quickly, as he and his partner, carefully loaded Penny on to the gurney.

He asked the question to Hayden. Probably because Hayden looked more like he was capable of intelligent speech.

"Cocaine." Hayden replied. He didn't need to ask. There was still white powder around Penny's nose, and Hayden had already established, what Randy's drug of choice was.

The other paramedic was checking Penny's pulse, and blood pressure.

"I'm a med student. I live across the hall. I wasn't here when it happened, but Randy…" Hayden began, referring to the stunned mullet in the room. "He came and got me, and I started compressions." He informed the two men. "Her pulse came up, fairly steadily."

The paramedic nodded. "We have to get her to the hospital. One of you can come with us, or if you want, you can follow us."

The other paramedic nodded. "Her pulse is getting stronger."

They obviously didn't make time for small talk. Hayden blinked, and then they were gone.

As soon as they left the lounge room, a ball of rage welled up in Hayden. "You arse hole" He screamed.

Randy staggered around the room, absolutely bewildered. "I didn't think this would happen."

"Of course it was going to happen! I told you it was going to happen! I told you to leave Penny out of this."

"I'm sorry…I didn't think…"

"You never think." Hayden screamed, not able to control his anger. "You have no idea what you've done!" He scolded him.

"I know." Randy sobbed. He was shaking uncontrollably, and he looked like he was going to faint.

"You said you wouldn't do it anymore. What is wrong with you?" Hayden yelled, venting his absolute fury. "She came to me, because she was worried about *you*… Then, this is the position you put her in?" He demanded.

"I'm sorry." Randy said, shaking his head again. "I thought it good quality stuff." Randy put his hands on his head, overwhelmed.

"People have reactions to drugs, you idiot!" Hayden screamed at him, not being able to contain his anger.

Hayden furiously ran his fingers through his hair.

He and Penny had slept together. They had been so close and intimate. Hayden should have been in contact with her since then. He should have followed up on this. He should have been, a better friend.

He had just let Penny shrug off their affair, like it was nothing, but it was something. It was a big deal to him, and maybe to her too.

Penny was vulnerable, and he wasn't there for her.

"I hate you Randy." Hayden screamed. "How could you ever do this? You treat people like they are there for your amusement. What the hell did you *think* was going to happen?"

"I don't know." Randy cried. "I didn't think this...I didn't think this would happen." He stammered, as he looked up. His eyes wide, with terror "What did you say before?" He asked suddenly, confused. "Did you just tell me that Penny's...pregnant?"

"Yes." Hayden said, exasperated. "Yes she's pregnant."

"How do you know?"

"I just do." Hayden murmured, without explaining.

"Well, is yours or mine?"

"What." Hayden screamed back, seething.

"Don't think I don't know, what happened, between the two of you." Randy rumbled.

Hayden could barely control himself. "It's yours Randy. It's barely a fertilized embryo. It's a couple of weeks old. Of course it's fucking yours! I haven't been with Penny in months."

"And how the hell did that happen?"

"Focus Randy!" Hayden demanded. "You almost just killed your girlfriend." He shouted at him. "I was with Penny at a vulnerable time, in both of our lives, but for whatever reason; she loved *you*."

"I know she did." Randy said, softly.

"Well then, get your act together." Hayden swore. "You have to go to the hospital."

"I can't believe this." Randy said, mumbling.

He didn't quite understand what was going on. "I know I screwed up, but I didn't mean to. I didn't' mean for this to happen. I don't know what to say." He stammered. "I know I can't fix this." He shrugged, aimlessly. "I have to get to the hospital." He said confused. Then he looked up. "Why didn't you tell the paramedics about the needle you put in her wrist?"

"Why the hell do you think?" Hayden screamed. "Because I'm not a doctor! Because I'm not licensed to practice medicine! Because I'm not insured to practice medicine! Because I'm not supposed to have a vial of adrenalin on me, or laying round in my fucking fridge."

Hayden walked round in a circle, he was so mad. "I put my career on the line for this, because she told me it would happen, and I believed her. It was supposed to happen to *you*."

"I wish it was me." Randy staggered.

Hayden looked at him with fierce contempt.

The stupid idiot was still high on the drugs that he had ingested, so it probably wasn't a bad batch. It was just that Penny had probably allergic to something in it. Or she took too much of it.

"Won't they notice that you gave her a needle?"

"They will only notice that she has taken a drug. It's called cocaine! Because of you! Adrenalin isn't a drug. It's produced naturally in the adrenal gland. I'm hoping they won't detect it, because they have no reason to look for it, and no way to test for it."

"Ok." Randy said exhausted. "Ok." He said again, clearly trying to get his thoughts straight. "I'm sorry. I'm sorry." He blubbered. "Thank you for what you did."

"Don't thank me just yet." Hayden swore again. "She could have lost oxygen. She could have brain damage. She could go into anaphylactic shock, and start convulsing her way into a coma." Hayden looked at Randy desperately. "She could still die. She is not out of the woods yet!"

"But you just saved her didn't you." Randy queried him. Staring vacantly.

Hayden shook his head, and looked at the ground. "I don't know."

Randy was shaking violently now.

"Just go be with Penny. Just go. Get out of my sight. I can't bare it any more. You make me sick."

Randy started to meander towards the door. "Are you coming?"

Hayden shook his head. "No. I'll be there later."

Randy stared at him for a long time. "Thankyou."

"Get out." Hayden bellowed.

He told Randy to get out of his own apartment.

"Wait." Hayden said suddenly. "Whatever you were using. Take it with you." Hayden explained to him. "The hospital can test it… And, I'm sure the police will want to talk to you." He exclaimed. "It will go much smoother, if you confess up front."

Randy reached into his top shirt pocket, and checked that the drugs were still there.

"Go be with your girlfriend." Hayden said quietly.

Hayden watched his neighbor leave. He felt full of fear, panic, and adrenalin, and it was all taking its toll.

This was something that was *supposed* to happen, in the trauma room, of the hospital. Not in his everyday life.

Hayden stood there for a few minutes, gathering his thoughts. A slight trace of Penny's blood was on the couch. There was one line of coke still on the coffee table.

It was so unnecessary. They were young and healthy. They didn't need this.

He couldn't understand why Penny had changed her mind about this.

Was *he* responsible for that?

Maybe it was because penny was now pregnant, and hormonal, and not thinking clearly.

Finally he turned around and left.

He closed the door to Randy's apartment, and went into his own apartment.

He sat down on the bed, and looked out the window. It was going to storm soon. He saw lightning in the distance.

Hayden curled up on the bed. Then the thunder boomed outside. He looked around bewildered, and then he started crying. Helplessly.

All of this was so overwhelming. Yet this was the life he always wanted: The life of a doctor.

Chapter 36

It was a rough 24 hours.

Hayden finally sat down at the computer, and connected to his board exam results, from the Australian medical licensing authority. His results were released yesterday, and if he didn't pass them, he didn't get his medical license.

Ordinarily, he would have been on the website, the second they were released, but yesterday he forgot.

Yesterday was one of his final shifts in the Operating Room, and then after that, he went to see Penny.

Penny was ok. She was embarrassed, and her pride was hurt, but she was ok.

She was grateful he was there, and she had learned her lesson.

It turns out she *was* hormonal. She was still upset about her dad, and her emotions were all over the place, so she tried to take the edge off.

Hayden spent hours talking to her. She told him everything that was going on, and how she felt about all of it.

Hayden just tried to comfort her, as best he could. Then, after that, he was exhausted. He came home, and went to sleep.

Right now, however, Hayden focused on the computer again. He jumped back to reality, and intensely scanned the commuter screen.

"Yes!" He screamed out loud, as the results page came up.

He read it again, to make sure he was reading it right. Then he relaxed. He had passed his boards! In fact, he had done well on them.

Hayden sighed a sigh of relief.

After that, he drowsily made his way to his email page. There were about 200 neglected emails, because he hadn't checked them lately. Almost all of them were advertising related, but there were a few interesting ones.

He was on email number 196, when there was another knock at his door.

He was surprised that time it was Kara.

"Hey Kara." He said modestly.

He looked closely at the girl, and she was pale again. Hayden knew instantly what was wrong with her.

"Hi." She said softly, as she walked in.

Hayden followed her in, and stared at her.

Kara saw his glare, and tried to explain.

"I changed my diet, and it worked." She began softly. "For the last few months, it's been really good. Hardly any pain at all" She said cryptically. "But there are so many yummy foods out there, and they all have gluten in them, or lactose."

"So you're sick again." He said, referring to her severe period pain, which neither of them wanted to say out loud.

She looked around disorientated.

Hayden leaned over and kissed her on the cheek. It was the first time he had kissed her, in such a long time.

Kara blushed, then staggered to the couch, and lay down on it.

She smiled at him, even though she was clearly in major discomfort.

Hayden thought she still looked pretty, even when she was so ragged. He lifted her shirt, and put his hands on her stomach.

"Lactose" He told her. "You're still eating chocolate."

"No one *willingly* gives up chocolate." She said frustrated. "I just had a little bit."

"Really." He said, trying to be nice about it.

"Ok, maybe a lot."

He looked in her eyes, then he leaned down and kissed her tummy.

Kara smiled.

He leaned down and kissed it, a few more times.

"Keep going." Kara snickered.

Suddenly he moved his hand to the side of her head. He slowly figured out the other part of the problem.

"Your pituitary gland." He explained slowly. "It's launching stress hormones."

Kara looked at him.

"You wrap yourself up, in so much stress Kara." He told her, exasperated. "What are you so stressed about?" He looked her in the eyes. "When girls put themselves under this much pressure. They make it so much worse for themselves."

"Yeah, cause we have so much choice about that." Kara said, sarcastically.

"Yeah, I know. I'm sorry."

Kara raised her eyebrows. "I don't mean to stress myself out. I just do it." She commented.

Hayden kneeled down, next to the couch, where she was lying. He grabbed her hand, and then settled himself on the floor.

Kara smiled. Then stayed quiet for a moment.

Finally, she spoke. "When I'm with you… It feel like you're taking the pain away." She noted, softly.

"If there is so much of it." He commented. "It would be nice if we could share it."

Kara closed her eyes. Then she opened them, and quickly looked into his face.

"Wow." She said startled, and instantly took her hand away. "You *are* taking my pain away." She looked at him exasperated. "Don't do that." She argued. "It's meant for me, not you."

"We can share it." Hayden grabbed her hand again, and wouldn't let go. He used his, somehow magic empathy, to take her pain away again.

"Why are you doing that?" She smirked, at him. "Why are you so good to me? How are you even doing that?"

Hayden took another deep breath in, and then shrugged. "It's like electricity. It flows through you, and in to me."

Hayden curled up against the side of the couch. He could feel it now. The pain was overwhelming him.

He still didn't know, how girls lived like this.

He focused on his breathing, for a few minutes.

"Will you come with me?" He asked her suddenly, out of nowhere. He had meant to ask her this question for a long time, but he kept putting it off. "To my university graduation?"

Kara was taken aback for a moment. "Yeah."

"Good." He said, relieved. "Thankyou." He nodded at her. "What are you so stressed about?" He asked again.

Kara looked away, and stared out the window, for a length of time. "Penny, and you, and everything's going to change soon." She barely whispered.

Hayden nodded, because she was right.

"Penny's pregnant."

Kara gulped down a lump in her throat. "Really." She asked.

"Yeah." Hayden replied.

"Is it yours?"

"No." He said, rolling his eyes.

"We're talking about the same Penny, who's currently in the hospital, right?"

"Yeah." He replied, idly. "She only just found out yesterday."

"After she overdosed."

"I don't want to talk about that." Hayden said frustrated. "The girl does one stupid thing in her life, and… this is what happens."

"Yeah, I get it." Kara murmured. "What about Randy?"

"Charged with Possession." Hayden answered. "But because he was fully cooperative, and he agreed to go to rehab. They let him go with a good behavior warning."

"The rumor mill was working overtime." Kara told him, desperately. "I didn't know what had happened… All I knew, is that you were there to save her."

"It was nothing." Hayden brushed her off.

"It never is, with you."

"Penny wants the baby." He said suddenly, changing the subject. "She's happy about it."

"I would imagine she would be." Kara nodded. "She's very maternal. I've always known that about her."

"Yeah, she'll be a great mum." Hayden proclaimed. "Now that I've finished med school. I can be there for her. I can be a better friend to her. I haven't been a good friend lately."

"Penny knows how hard you work… Like I do. Trust me. She knows you're there." Kara tried to persuade him.

Hayden shrugged. "I hope so." He mumbled.

Kara shook her head, and spoke forcefully all of a sudden. "Let go of my hand." She cried. "Go check your emails. I can see them on your lap top, from here." She told him. "I didn't want to disturb you. I just wanted to see you." She told him earnestly. "You should finish what you were doing, before I got here…I don't want to demand your time like this."

"You don't demand anything, I don't want to give."

"Well you've taken my stress away. Just by the sound of your voice." She told him. "You should let go of my hand." She said again, trying to take it back.

Hayden thought about it for a moment, and finally let go. He instantly felt a wave of pleasure go through his body. The pain relinquished.

He groggily got up, and made his way to the computer.

"I have one more day left as an intern." Hayden said suddenly, as he mindlessly deleted his unwanted emails. "My last shift is tomorrow." He told her.

He was glad he could tell her, because he had to tell someone. It was another momentous event.

"Yeah. I know." Kara nodded.

"I don't want to screw up tomorrow."

"You won't." She smiled, although Hayden was perfectly serious.

"It does feel like everything is going to change." He admitted.

"Yeah, why do you think I'm so stressed?" Kara exclaimed.

"I don't know what position I'm going to get, and I don't know what hospital, I'm going to go to."

"Will you have to move?"

"I don't know." Hayden said, nervously.

Kara thought about that. She didn't speak for a long time. Then she noticed something in the corner of the room, and looked around distracted, for a moment.

"I've never seen your guitar in here before." She said suddenly.

"It's usually in the spare room." Hayden answered.

"But you've been playing?"

"A little bit." He admitted. "

"Would you play it for me?" She asked timidly.

Hayden froze. He felt somehow embarrassed, because he wasn't good enough. "What do you want to hear?"

"Something you wrote yourself."

Hayden huffed. "How do you know I write my own songs?" He said, frustrated.

"Lucy told me." Kara shrugged. "At least, when she was still talking to me."

"Sorry."

"Not your fault." Kara replied. "She's slowly coming around… In fact she rang me the other day."

Hayden finished his emails off, and shut down the computer.

"Please Hayden." She pleaded with him.

Hayden sat frozen, for a while longer.

He very slowly got up, grabbed the guitar, and sat down on the recliner. He sat with the guitar in his lap, and started strumming some chords, on the strings.

Then he started singing, very softly. Very nervously.

The night shines bright
Hayden stuttered, at the start, as he sang.
And the world turns on its axis

And the star outside the window, shining brighter than the brightest star you've seen
And the mysteries of the world, you want explained.
When yesterday, you were smiling at the rain.
I know you
You believe in all the things you've never known
All the exciting seeds, you've never sewn
The playground of the world, you want to know
And nothing stops. Cause that's how far you'll go
So don't wake up
The dream's still there at sunrise
And if you fall, you'll fall in my arms. Like you always have before
You know it girl, like you've always done before.

Hayden stuttered again, and blushed, terribly embarrassed. "It's not finished."

Kara closed her eyes for a moment. "That was beautiful, Hayden."

Hayden shook his head.

"No really. It was beautiful." She told him, trying to look in his eyes, but he looked away.

"I'm just an amateur." He insisted, then changed the subject. "You should rest Kara."

Kara smiled at him, as she lay curled up on the couch. There was a look of longing in her eyes. Hayden could feel it too.

Kara grimaced as she got an agonizing cramp again. "Let's see how far we'll both go." She said softly.

Hayden nodded. He just liked that she was here. So he could watch over her. In a very temperamental world.

Chapter 37

Hayden looked at Kara, as he strolled the grounds, of the university campus. It was so reassuring, to have her next to him, on this particular, historic day.

They had just attended his graduation ceremony, and he was walking around humbly, with his cap and gown on.

Finally, after all the work, and all the study, and all the toil – he had actually graduated medical school. The victory of it all, tasted so good on his lips.

Today, he and Kara, were walking around in the fresh air. It was a bright summer day.

Kara sat down at a table, at one of the nostalgic café's on campus.

His mum and dad were both at the ceremony too. Being in the auditorium, was the first time they had been in the same room, in over a decade.

He was going to meet them later, for a graduation dinner. He already had his official photos taken with his parents, and a couple with Kara too.

Currently, he was focusing on being with Kara now. He was so curious about her.

"Why were you avoiding me at the club on Saturday?" Hayden enquired suddenly. He settled down, into the chair, at the table. "I didn't know if I was going to see you again."

"Are you serious? I was avoiding you on Saturday night, because I was sad. It was your last shift at the club. I knew everyone was going to miss you." She said wistfully. "But you *had* to see me again, because I was coming to your graduation today."

"Yeah, I worried you wouldn't show up."

"Of course I was going to show up." She proclaimed, and lightly punched him.

Hayden laughed. "I'm glad you're here. It's good to have you as a buffer against my parents."

Kara giggled. "Glad to play the role." She grinned, but then, suddenly, her face went more somber. "On Saturday night." She began slowly. "I was giving you your space. I didn't want to crowd you." She informed him. "You have to make up your own mind now." She told him adamantly.

"About what?"

"About your future, and what you *choose* for your future."

"I choose you." He said bluntly.

"What are you talking about?" Kara said annoyed. "Don't you get it Hayden?" She asked him. "You're the one going places. You're a doctor now, and I'm a bar maid, and a waitress."

"What's wrong with that?"

"Nothing." Kara said softly. "But I lowered my expectations, when my parents lost all that money." She told him. "Now I don't know what I want, or what I'm capable of."

"Kara you're just a kid. " He replied. "You have your whole life in front of you."

Kara shook her head. "Don't patronize me." She pouted. "We both know how volatile the world is. You're the one who explained it to me. It scares me sometimes."

"And you don't think, that working in an inner-city emergency room, scares me?" He asked incredulously.

"Yeah, but it's not the same." She grimaced. "You're the one who's going to take the world by storm. You already have."

Hayden sat forward, and grabbed her arm.

Kara shook her head. "How are my insides looking these days?"

Hayden shook his head. "That wasn't what I was doing." He said indignantly. "I just want to talk to you."

"But you're reading me right now."

Hayden smiled at her. "You seem pretty healthy to me." He paused. "Although, I don't know what's so heavy, on your mind." He said carefully.

Kara looked at the menu, on the table. "I know you care about me, but there has to be other girls, right?" She proclaimed. "Probably girls in your med school class, who are prettier, and smarter than me. People who you have more in common with, than me."

"No." He said. "Not that I've noticed, and I don't want any other girl."

"Why?" She asked, bluntly. "Because you rescued me that one time? On the steps of your apartment building? That doesn't mean we are destined for each other." She exclaimed.

Hayden shook his head bewildered. "You know me inside and out. You rescued me that night."

"I gave you a life, so you would know what's out there. So you could decide for yourself."

"And I decided on you." He smirked, because she was grinning at him. "Would you stop baiting me, Kara?" Hayden yelled at her, because she was toying with him again. "And don't forget - you're the one, who will be at this university next year. I'll be out in the *wild world*."

Kara shook her head, and laughed at him. "So I'll be moody and evasive."

Hayden grinned. "Ok, point taken, but let's talk about something else." He said quickly. "You never told me much about your holiday." He enquired.

"The most beautiful place I've ever seen." Kara said, talking about the Great Barrier Reef. "But it was kind of sad too. Coral Bleaching is tainting it."

"Yeah, climate change is part of our lives now."

"Yeah, just one of many issues."

"Yeah." Hayden nodded. "Huge drought. Wild fires. Storm surges, and melting polar ice."

Kara looked down at the ground.

"But we've talked about this before." He insisted. "Nothing's changed Kara. It's always been that volatile. Don't forget, that necessity is the mother of invention." He took a deep breath in. "Innovation, and new technology, are always driving this world forward. Technology is moving so fast these days... We have no idea, what is around the corner."

"Yeah. I have noticed that."

"Besides..." He shrugged. "This world is only about you. It comes down to the individual now. It always did." He tried to get her to smile. "It's like Gandhi said: '*You have to be the change you're looking for.*' He shrugged. "You have to make the difference."

Kara grinned at him. "Well isn't that the point?" She exclaimed. "I feel like I just sit back and let all these geniuses, and scientists, and smart people, change the world for me."

"Knowledge builds on top of knowledge." Hayden exclaimed. "Advancement comes from previous knowledge. No genius ever starts from scratch."

"Do you even know what you're talking about?" Kara asked, calling his bluff.

"No, not really." Hayden grinned, and laughed at her again.

Kara giggled to herself. "It's so confusing." She shrugged. "How do these geniuses emerge? Sometimes it doesn't feel like everyone has the same chances in life."

"Well, sometimes that may be true." Hayden chewed on his lip. "I think some places around the world, bring it on themselves. They refuse to modernize, and you know where a lot of that starts?"

"Where?" Kara asked, fully absorbed.

"Women's rights."

"Women's rights." Kara said surprised.

Hayden nodded. "Women who control their lives, control their bodies. Control their destinies. They can gain access to resources. They can be a huge part of negotiations. They can be educated. They can be part of the process. They can have children later in life, and control how many children they have. They can inform the countries that do well." He shrugged. "Most of the countries, and regions, that don't advance; are the ones where women don't have rights."

Kara nodded. "So it comes down to women's rights?" She reflected. "Poor countries are poor, because they don't treat women well?"

"Obviously not always, but there is a lot more corruption, anger, violence, and bad will in countries that mistreat their women."

Kara sat back in her chair, and thought about that for a moment.

"So girls like me. Who do have freedom… have to make it count?"

"All you have to do is be a good person." Hayden reached over, and touched her hand. "Which I know you are."

"But wait…" Kara shook her head. "Didn't you once tell me that the corporate world is taking over now?" She asked, thoughtfully. "What did you mean by that? Tell me about the world now"

Hayden glared at her.

She even wanted to hear one of his lectures, on his graduation lunch.

"Well." He began slowly. "What I told you, on our first date, *or non-date*: All about the World Bank, and the IMF, and decolonization." Hayden tried to explain. "Just forget all that at the moment. That regime, is still at the core of global politics, but the world is different now." He continued. "It's run on free-trade agreements, and conglomerates lead the way, and global crime syndicates have moved in, creating terrible monopolies, but at the same time; global charities, organizations, and law enforcement agencies, reach out, and coordinate, through interconnected channels."

Kara flicked her eyelashes twice. "Ok." She said

Hayden sighed to himself, and put the menu down.

"So it's good and bad, but the world is slowly gaining cooperation, and a global conscience." He inferred. "And don't forget." He added quickly. "Things like conglomerates aren't always a bad thing. Disney is a conglomerate, and it bring a lot of joy to the world. Just like many other conglomerates, who have entertainment, and media divisions." He paused. "So global communication, and things like multinational corporations, are a natural progression of the market economy, good or bad."

"Ok."

"But it's more concentrated now, and it's hard to measure the effect." He said, not really sure, if he was explaining this properly.

"Ok." Kara said again.

"The world is divided." He continued. "The richest one percent, making decisions on behalf of thousands of people. Lobbyists for corporations, beating back environmental policies. Wall Street rigging the system, to stay on top. Those who have money, wasting it on things they don't need. Then, those who *don't* have money struggling to afford the bare necessities. We don't see how bad it gets, for the other half of the planet."

Kara nodded. "No. We don't."

"But the individual, and philanthropist, and the charity, and the good will of people, can change all that." He exclaimed. "As we have talked about, some geniuses out there, can, and have, innovated entire infrastructures. With the help of groundbreaking new technologies." He smiled at her. "They've done it in all different fields. In all different ventures." Hayden looked at her for a long time. "That's the way it's always been."

Kara looked in his eyes, and then nodded. "That sounds good."

"Well it is… but…"

"But what." Kara asked, concerned again.

"I think there is one thing, we can't control though." Hayden said suddenly, disheartened.

"What is that?" Kara asked, concerned at his tone.

"Overpopulation." Hayden said, flatly.

Kara waited patiently, for him to explain.

"The places that are in the most trouble…" He started to say. "The Rohingya, Sudan, Yemen, much of Africa, some of Asia, and the Middle East." Hayden nodded "It's not uncommon for many of the women there, to have about ten children each." Hayden proclaimed. "Even in the worst conditions." He grimaced. "Those children grow up in abject poverty, and they suffer sometimes, with malnutrition, and Poor living standards." Hayden shrugged. "If the population of any country is too high, then of course they are going to run out of food. Of course they are going to run out of land. Of course they are not going to have enough jobs. Of course they are going to get into a war, over resources."

He took another, breath in. "That goes for any one country, or between countries." He told her. "All those problems are already clear. Many nation's populations are massively spilling over their borders. Especially into Europe, but we also take them in as refugees, and immigrants, in Australia, and the rest of the world."

Kara nodded.

"But that's a politically correct area." He shrugged. "Should *we* be responsible for if they want have ten, or more, children?" Hayden grimaced again. "A lot of those children are Muslim too. So the girl get married off at an early age, and then the cycle continues."

"So they don't use birth control, in those countries?" Kara asked, profoundly absorbed by the conversation.

"Well, that's the question." Hayden sighed. "Many of those women, don't have rights, so they don't get a say. But, as for the rest… Do they not *want* birth control? Or do they not have access to it?"

Kara nodded, still profoundly stirred by the conversation.

Hayden took a deep breath in. "Then there is the media's role, in how the world works."

"Yeah." Kara giggled. "I shouldn't get you started on that." She smirked, again.

"Well" he shrugged. "The media can expose injustices, and inform us, and be a valuable source of information." He explained. "But they can also steer us *away* from anything their advertisers don't want us talking about, and that's a lot of stuff."

"Like the environment." Kara asked, softly.

Hayden nodded, sadly. "Exactly, like the environment." He sighed. "Mostly about the environment." He sighed again. "In fact, almost entirely, about the environment." He grimaced. "Free trade deals, can do the same thing."

"For instance…"

"No country wants to upset their trade with China, by talking about China's black market trade in ivory, and rhino horn."

"Oh, Ok." Kara said, saddened by that analogy. She looked at him dismayed. "And the bear bile trade, too." She whispered.

Hayden looked up, suddenly. "You know about that?"

"Yeah." She said softly. "I saw that you had a letter, from *Animals Asia*, once." She explained. "So I went to the web site, and researched it." She shook her head, sadly again. "It was vile." She grimaced.

He looked at her, and they each gave a mutual moment of silence, for the Moon Bears, Sun Bears, and even the Brown Bears that were being tortured by the Asian bear bile industry.

Hayden looked up. "I'm sorry Kara." He paused. "This is a heavy subject for lunch."

"No. I asked you to tell me." Kara blinked twice. "That's why I love you."

Hayden nodded. He looked closely at girl with turquoise eyes and red hair. At long last he could ask the question that had been on the tip of his tongue, for over a year. "Will you go out with me Kara?"

Kara smiled despite herself. "Yes."

Hayden stared at her. "We cannot know what tomorrow brings, but I need your help to face it."

Kara nodded. "I'm ok with that. That's half the fun."

Hayden nodded. "And you know how volatile *I* can be? You know what you're getting into?"

"Yeah, well, I can be kind of volatile myself some days." She teased him.

"So, I'll be there for *you*." He assured her.

"Like only *you* know how to be." She looked in his eyes. "We'll figure out this world together."

"No backing down now." Hayden contemplated.

"Cause that's how the world works." She smiled at him.

www.ingramcontent.com/pod-product-compliance
Lightning Source LLC
Chambersburg PA
CBHW060525180626
46817CB00002B/486